Caleb's Calling

Stoltzfus Brothers Book One

Emma Schwartz

Contents

Foreword

A Letter to You, Dear Reader,

Gut day, Amish Romance fan. I am Bishop John Yoder of Grace Hollow, a community that stands at the crossroads of tradition and change. It brings me great joy to welcome you here, to this story of faith, love, and the challenges we all face, no matter our way of life.

As you read this tale, I ask that you remember one thing: we Amish are not so different from you. While our Ordnung sets boundaries to guide our lives, we are still human—full of joys, struggles, and, *jah*, even flaws. The world around us is changing faster than a horse can trot, and many among us have embraced tools and ways once thought impossible.

Our hearts, too, are not untouched by these changes. Love blooms in unexpected places and often takes paths we cannot predict. You may find yourself surprised by the journey of Caleb Stoltzfus and Sadie Miller, as they navigate what it means to truly know one another and find *Gott's* purpose for their lives.

Let me remind you, this is a story. It is not an exact reflection of life in our communities, but a tale crafted to entertain and inspire. If you are tempted to compare it to what you think you know of the Amish, I urge you to reflect on this: just as the *Englisch* world holds infinite variety, so too does ours. Some among us cling to tradition with both hands. Some carry cell phones in their pockets. Others embrace a combination of new and old ways. Many wrestle with faith, love, and life's complexities in ways that might surprise you.

This book does not shy away from exploring those complexities. And yet, at its heart, it holds the same truths we teach in our homes and churches: faith guides us, love redeems us, and grace surrounds us.

So, I invite you to step into Grace Hollow, Minnesota. Learn from Caleb and Sadie's story, and let it remind you of the beauty and messiness of human connection. Thank you, dear reader, for joining us here.

With blessings,
Bishop Yoder

Chapter One

CALEB

I didn't think a morning could go sideways so fast. One minute, I was fixing the latch on the chicken coop, and the next, I was mid-sprint, chasing a squealing pig through the barnyard.

"*Ach*, Levi!" I shouted, dodging a bucket as the pig barreled past me. "Get that gate closed before he—"

Too late. The pig wriggled past the gate and tore through the yard with all the freedom of an escaped convict. And, just my luck, my five younger brothers had gathered in time to "help." If you could call Levi's grinning face and Micah's half-hearted gestures at the pig helping. Seemed they were getting far too much personal entertainment from my pain.

The yard stretched wide around us, bordered by sprawling green fields that rolled up to the tree line in the distance, where a winding creek marked the property line. The main barn, a deep, worn red with weathered wood siding, stood at the heart of the farm like an old sentinel, its doors open to reveal the shadows of stalls and stacked bales of hay. Beside it sat our family's vegetable garden, neat rows of beans, carrots, and corn just starting to stretch toward the sun, the earthy smell of freshly tilled soil mixing with the scent of hay and warm livestock.

A handful of chickens strutted across the yard, pecking at the dirt, seemingly unfazed by the pandemonium unfolding around them. Beyond the barn, our modest white farmhouse stood proud, its shutters painted a crisp blue, smoke drifting lazily from the chimney as if it had all the time in the world. *Mamm* kept the flower beds neat, filled with bright bursts of peonies and daisies lining the porch, a touch of softness in a life ruled by hard work.

And here I was, face-to-face with chaos in the form of a squealing, mud-streaked pig determined to make a break for it. Levi was still leaning against the fence, watching me with a smirk, clearly in no rush to lift a finger. Behind him, Samuel was waving his arms, more like he was cheering the pig on than trying to catch it.

Levi leaned on the fence post, smirking. "Looks like you've got a real mess on your hands, Caleb."

"Could use a hand instead of that smug look," I shot back, trying to corner the pig without stepping into the mud... or worse.

"Relax, big brother," Levi said, chuckling as he made no attempt to move. "Can't catch a pig without a little fun, *jah*?"

The pig squealed again, darting left, then right, zigzagging in pure defiance. I muttered under my breath, hands up and ready, hoping I didn't have to spend my whole morning chasing one stray hog. But if I didn't corral this headstrong animal, it could do major damage.

"Might be easier if someone closed the gate, *dummkopp*!" I barked, the Pennsylvania Dutch slipping out in my frustration. The oldest twin, Ezra, burst out laughing, and even Levi couldn't hold back his grin.

"Don't strain yourself, Sheriff!" the other twin, Elias, called, wiping a tear of laughter. "We're just following orders!"

Following orders—right. They'd done about as much following as a herd of cats, and this pig was already smarter than all six of us combined. My little brother's use of my annoying nickname rankled almost as much as my inability to get the pig back in the enclosure. I didn't ask to be the "sheriff." The name just stuck because, being the eldest brother, I ended up being the one who took charge, whether I wanted to or not. But it wasn't some badge of honor. It was a title that clung like a burr, making me feel more like a foreman than family. The hardest part was, I wasn't sure how to let go, or if anyone would even let me try.

With another lunge, I tried cornering the pig, but it darted past me in a pink flash, leaving me empty-handed and feeling like the fool. This was my life—wrangling pigs and herding brothers who thought they knew better, all while my own patience wore thin. I felt that tug of duty like a yoke around my neck, keeping me tethered to every little mess around here. And right now, it wasn't just the yoke weighing me down.

The weight of the farm sat heavy on my shoulders, its demands as endless as the rows of corn stretching toward the horizon. It wasn't just my father's fields I was tending these days—*Grossmamm* Eliza's farm needed care, too. Her health had been failing, her once-strong frame now frail, her voice softer with every passing season. My father, unable to do much after a back injury when he fell off a barn roof over a decade ago, still found ways to help where he could, but the real labor fell to me. It was a labor of love, sure, but that didn't ease the ache in my back or the resentment that sometimes crept in when I thought of Eli.

The youngest of my grandma's five children, Eli was more shadow than man, always disappearing when work needed doing. A single man who could easily be working his mother's farm instead of me. The man was good at taking—money, food, time—but giving? That wasn't in his nature. And maybe that was what bothered me most—that he could look at all we were doing and not feel the tug of duty. It left me with too many long days and not enough sleep, the kind of burden that made a man question just how much weight one set of shoulders could bear.

But there was no time to think about that, not with this runaway pig and my brothers watching, clearly enjoying the spectacle. If I had my way, they'd be chasing the hog while I put my feet up and enjoyed some quiet. But if I didn't wrangle this pig soon, I'd never hear the end of it.

The animal was mocking me. I could see it in the way it zigzagged, dodging my every move like this was some game we'd both agreed to play. And when it stopped a few yards away and made eye contact, I could swear it smiled. Except only one of us was having any fun, and it wasn't me.

"Levi, Samuel, quit standing around like fence posts!" I hollered, motioning wildly toward the open gate. "If this pig gets into the field, I'll have the both of you filling that hole all afternoon!"

Levi, the charming, flirtatious brother born second in line, had no sense of urgency. He raised an eyebrow, a smirk tugging at the corner of his mouth. "What's the rush, Caleb? He's just stretching his legs. You could learn a thing or two about that."

"Yeah, Caleb," Ezra piped up, his face red from laughter as he mimicked Levi's casual stance. "When's the last time you let loose?"

I ignored them both, crouching low as the pig trotted in a circle, eyeing me like it knew it was winning this fight. I lunged forward, trying to cut it off before it bolted for the gate again. But my boots slid in the mud, and I barely caught myself in time. Levi let out a low whistle, clearly impressed with my less-than-graceful display.

"Careful there, Sheriff," Levi called, grinning wider. "Wouldn't want you to land face-first in the manure pile. Again. Remember last time? Ten baths couldn't rinse the stench off of you."

"Stifle it, Levi," I muttered, swiping a bit of mud off my sleeve. "If something happens to me, remember who's next in line to take on the majority of the workload."

I could feel my patience slipping faster than my boots in this muck. Every command I threw at them bounced back like they had some immunity to authority. And for once, I wished they'd take something I said seriously.

The pig zigged left, then zagged right, as if testing just how long I'd keep up this chase. My brothers' laughter echoed across the yard, adding insult to my already bruised pride. It didn't help that every time I yelled, they just laughed harder.

"Fine," I said under my breath, a new plan forming. "Let them laugh. I'll get the last word."

I edged forward, my focus narrowed on that squealing menace. "Alright, boys, I'm taking this pig down with or without your help." I gritted my teeth, crouching low for another go. I lunged again, but the pig ducked at the last second, sending me sprawling forward. I stumbled, righted myself, and caught Levi's eye just in time to see him stifle a chuckle.

The youngest, Micah, sat on the fence, shaking his fist in solidarity for me. "You've got this, Caleb!"

"If you two don't want to spend your whole day mucking the barn," I said, my voice sharper than I intended, "close the gate, *sofort*!"

Ezra, still grinning, managed to swing the gate halfway shut, but the pig—ever the opportunist—sprinted past him with a triumphant squeal. I darted after it, but my boot slipped in the mud, and I hit the ground hard, hearing Levi and Micah's laughter reach new heights.

For a brief, shining moment, I considered throwing my hat at them. Or the pig. Or maybe both. But instead, I pushed myself up, wiped the mud from my sleeve, and kept my gaze fixed on the hog as it pranced off.

"Get it together, Caleb," I muttered to myself. "You're the eldest. Set an example."

The pig had one last laugh before it made its final sprint toward freedom. I dove for it, arms outstretched, determined that this chase would end here and now. But just as I lunged, the pig dodged right, and I… didn't.

Instead, I sailed straight into the nearby manure pile.

The world went quiet for a second. All I heard was the soft squish as I landed, face-first, in the most undignified position possible. The smell hit me next, sharp and immediate, filling my senses and reminding me just how low a morning could sink. Somewhere in the distance, I heard Ezra lose himself in a fit of laughter, and Elias wasn't far behind.

I pushed myself up, wiping a glob of… something off my cheek. "*Wunderbaar*," I muttered, feeling the heat rise to my face. Just what I needed to cement my image as the "sheriff" around here—a sheriff who couldn't catch one stubborn pig without it costing a bit of his dignity.

I should lose my badge.

Laughter erupted around me like a chorus, echoing off the barn walls as my brothers cackled, their voices filled with far too much delight. Ezra had doubled over, clutching his sides, and Levi leaned against the gate, gasping for breath between laughs.

"Nice dive, Caleb!" Micah called out, his face red as he struggled to compose himself. "Didn't know you were aiming for the manure pile all along! I swear, you like having all the girls pinch their noses when you're around. At this rate, you'll never get married, so you can grow a beard over that baby face of yours."

"Oh, I was aiming for the manure pile," I said dryly, struggling to regain any shred of authority. "Thought it could use my personal touch." I stood up, brushing off what I could, though it was a lost cause at this point. "Glad

I could give you all a show," I added, doing my best to ignore the warm, sticky mess I'd ended up in.

Levi sauntered over, still grinning from ear to ear, and offered me a hand. "Guess even the sheriff has an off day, huh?"

I accepted his help, muttering under my breath, "Funny, I don't see you stepping up to take over."

Levi shrugged, unbothered. "*Nee*, wouldn't want to steal your thunder." He nodded toward the pig, who had found a comfortable spot to sit, watching us with what looked like sheer satisfaction. "Guess that one's smarter than he looks."

Ezra finally straightened, wiping his eyes. "*Ach*, you'll never live this one down, Caleb. Not for as long as I'm around."

I took a deep breath, feeling the familiar weight settle over me. It wasn't just the manure clinging to me; it was the sense that every bit of order, every bit of responsibility, had somehow fallen squarely on my shoulders. I was the eldest of six sons, the one everyone looked to, the one who had to set the example—even if that meant wrangling pigs in a less-than-dignified manner.

As I brushed off the last bit of my pride, I noticed the others weren't even attempting to help with the runaway hog. They were just watching, amused, leaving me to clean up the mess as usual.

"Figures," I muttered, squaring my shoulders as I prepared to chase down that pig one last time. "They're always watching just when I fall face-first."

I was about to make one last attempt at corralling the pig when I heard the sound of our front door swinging open. My mother—*Mamm*—stepped outside, a quiet sigh escaping her lips as she took in the scene.

"Well now," her voice carried a mix of patience and exasperation. "Looks like my boys have things well in hand." Her gaze fell on me, still covered in manure, and I saw the faintest twitch of a smile tugging at the corner of her mouth while the breeze flittered the strings of her *kapp* around her face.

I tried to stand a little taller, wiping one last smear of manure from my sleeve. "Just another day keeping the peace," I said, attempting some dignity despite the situation.

Mamm shook her head, clearly amused, and walked over to me, holding out a clean rag she must have brought from the kitchen. "The sheriff of Grace Hollow," she murmured, passing it to me with a gentle smile. "And you wonder why we don't call you Caleb anymore."

"'Sheriff' isn't exactly the name I'd choose," I muttered, taking the rag and wiping off what I could.

Mamm placed a hand on my shoulder, her eyes warm but full of that knowing look only mothers seem to have. "You're doing well, Caleb. Holding it all together for us." She nodded toward Ezra and Elias, still grinning behind me. "They don't always show it, but they look up to you. You're a good *sohn* and a good role model for your *bruders*."

I didn't respond. There wasn't much to say to that. I felt the weight of her words settle in the familiar place I'd carried it for years, a mix of pride and obligation that somehow felt as heavy as any burden could.

Mamm gave my shoulder a final pat and turned to head back inside, tossing one last comment over her shoulder. "And don't worry too much about that pig. They'll be telling the story long after the manure's washed off. Use the creek for that task, will you?"

I let out a low chuckle, watching her disappear back into the house. She was right, of course. They'd keep telling this one for years—Caleb, the sheriff, diving into the manure pile, stinking to high heaven. But that was the way it went, wasn't it? I was the one everyone counted on, the one holding things steady, even when it meant taking a dive head-first into chaos. Most days I held it together like Mamm indicated, but some days... I almost wish I'd been born in the middle so I could get lost in the shuffle like my twin brothers, Elias and Ezra.

As I squared my shoulders, I felt that itch for something more, a flicker of a desire I couldn't quite put a name to. I was grateful, of course—grateful for my family, for the farm, for the life I'd been raised in. But standing there, mud-streaked and smelling of manure, I wondered if maybe there was something out there waiting beyond my role as "sheriff." Just the faintest whisper of a question, nothing more. Because at the ripe old age of twenty-seven, I was starting to lose hope.

With one last look at my brothers, who'd returned to their casual, unbothered state, I let out a sigh and readied myself for the next thing on my endless list. Because, sheriff or not, someone had to keep things in line. And if that someone had to be me, then so be it.

Chapter Two

SADIE

The morning sunlight spilled in through the wide windows of my family's General Store, casting a warm glow across the shelves as I bustled from one end to the other, humming "How Great Thou Art" under my breath. I straightened a crate of apples and ran a hand along the edge of the shelf, wiping away any stray dust. The whole store smelled of fresh herbs and vegetables, like rosemary and mint mingling with the earthy sweetness of carrots and potatoes. I always thought the place felt a little like a patchwork quilt—bright, familiar, and comforting, even in the early morning quiet.

We carried all the necessities here, from jars of homemade jams to neatly folded quilts and baskets of dried flowers. Rows of dark wooden shelves held jars of preserves, cornmeal, molasses, and a few treats for the young ones—molasses candies wrapped in wax paper that I knew would be gone by sundown. I'd helped my father build these shelves myself, painting and sanding each one until it was smooth as glass. And it was worth every sore muscle to see neighbors stopping by, their hands brushing along the wood as they picked up what they needed, feeling that same pride in our work.

I adjusted my *kapp*, feeling a loose strand of hair brush my cheek, and pulled it back into place. I wasn't one to think much about my appearance, but folks often told me I had a "glow"—though I'd always thought that was more a reflection of how I felt here. My dress was a plain, modest blue, and I'd made sure my apron was freshly pressed this morning. Not that anyone would notice, but somehow it made the day feel like it was starting right.

A few customers milled about, and I greeted each one with a smile and a warm "*Gut morge*." They returned my smiles, stopping to chat about this or that, some asking for advice on what to make with the rhubarb in season, others just stopping to catch up on the latest news. I liked to think I made this place feel like home for anyone who walked in. Sometimes people just needed a friendly face or a kind word to make their day a little brighter, and if I could be that for them, then I'd done my work well.

The bell above the door chimed as Mrs. Schwartz came in, glancing around with a twinkle in her eye. "Got any of that bread with the molasses crust, Sadie?"

"*Ach*, I know it's your favorite," I said, reaching behind the counter to bring out a fresh loaf. "I kept it warm just for you."

I handed her the loaf, smiling as she tucked it under her arm. After paying me, she looked around, gave me a wink, and whispered, "Keep singing, Sadie. The store always feels a little better when you do. You have the voice of an angel."

I laughed, feeling that warmth fill me again. For all the hard work, this place was more than a store—it was a meeting place, a haven, a bit of light on a busy day. And if I could be even a small part of that, it make my heart happy.

The bell above the door jingled again, and I looked up, my smile already in place. But as soon as I saw the familiar stooped figure, her face pinched like she'd tasted a sour lemon, I braced myself.

Edna Zook. Gossip extraordinaire and unrelenting critic of anything new.

"*Gut morge*, Edna," I said, keeping my voice light as I arranged a small stack of clothespins. "What brings you in today?"

She glanced around the store, her sharp eyes taking in every corner, as if waiting to catch something out of place. "Oh, the usual, I suppose," she said, her voice carrying that toxic and permanent judgmental tone. She sniffed, eyeing the vegetables I'd just restocked. "I heard some folks over in the next district have been having trouble with pests in their gardens. Wouldn't surprise me if we had the same problem here. Seems to follow folks wherever they're too... modern."

I swallowed back a sigh, turning to face her with a polite smile. "Well, if the pests come around, we'll know what to do. Many community members have already put up some new fencing, and it's keeping things pretty neat and tidy."

"Hmph. Fencing. Solar panels. Wonder what's next." She huffed, eyeing a display of dried herbs like they were to blame for all the woes of the world. "Seems like people around here are forgetting the old ways, getting too big for their britches."

I leaned against the counter, determined to keep things friendly. "Now, Edna, I think those solar panels are mighty helpful over at the Stoltzfus farm. It's saving fuel and keeping things running smooth."

Edna's expression didn't soften. If anything, it hardened. "You don't say. Well, I'll stick to my lantern and wood stove, thank you very much. Least I know it's reliable, not like all these newfangled gadgets. Pretty soon our young people will have Satan's cellular phones stuck to their palms like those nasty *Englischers.*" She shook her head, crossing her arms. "Folks need to be careful, Sadie. Progress doesn't always mean improvement."

I nodded, resisting the urge to roll my eyes. If there was one thing I'd learned growing up in Grace Hollow, it was that Edna Zook wouldn't change her mind, no matter how many benefits you listed off. She'd rather walk the long way around just to prove a point.

"Well, I'm sure Abraham Stoltzfus wouldn't have installed them if he didn't think it was for the best," I replied, trying to keep my tone even. "And they seem to be doing just fine, keeping things running without any trouble."

"*Jah*, until they do have trouble," Edna muttered, her gaze sharp as a hawk's. "Who has only six *sohns* and no *dauchtahs*, I ask you?" She turned back to the shelves, rearranging a few jars of jam as if to put them in proper order, though they were already perfectly lined up. "It's not natural."

I could feel the tension tightening around my shoulders, but I kept my face pleasant, hoping she'd move on soon. Some folks came into the store for conversation and fellowship. Edna Zook came in to poke around, find fault, and hand out uninvited opinions like they were candy on *Sunndaag*.

I gripped a jar of pickles a little tighter than necessary, my smile still in place as Edna continued rearranging the shelves to her liking. Part of me wanted to point out that everything was already where it should be, but I held my tongue, counting to ten in my head. I'd been dealing with Edna Zook's "help" since I was old enough to stand behind this counter, and if there was one thing I'd learned, it was that she was as set in her ways as the store itself.

"Sadie, dear, you know folks around here could use a little guidance now and then," Edna said, giving me a look that suggested she was only trying to help. "Not everyone's got sense enough to avoid modern nonsense. Some might even say that you, for example, could use a bit more of that sense yourself."

I raised an eyebrow, biting back a laugh. Oh, I had plenty of sense. More than enough to know that getting into an argument with Edna was as pointless as trying to convince the rooster it didn't have to crow at dawn.

"Well, Edna," I said, keeping my tone as gentle as a lamb's, "I'll take that to heart." I leaned in with a conspiratorial smile. "Besides, if everyone was perfect, what would we have to talk about?"

Her eyes narrowed, trying to find a hidden meaning in my words, but I just kept smiling. I could tell she wanted to find some barb in my response, some slight to correct me on, but all she found was a polite smile and an innocent shrug.

She sniffed, clearly dissatisfied. "If only the young people around here listened like that more often." She eyed me with a look that seemed to weigh my soul and find it barely passable. "You'd do well to remember that, Sadie. Stick to what's tried and true, and don't go getting ideas. One day, when you're married and have a family of your own to protect, you'll tell me *denke*."

"Of course, Edna," I said with a nod, my voice sweet as honey. "I'm all for sticking to what's best for Grace Hollow while utilizing your infinite wisdom."

And in some ways, it wasn't a lie. I loved our town—the tight-knit, well-worn familiarity of it. I loved how the whole town came together—whether for *Sunndaag* services, events at Grace Hall, tending the community garden, or simply sharing a fresh cinnamon roll at the Baker's Nook. We shared meals, laughter, and our troubles too. But I also knew that every change, like those solar panels Edna frowned at, wasn't the end of the world. If anything, they helped keep Grace Hollow the place it had always been.

Edna looked around, her gaze sweeping over the store as if she had a duty to inspect every inch of it before moving on. Her eyes landed back on me, and I could feel her judgment like a weight on my shoulders. I let out a small breath, reminding myself that her grumbling wasn't personal. She'd been that way for as long as I could remember, raining on every parade that crossed her path.

Still, it took a good bit of patience to keep that smile in place. Behind my polite nods, I was counting down the minutes until she moved on, hopefully to find another target for her endless stream of "advice."

Edna's eyes flicked over me, then narrowed in that way that always meant she was about to spill some bit of gossip, as though it were a serious matter of importance. I braced myself, holding my breath, hoping it wouldn't be about anyone too close to me. But of course, that kind of luck wasn't on my side today.

"Sadie, dear," Edna started, leaning in, her voice dropping to a dramatic whisper. "Speaking of the Stoltzfus farm. Did you hear about that little incident over there? Something to do with a certain manure pile... and a certain Caleb Stoltzfus?"

My stomach did a little flip. I tried to keep my expression neutral, careful not to give away any interest. I already knew she had enough details to make anyone blush—details I didn't need her airing out right in the middle of the store.

"Oh, now, Edna," I said, feigning a casual chuckle as I reached up to adjust a jar on the top shelf. "You know Caleb's probably too busy to get up to much excitement." I kept my tone light, even though I was itching to redirect the conversation before she dug in any deeper.

Edna's eyes sparkled, a satisfied gleam that said she knew just how to hold onto a story like this. "Busy, is he? Busy getting himself into trouble, you mean. They're still talking about it all over town—the mighty sheriff Caleb, face-first in the manure pile!"

I suppressed a laugh and kept my voice as gentle as I could manage. "*Ach*, you know he's always trying to lend a hand. I'm sure he just wanted to give the pigs a closer look." I shrugged, throwing her a warm smile. "It's just one of those things, I suppose."

Edna crossed her arms, giving me a look that said she wasn't fooled in the least by my efforts to brush it off. "One of those things," she repeated, unimpressed. "He should've known better. Why, if I were his *Mamm*, I'd tell him to start paying attention to the things that matter. He'll never catch a *frau* when he stinks like that all the time."

I bit my tongue, feeling a spark of protectiveness that surprised even me. Caleb and I weren't even friends, were we? We'd known each other since childhood, and spent time together over the years in large groups. But the man had never looked twice at me, despite my little crush on him. Despite his grumpiness. Edna might have a sharp tongue, but there was no need to start picking apart Caleb's every move. "Well," I said, doing my best to sound casual, "I'm sure he's doing just fine. There's no harm in a little mishap now and then. It's *gut* for the character."

She pursed her lips, looking like she wanted to say more, but I was already moving on, stacking a row of bread loaves on the counter with a finality that I hoped sent a message. "Now, Edna," I added, offering her a sweet smile, "let me know if there's anything you need today. I'd be happy to help."

Edna gave me a final, searching look before relenting, but I could see the glint of intrigue in her eyes. "Well," she said with a huff, "I suppose I'll leave you to it, then." She turned to leave, her footsteps echoing across the floor, but not before I caught one last mutter about "young folks these days."

As the bell above the door jingled, I let out a quiet sigh of relief, feeling a weight lift with her departure. With Edna finally gone, I couldn't help but think about Caleb—how he must've felt with the whole town buzzing over that silly nickname.

I stood there for a moment, staring at the door as it swung shut behind Edna. The air felt a little lighter now, like the room itself had taken a breath. Edna had left behind her usual trail of meddling, leaving me to wonder how many people she'd spin that tale to before the day ended. If it were up to her, Caleb would be the talk of Grace Hollow, and that nickname of his, Sheriff, would probably stick even longer.

The thought tugged at me, bringing a little pang of sympathy. I knew Caleb could handle himself just fine, but Edna's words had a way of stinging, settling in like a thorn you couldn't quite pluck out. And Caleb, for all his stubbornness, was the type to bear things silently, to shoulder burdens alone.

A part of me wanted to find him, maybe to tell him not to worry, that nobody took Edna's stories too seriously. But what right did I have to offer comfort like that? Caleb and I... we were neighbors, sure, but it wasn't as if he'd ever asked for my opinion, let alone my help.

He was aloof. A loner.

Still, it was hard not to feel something—a pull, a quiet urging. He might not need me, but I couldn't help but wonder if maybe he could use someone to remind him that he didn't have to do it all alone.

My gaze drifted over the image of him in my mind, a figure as solid and unyielding as the land he worked. Caleb had a strength about him, one that went deeper than his broad shoulders or the roughened hands that bore the marks of farm work. His jaw was square, always set with that hint of determination, and his steel gray eyes held a quiet intensity, like he was always carrying something heavy inside, even if he'd never say a word about it.

And despite his constant gruffness, there was something about him that pulled at me, an honesty in the way he moved and spoke that made me want to know more, to see past the walls he kept so firmly in place. He probably thought he was just being practical, keeping us all at arm's length. But all I saw was a man who'd chosen to stand alone, even when he didn't have to.

Before I knew it, I'd straightened the same jar of pickles three times, my mind wandering to thoughts I'd never dared let in before. Thoughts of what it might be like to see Caleb let down his guard, even just a little, to catch a glimpse of what lay beneath that quiet strength.

I took a deep breath, pushing those ideas back where they belonged. This wasn't the time to be mooning over the town's most serious man, especially not when I'd barely said two words to him outside of quick exchanges at church or here in the store. But no matter how much I tried to ignore it, the feeling stayed—a small, persistent whisper that maybe he was as lonely as he was steady.

As I finished stocking the last of the shelves, I glanced out the window, almost expecting to see him there, maybe walking past with that determined set to his shoulders. But the street was empty, the stillness settling like a secret between us.

Well, if he wasn't about to ask for my help, then maybe it was up to me to look out for him anyway. After all, we all needed someone to lean on, even if they didn't know it yet. And as much as Caleb tried to hide it, I had a feeling that deep down, he was looking for a little light.

Chapter Three

CALEB

I pushed open the door to the General Store, already calculating how fast I could get in and out. The place was busier than usual, the familiar murmur of folks chatting about this or that making it impossible to grab anything without someone trying to make conversation. And outside of my family, I'd never been much good at socializing. I just never knew quite what to say. I scanned the shelves, focusing on the supplies I needed and hoping I could dodge any delay.

Of course, my luck ran out the second I spotted Sadie Miller behind the counter. She was in the middle of explaining something to an *Englischer*, who was watching her with rapt interest while Sadie gestured toward a shelf of quilts and canned goods, speaking with a kind of patience that had never come naturally to me. The woman nodded along, clearly fascinated by every word.

Sadie looked particularly pretty today. Not that I'd ever admit it, not even to myself most days, but there was no denying it. Her *kapp* framed her heart-shaped face just right, her thick chestnut hair was pulled into a bun at the nape of her neck, and her cheeks were flushed from the bustle of the store. That smile of hers was warm enough to melt the morning frost. She moved with an ease I couldn't fathom, like she belonged in every corner of the room at once, brightening it just by being there. It was maddening, really—how she made it all look so effortless. And yet, there she was, shining like a ray of sunshine in a world that didn't leave much room for light.

I shook the thought off as fast as it came, forcing my attention to the shelves in front of me. Whatever charm Sadie had, it wasn't something I had time to think about. A woman like her deserved a different kind of man. A happy man. Not a surly man like me obsessed with his never-ending to do list.

I gave an inward sigh, mentally running through the slate of farm chores I'd been trying to finish all morning, wishing I'd wrapped them up sooner. It wasn't like I had time to linger in town, but apparently, half of Grace Hollow had decided they needed something from the store today. Typical.

The air smelled like fresh bread—the Grace Hollow ladies must have delivered their loaves for sale—and the scent was strong enough to tempt anyone, though I wasn't about to let myself get sidetracked. I shifted my weight, hands clenched at my sides, hoping Sadie wouldn't notice me in the back of the line. Of course, as soon as she glanced up, her eyes found mine, and that infuriating grin spread across her face.

Her look was like a silent dare, and I muttered a quiet prayer for patience, wishing the line would just hurry up. She didn't have to say a word to get under my skin. That grin of hers could do it just fine. While I never felt much like smiling, Sadie Miller's face always seemed to be stretched wide.

As I watched, she handed the *Englischer* woman a small tin of herbs, explaining with that bright tone of hers. "It's for soothing sore muscles." Her voice was loud enough to carry to throughout the small space. "Perfect for anyone doing hard work—like a good day's chores."

I gritted my teeth. Why did it always have to be her behind that counter? If it was anyone else, I'd be in and out, no fuss, no second glances. No *thoughts*. But Sadie was all sunshine and light, always ready with a smile or a friendly word, something that kept folks lingering far longer than they should.

I shifted again, trying to tune out her chatter. The last thing I needed was to get caught up in Sadie's world of endless cheer. Just a quick grab-and-go, that's all I wanted, so I could get back to worrying and ruminating.

By the time the line moved enough for me to get closer, I could feel her gaze on me, still bright as ever, as if my scowl was some source of amusement for her. I let out a sigh, keeping my head down, hoping—futilely—that maybe she'd skip the comments today. But I wasn't about to bet on it.

Finally, I got close enough to the counter to reach for my list and start piling supplies, hoping Sadie would just ring them up without the usual chitchat. But as soon as she finished with the *Englischer*, she turned that knowing smile straight on me.

"Well, if it isn't the Caleb Stoltzfus," she said, her voice laced with that hint of mischief I'd come to dread. "Looks like you've lost your smile again." She leaned over the counter, one eyebrow raised, not even trying to hide her amusement. "I'm starting to think you don't have teeth, since I never see them."

I frowned, shoving a bag of oats onto the counter. "I'm here for supplies, Sadie, not a personality assessment."

But she didn't miss a beat. "Oh, I know, but it's hard to ignore when you walk in here like you've been hauling a buggy uphill all day." She placed her hands on her hips, her eyes twinkling with that relentless cheer. "Did that frown come free with the supplies, or do you just like making everyone's day a little darker?"

I took a slow breath, reminding myself that snapping at her would only make her more insufferable. Sadie loved nothing more than getting a reaction out of people, and I wasn't about to hand her one on a silver platter. Still, there was something in her expression that made it hard to hold back.

"Some of us have work to do," I replied, deadpan, reaching for a sack of flour. "Not everyone has time to chat all day."

"For your information," she said, her tone light as a feather. "I am working. And yet... I'm not scowling."

My lips twitched in spite of myself. She just wouldn't let it go. "It's a wonder you get any work done at all, with all the talking and smiling you do."

She laughed, brushing off my comment as if it were a compliment. "See, I knew you had a sense of humor hiding in there somewhere, Caleb."

I grunted, trying not to let her words sink in too far. "It's not hiding. It's just reserved for people who don't make a habit of poking at me."

Sadie leaned in, folding her arms on the counter, her voice dropping a notch. "Maybe you just need the right woman to poke at you once in a while. You know, to keep you from turning into a grumpy old man too soon."

She was relentless. And for some reason, instead of walking away, I stayed put, letting her ribbing continue. Maybe it was because she had a way of making everything seem a little lighter, even when she was being annoying. Or maybe, deep down, I liked the challenge. Not that I'd ever admit it.

She glanced at the flour sack and then at me, one last quip on the tip of her tongue. "You know, a smile wouldn't hurt you. It might even keep folks from thinking you're part bear."

I narrowed my eyes, unable to help myself. "I think you talk enough for the both of us, Sadie."

She only grinned wider, clearly satisfied. "Well, then, I'll just keep smiling for the both of us, too."

Sadie rang up the last of my items, still smiling like she had all the time in the world, while I just wanted to grab my things and get back to the farm. But as I reached for the sack of supplies, she tilted her head, her expression softening in a way I didn't expect.

"You know, Caleb," she said, her voice quieter than usual, "being just a smidge softer once in a while wouldn't hurt you. People might start to think you're, well... approachable."

There was no teasing this time, no sly grin, just a warm look that made me shift uncomfortably on my feet. I wasn't used to this—the way she looked at me like she actually believed there was something worth uncovering underneath all the gruffness.

I scoffed, trying to brush her off. "I don't think 'approachable' is exactly what folks expect from me."

And I'm all about meeting everyone's expectations.

Sadie just shook her head, undeterred. "That's where you're wrong. People look up to you, Caleb. You carry yourself like... like you're everyone's big brother. But sometimes, it's okay to let people know you're human too. It might make them feel like they don't have to be as perfect as you."

Her words hit me harder than I wanted to admit. I'd spent years building up walls, keeping folks at arm's length because it was easier that way—easier not to get tangled up in other people's troubles. But the way she looked at me, like she could see something deeper... It left me feeling unsteady, like my footing was suddenly less sure.

"I don't think people need to worry about me," I said, my voice gruff. "I do just fine on my own."

She nodded slowly, her eyes never leaving mine. "Maybe. But doing fine isn't the same as being happy."

Happy. The word landed like a weight in my chest, heavier than I wanted it to. I hadn't thought much about happiness in a long time—there wasn't any point to it when there was work to be done, responsibilities to shoulder. Happiness was for other people, the ones who didn't have half a dozen brothers and two farms to keep running.

But looking at Sadie now, I felt something shift. Her words had slipped past all my defenses, leaving me feeling raw and exposed in a way I didn't quite understand.

Before I could respond, she reached across the counter, her fingers brushing mine as she handed over my change. "Anyway," she added with a soft smile, "just something to think about. I'll leave you to it since I know how badly you want to escape."

I took the change, swallowing against the strange tightness in my throat. For a moment, I couldn't find the words to respond, so I just nodded, hoping that would be enough. The silence stretched between us, filled with something unspoken, something I didn't have the courage to address.

Finally, I cleared my throat, gripping the sack of supplies like it was my lifeline. "*Denke*, Sadie," I muttered, feeling the weight of her gaze as I turned to leave.

As I stepped outside, the warmth of the store faded, leaving me with a lingering sense of... something. I wasn't sure what it was, but whatever Sadie had managed to stir up, it wasn't going away anytime soon.

I stepped onto the dirt road outside the store, the weight of Sadie's words staying with me, like a burr stuck to my thoughts. I'd told myself for years that I was fine as I was—steady, grounded, dependable. It was all I needed to be. Yet there was Sadie, so certain that there was more to me, some hidden potential for... what, exactly? Lightness? Joy?

The morning sun was bright, casting long shadows across the path, and for once, I wasn't in a hurry to get back to the farm. I stood there, gripping the sack of supplies, feeling like I'd missed something important, though I couldn't say what.

Her words echoed in my mind, lingering in a way that made my chest feel tight: "Sometimes, it's okay to let people know you're human too."

I shook my head, trying to shrug off the nagging feeling. But the harder I tried, the more it clung, her voice mixing with the warm scent of the store and the quiet laughter she'd left behind. The lightness she carried seemed to follow me, a lingering reminder that, for once, I didn't have all the answers.

And there was something else, too—a question I couldn't quite shake: what did she see in me that I couldn't see in myself?

As I stared at my horse and buggy, I tried to focus on the routine waiting for me—fences that needed mending, a few sheep that had gone wandering again. The chores were familiar, grounding, and safe. They were enough, weren't they? They had to be.

But a stubborn part of me, the part I usually ignored, kept circling back to Sadie's smile, to the way her eyes softened when she looked at me, like she saw something worth noticing. I hated how it made me feel, like she was opening up a part of me I'd tried to keep shut tight, a door I wasn't ready to crack open.

Maybe that was why I couldn't help glancing back, half-expecting to see her watching me from the store window, though I knew better. Sadie had already moved on, chatting with the next person in line, her laughter spilling out into the morning air like sunlight. She wasn't holding onto our exchange the way I was. She didn't have to.

I wasn't special. At least not to her. She treated everyone like that, and I would do well to remember it.

Despite my mental warning, it still felt like something had shifted. Sadie's words had left a mark, like a quiet echo that would follow me no matter how hard I tried to outrun it. And the worst part?

Deep down, I wasn't sure I wanted to.

Chapter Four

Sadie

I spotted the tilt of the buggy wheel just before I heard *Dat* curse under his breath—a rare enough occurrence to make me glance over sharply. Sure enough, the back wheel was sagging worse than the bread I'd tried to bake last week. We hadn't even made it halfway through the morning deliveries.

"*Ach*, this is no good," *Dat* muttered, climbing down to inspect the damage. He crouched by the wheel, shaking his head like it was the worst thing he'd seen in years. "We can't go anywhere with it like this. *Gut* thing we left your *mamm* behind to man the store all day."

I stayed perched on the buggy seat, shielding my eyes against the bright sun. "Do you think we can fix it?"

"Not without a miracle and a better axle," he grumbled, brushing dirt off his hands. "And I don't see either coming down the road. We're just going to have to sit here and wait for a savior."

He barely got the words out before, as if summoned by Providence itself, a familiar buggy rounded the bend. I recognized Caleb Stoltzfus right away—broad shoulders, steady hands on the reins, and that eternal scowl carved into his face like it was part of his anatomy.

Dat waved him down, and Caleb pulled up with a sharp tug of the reins, his expression already somewhere between suspicious and resigned.

"Need help?" he asked, though it was less a question and more of a statement, like he already knew he wasn't getting out of this.

I tried to ignore the way my stomach knotted as my gaze swept over Caleb. If he could've kept riding without so much as a glance our way, I knew he would have. And that stung more than I cared to admit. I didn't know why Caleb Stoltzfus seemed to dislike me so much. I'd never been anything but friendly—maybe too friendly—but that was just who I was. And yet, every time we crossed paths, his restrained demeanor felt like a wall I couldn't scale, no matter how hard I tried. The thought burrowed deep, leaving me wondering if there was something about me that rubbed him the wrong way. And why did that bother me so much? Caleb's opinion shouldn't matter, but somehow, it did. Too much.

"*Jah*, we've had a bit of bad luck," *Dat* said, gesturing to the wheel. "Think we'll need to transfer these supplies to your buggy, if you don't mind. Some of them are perishable."

I caught the way Caleb's mouth tightened, like he was about to protest, but then *Dat* added, "Sadie can ride along and help with the deliveries while I stay back and wait for someone to bring me to town to fetch tools for the repair."

Caleb glanced at me, and his frown deepened, which I hadn't thought possible. "Right," he muttered, climbing down from his buggy with the enthusiasm of a man being sentenced to hard labor.

I hopped down too, dusting off my apron. "Now, now, Caleb, don't look so thrilled. You'll scare that flock of crows over there."

He shot me a glare, but it didn't have much heat. "Apparently, I'm just here to get the job done whether I like it or not."

"And what a cheerful helper you are," I said brightly, earning a muttered response I didn't quite catch—but judging by his tone, it wasn't exactly complimentary.

We worked in relative silence, loading sacks of flour and crates of canned goods into Caleb's buggy, along with freshly baked items and medicines. Well, he worked in silence. I filled the space with commentary, mostly to see how far I could push him.

"You know, you should be flattered, Caleb. Not everyone gets the honor of being my delivery partner."

He paused, giving me a look that could've curdled fresh milk. "I'm here because your *dat* asked."

"A noble sacrifice." I clasped my hands dramatically. "Truly, Caleb, you're an inspiration."

His sigh sounded long-suffering, but when he turned away to grab another sack, I caught the faintest twitch of his mouth. Wouldn't it be a plot twist if I was wearing him down.

Once the supplies were loaded and the buggy creaked under the extra weight, *Dat* gave Caleb a firm pat on the shoulder. "Appreciate this, Caleb. I'll get this wheel sorted and meet you back at the store later."

"Of course," Caleb said, his tone as flat as the broken wheel. He climbed up into the buggy and adjusted the reins with a practiced hand. Meanwhile, I was brushing my skirt off, readying myself to climb up beside him.

"Don't keep him out too long, Sadie," *Dat* added with a smirk. "You'll scar him for life if you chatter his ear off."

I tilted my head, feigning innocence. "Who, me? I'm the very picture of restraint."

Dat chuckled and waved us off as I climbed up onto the bench. Caleb didn't wait for me to settle before snapping the reins, sending the buggy lurching forward with a jolt.

"Easy there!" I shot him a look as I adjusted my seat. "Trying to toss me off already?"

"Just testing your balance," he muttered, eyes fixed on the road ahead. "Figured you'd be used to rough rides."

"Oh, I'm plenty used to rough rides, Caleb," I shot back with a grin, leaning slightly toward him. "I just didn't expect my company to be so... enthusiastic about seeing me eat a mouthful of dirt."

He grunted, his usual response to anything he didn't feel like answering. I let the silence stretch for a moment, studying his profile. The sharp line of his jaw, the way his hands gripped the reins like they were his anchor in the world—everything about Caleb Stoltzfus screamed control, steadiness, and an utter lack of patience for distractions. Which made teasing him all the more satisfying.

"So," I began, breaking the silence. "What's it like being the community's knight in shining armor? Saving damsels, fixing broken buggies—next thing we know, you'll be rescuing kittens from trees."

Caleb shot me a sidelong glance, his brow furrowed. "I'm not a knight."

"No," I agreed with mock seriousness. "You're more like a grumpy farmer who can't take a joke."

"I don't have time for jokes," he replied flatly, his eyes still on the road. "I would think you would know that by now. And stop trying."

"*Ach*, Caleb," I said with a dramatic sigh. "If you don't learn to loosen up, you're going to give yourself wrinkles before your time."

"Better wrinkles than wasting time," he muttered.

I smirked, undeterred. "You're just lucky I'm here to brighten your day."

"Is that what you're calling it?" he shot back, his tone dry as toast.

"*Jah*, I'm like sunshine breaking through storm clouds," I said with a grin. "Admit it—you'd miss me if I wasn't here."

Caleb rolled his eyes and kept his focus on the road ahead. "Where are we going? Your father didn't give me a map, and I'd rather not drive around all day guessing."

"Oh, of course," I said, shifting on the bench to face him. "We've got three stops before we head back to the store. First is the King farm—they ordered the flour and sugar sacks. After that, it's the Lapps for their crate of preserves and fresh produce. Then we finish with the Troyers, who needed fresh herbs for tinctures."

He nodded, his grip on the reins firm and steady. "Which one's closest?"

"The King farm." I pointed down the road. "Just past the second split, take a left at the old oak tree. You'll see their barn with the red trim."

Caleb gave a curt nod. "And after that?"

"From the King's, we head back toward town but take the eastern road to the Lapps. Their place is easy to spot—white house with blue shutters and a big flower garden out front."

"And the Troyers?" he asked, his tone clipped but practical.

"They're past the Lapps, closer to the creek. You'll see their little bridge—painted green—and their barn is to the right of it."

Caleb mulled over the route, then glanced at me with a raised brow. "Any surprises I should know about? Detours? Cows wandering across the road?"

I laughed, shaking my head. "No detours today, though I can't make any promises about the cows. But from what I've heard, you should be more concerned about loose pigs."

"Hmph," he grunted, his eyes flicking back to the road after he tossed me some very crabby side-eye. "Let's just get this done."

"Oh, Caleb, you make it sound so dreadful," I teased. "We're making deliveries to our friends and neighbors, not preparing for battle."

"Feels the same," he muttered under his breath.

I stifled a grin, leaning back against the seat. "Don't worry—I'll make sure you don't get lost. It's a simple enough route, even for you."

He cast me another sideways glance, his expression unreadable but tinged with what might've been mild annoyance. "Just tell me when to turn."

"Don't worry, I will," I replied, my tone light. "You'll be back to your brooding farm life before you know it."

His only response was another grunt, but I caught the slightest twitch at the corner of his mouth. If Caleb Stoltzfus thought he could keep his walls up forever, he clearly didn't know who he was dealing with.

The road stretched out ahead of us, winding through fields of tall grass and patches of wildflowers. The gentle sway of the buggy and the clip-clop of the horse's hooves filled the spaces between our banter. Despite Caleb's gruff exterior, I could sense he wasn't entirely immune to my efforts. There was a flicker of something—amusement, maybe—that he tried very hard to hide.

But I'd seen it. And I wasn't about to let it go.

For a moment, as the buggy rolled along, I let myself imagine what this might feel like if things were different. If Caleb weren't so set on keeping everyone at arm's length. Sitting beside him, the steady rhythm of the horse's hooves almost felt... intimate. Like we could be courting, like this was the start of something instead of just a favor he'd been cornered into. The thought left an ache in my chest I didn't know how to name. I shook it off, but not before the weight of it settled deep. Caleb Stoltzfus wasn't the type to notice someone like me—not in that way. And yet, sitting here beside him, it was hard not to wonder what it might be like if he did.

The first stop on our route wasn't far—just a little farmhouse nestled at the edge of Grace Hollow. The kind of place where vines climbed the porch posts, and curtains swayed in the windows like friendly waves. Caleb pulled the buggy to a halt with his usual precision, hopping down without so much as a glance my way.

"I'll grab the sacks," he muttered, already moving to the back.

"Don't strain yourself," I said, following him with a grin. "Wouldn't want you pulling a muscle before we've even started."

He ignored me, hefting a sack of flour like it weighed nothing while I admired the stretch of his shirt across his back. I grabbed a smaller box of canned goods, mostly because I didn't feel like wrestling with the flour myself, and followed him up the front steps.

The door opened before we knocked, and there she was—Esther King, as if she'd been waiting all morning just to catch sight of Caleb. Her golden hair framed her face in soft waves beneath her *kapp*, and her smile lit up like the sun breaking through clouds. "Oh, Caleb! What a pleasant surprise."

I blinked. A *pleasant* surprise? That was one way to describe him.

Caleb cleared his throat, shifting the heavy sack of flour from one hand to the other. "Delivery," he said, his voice clipped, as he set the sack down on the porch. Esther tilted her head, her smile widening like she'd just been handed a basket of wildflowers.

"Such a gentleman," she said, stepping closer and placing her hand lightly on his arm. "Always helping those in need."

Caleb stiffened, glancing down at her hand like it was a bee about to sting him. "Just doing what needs doing," he said gruffly, stepping back ever so slightly, but not enough to escape her reach.

"Oh, you're too modest," Esther cooed, following his retreat with an easy step forward. Her hand lingered on his sleeve, fingers brushing the fabric like it was the finest silk. "You've always been so kind, Caleb. I can't help but notice it."

I bit the inside of my cheek, trying very hard not to roll my eyes. Caleb? Kind? Clearly, she hadn't seen him standing in the middle of town square barking orders to his younger brothers like a drill sergeant.

"We've got more stops to make," he said, his tone almost desperate now as he gestured toward the buggy. "Busy morning."

"Oh, of course," Esther said, her voice as soft and sweet as honey on fresh bread. "But surely you've got a minute to come inside? I've just made a fresh coffee cake, and the lemonade's cooling in the springhouse."

Her words hung in the air like a lure, and Caleb, to his credit, looked like he wanted nothing more than to sprint for the buggy. "*Nee, denke*," he said quickly, his gaze darting toward me for the first time since we'd arrived. "Sadie and I need to keep moving."

"Oh." Esther blinked, her smile faltering for half a heartbeat before she smoothed it back into place. Her eyes slid to me for the first time, as though she were only just noticing I existed. After a sweeping gaze of my entire body, for the first time her lips twisted. Like she'd just sucked down one of those lemons she used to make refreshments. "Sadie, of course. How nice of you to come along."

"Very nice," I said with a tight smile, my words sharp enough to cut glass. "Since your order came from my families store."

Caleb, oblivious as ever, tried to soften the moment by adding, "Sadie's been a big help this morning."

Esther didn't even look my way as she replied, "I'm sure she has."

The dismissal was as clear as the summer sky, and my stomach twisted. Before Caleb could make any more polite excuses, I stepped forward. "We'd best be going. There's plenty left to deliver."

Esther gave Caleb one last lingering look, her gaze practically dripping with admiration. "I'll see you at the next singing, Caleb."

As we turned to leave, my heart was a swirling mess of emotions I couldn't quite name. Why did it bother me so much? Esther King was everything an Amish man like Caleb would want in a wife—sweet, demure, and beautiful in that understated way that turned heads without trying. And me? I was just Sadie Miller, the neighbor girl who couldn't seem to stop annoying him. Who everyone talked to about their troubles, but who no man seemed to want to make a commitment to.

As Caleb turned to rearrange the deliveries inside the buggy, shifting the items to distribute the weight more evenly, I caught Esther's eye and offered her a polite nod. Esther's smile didn't waver as her gaze lingered on Caleb. She stepped off her front porch and trailed after us.

Caleb's back stiffened as he finished adjusting the load. He turned, glanced at Esther with a tight nod, then surprised me by extending his hand toward me. "Sadie," he said, his tone firm but unreadable.

I hesitated, my pulse fluttering as I stared at his outstretched hand. He didn't look at me, his eyes fixed somewhere over my shoulder as though this was just another task to check off his list. Still, it was Caleb, and he was offering to help me up into the buggy. I was going to touch Caleb for the very first time that wasn't by accident. The heat rose to my cheeks as I took his hand, his grip steady and strong as he boosted me onto the bench.

"*Denke*," I murmured, barely able to meet his eyes.

"Don't mention it," he replied briskly, walking around to the other side of the buggy. He climbed in without a glance back at Esther, flicking the reins with a sharp, deliberate motion. The buggy started forward with a lurch, leaving Esther standing in the dust of the driveway, her smile finally slipping.

I glanced over my shoulder at her retreating figure, then straightened, clasping my hands tightly in my lap. My thoughts churned as I tried to make sense of Caleb's gesture. I shouldn't make anything of it. It wasn't special. It wasn't meant to mean anything. He was just being polite, just showing Esther that he wasn't interested.

And yet... the warmth of his hand lingered, sparking a traitorous flutter in my chest that I tried desperately to squash. It wasn't fair. It wasn't fair that Caleb Stoltzfus could drive me to distraction with a single small act, while I barely seemed to register to him at all. For him, helping me was probably no different than hitching a wagon or stacking firewood—just another chore to complete before moving on. But for me, it was something I couldn't quite let go of, no matter how much I wished I could.

We rode in silence for a moment, the horse's hooves clopping against the dirt road. Caleb's jaw was tight, his hands gripping the reins with a little too much force.

"So," I said finally, unable to resist. "She's very... nice."

Caleb glanced at me, frowning. "Who?"

I tilted my head, giving him an exaggerated look of disbelief. "Esther. You know, the one practically swooning on the porch? The one who kept touching you when everyone knows that is totally inappropriate."

"She wasn't swooning," he said, his tone defensive.

"Oh, Caleb," I said, letting out a laugh. "You really are clueless, aren't you?"

The buggy swayed gently as we made our way back to the main road, but Caleb's grip on the reins looked like he was steering through a hurricane. I could practically see the gears turning in his head, trying to make sense of what had just happened at Esther King's doorstep.

"She wasn't swooning," he muttered again, as if saying it would make it true.

"Don't be so modest," I teased, leaning back against the bench with a grin. "The way she fluttered her lashes, touched your arm—she might as well have handed you a love note."

"She was just being polite," he said firmly, his tone leaving no room for argument. Or so he thought.

"Polite," I repeated, drawing the word out like it was something exotic. "Sure, let's call it that. And I suppose the way she looked at you like you hung the moon was just friendly admiration?"

His silence was answer enough.

I couldn't help but laugh, the sound breaking through the quiet of the morning. Caleb shot me a look that could've curdled fresh milk, but it only made me laugh harder. "You really don't notice such things, do you?"

"Notice what?" he asked, sounding genuinely perplexed.

"*Ach*, Caleb," I said, shaking my head. "You could have half the women in Grace Hollow falling at your feet, and you'd still think they were just being mannerly."

He didn't respond right away, his frown deepening as he focused on the road ahead. For a moment, I thought he might stay quiet for the rest of the ride. But then he said, almost to himself, "I don't see why it matters."

That gave me pause. There was something in his voice—something quieter, almost vulnerable—that I hadn't expected. It wasn't that he didn't notice; it was that he didn't think he was worth noticing.

The thought stuck with me as we made another stop to drop off supplies. This time, it was an older couple who welcomed us with warm smiles and friendly chatter. Caleb handled the delivery with his usual efficiency, speaking only when necessary and keeping his gaze steady on the task at hand. But I noticed the way the woman patted his arm as she thanked him, and how Caleb responded with a small, almost shy nod.

By the time we climbed back into the buggy, I couldn't resist needling him one more time. "You know, Caleb, you might just be Grace Hollow's most eligible bachelor."

He gave me a look that could've melted the frost off the barn, but there was no real heat behind it. "I'm not interested."

"Oh, I know," I said, leaning back with a satisfied grin. "But that doesn't mean *they* aren't. Esther wants you for herself, but Mrs. Lapp wants you for her *dauchtah*."

Caleb muttered something under his breath that I didn't catch, but the way his ears turned pink was answer enough. I let the silence stretch as we rode on, a quiet smile tugging at my lips. Maybe he didn't see it yet, but there was more to Caleb Stoltzfus than his scowl—and I wasn't the only one who'd noticed.

The sun was climbing higher now, casting a golden glow over the fields as we made our final delivery. Caleb's silence had grown heavier with each stop, but I wasn't about to let him brood his way through the entire morning. After all, what kind of delivery partner would I be if I didn't keep him on his toes?

As we approached the last house, a group of children darted out from behind a tree, their laughter ringing out as they ran toward the buggy. "*Mamm* said you'd be here today!" one of the boys shouted, his face bright with excitement.

"Sadie!" the littlest girl cried, her braids bouncing as she tugged on my skirt the moment I stepped down. "Did you bring the jam?"

"Of course," I said, reaching for the small box of jars. "Would I ever forget your favorite?"

The girl beamed and ran back to the porch, calling out to her mother about how "Sadie never forgets." Caleb was unloading a sack of potatoes, his movements efficient as always, but I noticed how he paused to watch the children for a moment, his expression softening just enough to be noticeable.

"You've got a fan club," I teased as we carried the goods to the porch.

He glanced at me, raising an eyebrow. "They're just excited about the jam."

"Or maybe they just like seeing you, Caleb," I said with a sly grin. "You know, you're not as intimidating as you think."

His grunt was noncommittal, but I caught the faintest flicker of something in his eyes—something almost like amusement. "Let's get this done."

The Troyer family thanked us warmly, and as we climbed back into the buggy for the ride home, I couldn't resist one last jab. "You're *gut* with *kinner*, you know. Bet you'll make a great *dawdi* someday."

Caleb turned to me, his expression unreadable, but the pink creeping up his neck gave him away. "You really don't know when to quit, do you? Why do you torment me so much, Sadie?"

"Seems I can't stop. Not when I'm having this much fun," I replied, settling back against the bench.

The road stretched ahead, peaceful and quiet, but the tension between us buzzed like a live wire. Caleb's hands were steady on the reins, his jaw set in that familiar line, but there was something different now—a charge in the air that hadn't been there before. I wondered if he felt it too.

As we neared the fork that would take him back to his farm, Caleb finally spoke. "Thanks for... helping with the deliveries."

I blinked, surprised by the unexpected gratitude. "Actually, you were the one who was helping me. And it is appreciated."

He nodded, his gaze fixed straight ahead. And then, just as we reached the turn, he added, almost too quietly to hear, "You're not as annoying as I thought."

I burst out laughing, the sound carrying over the fields. Caleb's expression didn't change, but I swore I saw the corner of his mouth twitch.

Just a little.

Chapter Five

Caleb

The buggy rolled steadily along the main path, the rhythmic clip-clop of the horse's hooves offering the kind of predictable comfort I usually welcomed. But not today. Not with Sadie Miller sitting beside me, her presence as loud in my head as the stillness was around us. I gripped the reins tighter than necessary, my knuckles white against the worn leather, trying to will away the frustration that had nothing to do with her chatter and everything to do with... her.

She made me feel things—confusing, unwelcome things. Things I'd worked hard my entire life to avoid. Sadie was like the spring sunshine, breaking through clouds that were better left undisturbed. And the worst part? I didn't know how to stop it. I'd always thought of myself as steady, unshakable, but one look at her easy smile and I felt like the ground wasn't as firm beneath me as I'd thought.

"You're holding the reins too tightly, Caleb," she said, her voice soft but edged with that teasing lilt that never failed to grate on me. "The horse might think you're angry with him."

"I'm not angry," I muttered, my jaw tightening as I avoided her gaze. "I'm focused."

She laughed lightly, the sound cutting through the air and somehow finding its way under my skin. "Focused, huh? Is that what you call it?"

I clenched my teeth and didn't respond, keeping my eyes firmly on the road ahead. She didn't understand—couldn't understand—what it was like to feel this kind of pull toward someone. It was maddening, like trying to resist the tide while knowing it was going to drag you under anyway.

And the worst part? I wasn't sure I even wanted to fight it.

I glanced at her again. She was so pretty. And that alone was a kind of quiet torment, the sort that crept in and lingered, refusing to be ignored. Sadie had a heart-shaped face, framed by soft tendrils of chestnut hair that caught the sunlight and gleamed like spun honey. Her skin, so smooth and luminous, reminded me of the silk threads *Mamm* used in her finest embroidery, flawless and untouchable. And her eyes—deep, expressive pools of blue-gray that could shift from teasing to tender in a heartbeat—seemed to see through every wall I'd spent years building.

It wasn't just her looks, though they were enough to undo me. It was the way her presence made my body tighten, like a taut bowstring, a tension that wasn't entirely uncomfortable but left me on edge. My pulse kicked up, my palms grew damp, and it wasn't from the reins I held. I'd never noticed a woman like this before—not in a way that made my thoughts stray to things they shouldn't. It wasn't right. It wasn't proper. But *Gott* help me, I couldn't stop myself

Sadie let out a contented sigh, leaning slightly to adjust something on her side of the bench. "You know, this has been a nice day," she said, her voice warm. "A little change of pace never hurt anyone."

I didn't respond. Change of pace wasn't something I welcomed. Routine was safe, predictable—free from the kind of feelings that Sadie Miller seemed determined to stir up every time she parted her full lips.

And then I felt it—the shift in the buggy's direction, subtle but deliberate. My grip on the reins tightened as the horse veered slightly off the main road onto a smaller, less-traveled path. Then I stared at Sadie's fingers squeezing the line.

"What are you doing?" I asked, my tone sharper than I intended.

Sadie blinked up at me, all innocence. "What do you mean?"

"This isn't the main road," I said, glancing at the unfamiliar stretch of lane ahead. "Where are you steering us?"

She shrugged, her expression far too casual for my liking. "Oh, just a quick stop."

My jaw tightened as suspicion flared. "A stop? Sadie, we're supposed to be heading back. I have things to do. A life to get back to."

"I know, I know," she said with a light wave of her hand. "But Mrs. Schultz lives just around the bend, and she hasn't been feeling well. I thought we could check in on her. It won't take long, I promise."

My teeth clenched as I pulled the reins tighter, slowing the horse. "So you got us off track on purpose?"

"On purpose is so harsh," she said, flashing me a grin that could've melted steel. "I call it creative navigation."

I let out a low breath, forcing myself to focus on the road ahead instead of her infuriating smile. "You could've told me first."

"Where's the fun in that?" she quipped, her eyes sparkling with mischief.

I shook my head, but my chest felt tighter than it should've. This was what Sadie did—steered people off course and made them feel like it was exactly where they were supposed to be.

The narrow lane curved gently ahead, and I couldn't shake the irritation simmering just under my skin. "This isn't how I planned to spend my afternoon," I muttered, my eyes fixed on the path, scanning for Mrs. Schultz's house. "Now I'm going to be behind on my chores."

Sadie leaned slightly closer, pointing ahead to a small white house tucked under a canopy of trees. "There it is," she said, her tone as light as if we were on a pleasant stroll instead of an unplanned detour. "See? That wasn't so bad."

I bit back a reply, pulling the horse to a stop in front of the modest home. The fence needed repairs, the garden was overgrown, and the front steps sagged slightly under the weight of time. It was the kind of place that tugged at your sense of duty, and I hated how quickly Sadie had used that to pull at my heartstrings.

Sadie hopped down before I could even get the reins tied, gathering a small bundle of goods from the back of the buggy. "I'll just be a minute," she said, shooting me a quick smile before heading toward the door.

I sighed, leaning back slightly on the bench. Of course she was taking the lead—this was Sadie Miller, after all. She could waltz into someone's life, rearrange it with a smile and a bit of sunshine, and leave them wondering how she'd managed to do it. It was both maddening and... impressive, though I'd never admit the latter.

The door creaked open, and Mrs. Schultz appeared, her face lighting up at the sight of Sadie. "*Ach,* Sadie, dear! You didn't have to come all the way out here. But I'm so glad to see you nonetheless."

"Nonsense," Sadie replied, her voice warm and full of that effortless charm. "We were in the neighborhood. I brought you a little something."

Mrs. Schultz reached out to take the bundle, her weathered hands trembling slightly. "You're a blessing, you know that? Always thinking of others. I wish I had a caring *dauchtah* like you."

I couldn't help but watch as Sadie handed over the bundle, offering a few soft words I couldn't quite catch. The older woman smiled, a deep, genuine expression that spoke of gratitude and relief. And for a moment, I forgot about the detour, the irritation, the interruption to my day. All I saw was the quiet joy Sadie had brought to someone else.

And I felt like a selfish heel.

But then Sadie turned, catching me staring, and I snapped back to myself, straightening on the bench. I busied myself with the reins, pretending I hadn't been paying attention.

"Mrs. Schultz says she'd love to see you," Sadie called, her eyes sparkling with mischief.

I frowned. "I'm fine right here."

"Suit yourself," she said with a shrug, though her grin told me she'd gotten exactly what she wanted. She turned back to Mrs. Schultz, her laughter carrying on the breeze as they exchanged a few more words.

I tightened my grip on the reins, ignoring the strange tug in my chest. Sadie finally bid Mrs. Schultz goodbye, her cheerful tone lingering in the air as she turned and made her way back to the buggy. She carried herself with a lightness I couldn't fathom, like everything in her world was as easy as breathing. It made me uneasy, that effortless warmth. It was so... opposite of everything I knew.

"Ready to go?" she asked, hopping up onto the bench beside me. She dusted her hands off on her apron, her smile as bright as ever.

I gave a curt nod, flicking the reins to get the horse moving. "You done spreading sunshine for the day?"

She laughed, the sound warm and unguarded. "If that's what you want to call it. Mrs. Schultz appreciated it, Caleb. This visit was probably the highlight of her week. Don't act like you didn't notice."

“I noticed,” I muttered, keeping my eyes on the road ahead. “I also noticed we’re now behind schedule.”

Sadie waved a dismissive hand. “*Ach*, we’ll make up the time. Besides, schedules are overrated. What’s the point of rushing through everything? The meaningful moments in life are meant to be savored.”

I clenched my jaw, resisting the urge to argue. To me, schedules were everything. They kept the day structured, predictable—something I could count on. Sadie’s carefree attitude toward time grated against every instinct I had, and yet... I couldn’t say she was wrong. Not entirely.

The road back to the main path stretched before us, lined with tall grass and a few scattered wildflowers. The sun dipped lower, casting a golden hue over the fields. I should’ve been thinking about the work still waiting for me, but instead, my thoughts were tangled up in the woman sitting next to me.

Sadie leaned back slightly, her gaze sweeping over the scenery. “You know, Caleb,” she said, her tone thoughtful, “it wouldn’t kill you to slow down once in a while. Take in the view, smell the flowers.”

I didn’t answer, but her words settled over me like a weight. I wasn’t sure what it was about Sadie—her insistence on finding beauty in every moment, or her relentless effort to drag me along with her—that left me feeling so off balance. All I knew was that her presence unsettled something in me, something I didn’t want to examine too closely.

I’d built a wall around myself long ago—a sturdy, unyielding thing meant to keep the chaos out and my focus in. It wasn’t pretty, but it worked. My life was simple, predictable, and I liked it that way. Walls didn’t ask anything of you. They didn’t challenge you or expect you to be someone you weren’t ready to be. They just kept you safe. And that’s all I wanted—emotional safety, the kind that came from keeping people at a distance. But Sadie... she had this way of brushing against that wall, not with force but with an ease that made it feel like she didn't even notice it was there. It scared me, the way she made me question whether staying behind it was worth the price.

The buggy jolted slightly as we hit a bump in the road, and Sadie's hand shot out to steady herself. Her fingers brushed against my arm, just for a second, but it was enough to send a jolt through me. She pulled back quickly, her cheeks pinking, and turned her face toward the fields as if she hadn't noticed.

I swallowed hard, keeping my grip firm on the reins. "You okay?"

"Fine," she said quickly, her voice light but a little too forced. "Thought I was losing my balance. Just wasn't paying attention."

Neither was I, apparently. At least, not to the road.

The horse settled into a steady rhythm as the buggy turned back onto the main road. I kept my eyes forward, pretending the moment back there hadn't thrown me. Sadie hummed softly beside me, her melody light and carefree, the kind of tune that could pull you from your own head if you let it. I wouldn't let it.

"Mrs. Schultz looked like she appreciated the visit," I said, breaking the silence more for myself than for her. My voice came out gruffer than I intended.

Sadie turned toward me, her expression soft. "She did. It's good for her to know she's not forgotten. Sometimes people just need to feel like they matter."

The words struck something deep, but I kept my face neutral. "She's lucky you stopped by."

"We," she corrected with a pointed look. "She's lucky *we* stopped by."

I snorted, flicking the reins lightly. "You mean she's lucky you dragged me off my planned route."

Sadie grinned, completely unfazed. "You're welcome, by the way. Admit it, Caleb. It wasn't so bad. Socializing with people."

I shook my head, a faint smile tugging at my lips despite myself. "You're impossible."

"And you're predictable," she shot back. "It's a good balance."

Her words settled between us, light but carrying more weight than she probably realized. Predictable. That's exactly what I was—and exactly what I thought I wanted to be. Predictable was safe, steady, responsible. But sitting beside Sadie, with her endless ability to see the good in everyone and everything, I felt anything but steady.

But predictable wasn't for someone like Sadie. She was light and laughter, the kind of brightness that made even the darkest corners seem less daunting. And me? I'd only dim that light. My steady predictability would weigh her down, snuff out the spark that made her so... Sadie. I couldn't risk that, not for a fleeting crush or feelings I barely understood. She deserved someone who could match her joy, someone who wouldn't see the world in black and white while she painted it in color. Admitting what I felt—pursuing it—would only lead to disappointment. For both of us.

As we passed a small stretch of wildflowers along the roadside, Sadie suddenly leaned forward, her eyes lighting up. "Stop the buggy."

I glanced at her, eyebrows furrowing. "What? Why?"

"Just stop," she said, her tone insistent but playful.

With a reluctant sigh, I pulled the reins, slowing the horse to a halt. Sadie hopped down before I could say anything else, darting toward the patch of flowers. I watched her with a mix of confusion and mild exasperation as she crouched to pick a handful of the brightest blooms.

"What are you doing?" I called after her.

"Making the world a little prettier," she replied, glancing back at me with a grin.

I rubbed the back of my neck, muttering under my breath about wasted time, but I didn't look away. The way the golden light caught her as she moved, the carefree energy in her every gesture—it was disarming. And it made me feel unsteady in a way I didn't like to admit. It made me want more.

More of her.

She returned to the buggy with her small bouquet, climbing back up with a flourish. "There," she said, placing the flowers carefully on the bench between us. "Now it feels more like spring."

I stared at the flowers, then at her, then shook my head. The sun cast shadows as the buggy creaked along the winding road. Sadie's humming had stopped, replaced by a quiet contentment that made the silence feel less like a void and more like... peace. I hated how much I noticed the difference.

The flowers she'd picked lay on the bench between us, their vibrant colors stark against the worn wood. I caught myself glancing at them more than once, and each time, my mind wandered back to the way she'd looked as she'd picked them, unbothered by time or expectation. So very breathtaking as the sun had warmed the planes of her face.

"You're awfully quiet," she said, breaking the silence. Her voice held that familiar teasing edge, but there was a softness beneath it.

"Just thinking," I replied, keeping my tone flat. "About how much time we've lost today."

Sadie laughed, a light, musical sound that I couldn't help but notice felt like it belonged here, in the stillness of the countryside. "You keep saying that, but I don't think you really mind. Admit it, Caleb. You've had fun."

"Fun," I repeated, glancing at her. "You think dragging me all over creation counts as fun?"

“Of course,” she said with a grin, leaning forward slightly. “You got to visit Mrs. Schultz, enjoy the scenery, and even pick up some flowers—oh wait, that was me.”

I shook my head, exhaling a quiet laugh despite myself. “You’re impossible.”

“And yet, here you are,” she quipped, her grin widening. "You probably wanted to throw me out of the buggy, but you refrained."

She wasn’t wrong. For all my grumbling, I was still here, still letting her pull me along on whatever tangent she dreamed up. And the strangest part was, I didn’t entirely hate it. That thought unsettled me more than anything else.

As we approached the fork in the road that would take us back toward town, Sadie turned to me with a sudden spark of mischief in her eyes. “You know, Caleb, I bet you’ve never just... stopped for the sake of it. Taken a moment to enjoy something for no other reason than because it’s there.”

I frowned, gripping the reins a little tighter. “What’s that supposed to mean?”

“It means,” she said, gesturing to the horizon where the sun was just beginning to set, “you could use a little more wonder in your life.”

“Wonder?” I echoed, incredulous. “You think I’ve got time for wonder?”

She didn’t answer right away, her gaze fixed on the glowing sky. Then she turned back to me, her expression softer than I expected. “Maybe not. But that doesn’t mean you don’t need it.”

The words hit harder than I cared to admit, lodging themselves somewhere I couldn’t shake. I stared ahead, refusing to let her see how much she’d gotten under my skin. But as we took the road back to town, her words stayed with me, echoing in the rhythm of the horse’s hooves.

Maybe it isn’t wonder that I need, Sadie Miller. Maybe it’s you.

Chapter Six

Sadie

The store buzzed with the familiar sounds of the afternoon—the low murmur of neighbors swapping stories near the counter, the occasional clink of coins on the register, and the soft shuffle of feet over worn wooden floors. The scent of fresh bread mingled with the earthy sweetness of molasses, wrapping the space in its usual comforting embrace. I stood perched on a ladder near the back wall, carefully rearranging jars on the top shelf to make room for the new shipment. The task required focus, but my mind kept drifting to…

Caleb Stoltzfus.

It had been three days since our delivery "adventure," and somehow, he was still taking up far too much space in my thoughts. I'd replayed every moment—his gruff words, the way he'd hoisted me into the buggy with a care that seemed so at odds with his surly demeanor, and that one fleeting expression I couldn't quite name when Esther had fawned over him. It wasn't interest, I was sure of that. But it wasn't indifference, either. The next time Esther wandered into this store, I might be hard-pressed to be nice to her.

I sighed, balancing a jar of honey precariously as I leaned forward. Caleb was… a puzzle. And not the easy kind with a picture of kittens on the box, but one of those impossible ones where half the pieces were missing and the picture made no sense.

He was so guarded, so determined to keep the world at arm's length. And yet, every now and then, he let something slip—a gesture, a glance, a word—that hinted at something more. Something that left me wondering if there was a reason he kept those walls so high. And why I couldn't seem to stop wanting to climb them.

The clatter of buggy wheels jolted me out of my thoughts. I glanced toward the window just in time to see the Stoltzfus buggy pulling up outside. Almost as if my stray thoughts had conjured the man, my heart skipped a beat as Caleb stepped down, his hat tilted low, one hand clutching a small bag. He moved with the same deliberate precision he always did, like he'd rather be anywhere else but was too honorable to turn away from a duty.

I froze, my grip tightening on the honey jar. Of course, Caleb would show up now, when I was perched ten feet off the ground, looking every bit as red, unkempt, and flustered as I felt inside. As my mouth twisted at the state of my apron and *kapp*, his broad shoulders caught the sunlight as he paused, scanning the storefront like he was bracing himself for battle. And then he walked through the door and the bell jingled.

"Afternoon," he said, his voice low and even, carrying just enough weight to pull every head in the room toward him.

I managed to squeak out a polite, "Afternoon, Caleb," before my foot slipped. The ladder wobbled beneath me, jars rattling ominously as my balance faltered.

"Whoa!" His bag hit the floor with a thud as he crossed the room in two strides, his hands gripping my waist just as I started to tip backward. The world tilted, and then his arms were around me, steady and solid, pulling me upright before I could crash to the ground.

I stared up at him, breathless, my hands braced against his shoulders. His eyes, those stormy gray eyes, locked onto mine for one unguarded moment. "Careful, Sadie," he murmured, his voice quieter now, almost... gentle.

Heat bloomed in my cheeks as I scrambled to regain composure, but his hands lingered for just a second longer than necessary, steadying me before he let go.

"Oh, my," I managed, my voice sounding far too soft for my liking. "*Denke*."

He only grunted in response, stepping back and retrieving his bag from the floor.

The silence between us stretched, charged with something I couldn't quite name. I should've said something light, something teasing, but for once, the words wouldn't come. Because for all his gruffness, for all his carefully constructed walls, Caleb Stoltzfus had just caught me like I was someone worth saving.

And that, more than anything, left me unsteady.

With his lips pressed tightly together, he didn't even glance at anyone. His gaze locked onto me like I was the only obstacle between him and his exit. So much for us having a moment. It must have all been in my imagination.

"You forgot this," he said, handing the bag to me.

I blinked. "I... oh!" Recognition dawned. That must've fallen out during our delivery trip. "Well, I appreciate you coming all this way to bring it back." I set the jar down and brushed my hands on my apron.

"I'm not," he muttered. "I just don't like things out of place."

"Of course not," I replied, unable to resist poking the bear. "It'd be a crime against Ordnung to have even the tiniest of messes."

He scowled, and the corners of my mouth twitched. Caleb's scowls were practically a second language, and I had become fluent in them. This one meant nothing, really. He was simply uncomfortable.

"So, I guess I'll be going now," he said, clearly eager to leave.

"Wait just a second. Since you're here, Caleb." I dragged out his name for good measure, "You can tell me how you liked being my delivery partner the other day. I mean... just in case I ever need another one."

His eyes narrowed, and for a moment, I thought he was about to bite back. But instead, he sighed, long and low, like he was resigned to my antics. "It was fine."

"Fine?" I pressed. "That's all I get? Not even a sliver of a compliment?"

"*Nee.*" He adjusted the strap on his suspenders, his jaw tightening. "Just fine."

I leaned on the counter, watching him like he was the most interesting thing in the room. Because, frankly, he was. Caleb Stoltzfus, always so serious, so determined to avoid joy like it was a sickness he might catch. And yet, there he was, bringing me back a forgotten item. Maybe he wasn't immune to a little human decency after all.

The thought made me grin, but I quickly covered it with a cough. "Well, I appreciate it, Caleb. Your kindness is noted. I'll be sure to write a hymn about it. And sing it. Loudly."

He rolled his eyes, but I swore, there was the tiniest twitch at the corner of his mouth. Maybe. Or maybe I was just imagining it.

Caleb shifted on his feet, clearly debating whether to stay long enough to respond or bolt out the door. The latter seemed more his style, but something held him in place. Maybe it was my grin, or maybe he was just too polite to walk out mid-conversation.

"You know, Caleb," I started, leaning against the counter with exaggerated ease, "you might actually enjoy conversing with more people."

He let out a short, humorless laugh. "And why would I do that?"

"Because it's good for the soul." I gestured to the people chatting around us. "You could start small. A smile here, a wave there."

Caleb's eyes flicked toward the nearest cluster of neighbors, then back to me. "I'll think about it," he said flatly, which was Caleb-speak for "never in a million years."

Before I could tease him further, the door swung open again, and in marched Edna Zook, a force of nature if there ever was one. Her *kapp* was tied tightly under her chin, and her sharp eyes scanned the store like she was on a mission.

"Well, if it isn't Caleb Stoltzfus," she said, her tone sweet but with an edge that made my stomach twist. "And Sadie Miller, of course. What a... pleasant *surprise* to see you two here together."

"Good afternoon, Edna," I said brightly, trying to preempt whatever she was about to unleash. Caleb just nodded, his jaw tightening as if he was bracing for impact. Then he actually stepped backward a few steps to place even more space between us.

Edna wasted no time. "I was just over at the Schrock place, and would you believe the things they're saying about the pig chase last week? Your *bruder*, Levi, couldn't wait to tell the story. I've heard it's the talk of the whole district. And you, Caleb, diving into the manure pile like a true hero! Perhaps you should step back even further, my boy, I doubt the stench has truly been washed away yet!" To make it even more dramatic, the woman tipped forward and took a huge breath, expanding her nostrils much like a bull might do. Then she flicked her wrist and waved her hand through the air. "Why, you're practically a breeding ground for bacteria!"

I stifled a laugh, but Caleb's ears turned red. He crossed his arms over his chest, clearly not in the mood for Edna's brand of storytelling.

"That was last week," he said gruffly. "Old news. And Levi should stop running his mouth."

"Oh, but these things stick, Caleb," Edna retorted with a pointed smile. "People love a good story, especially when it involves one of Grace Hollow's most eligible bachelors. What will all the young women say? What if you were courting one of our lovely young ladies and showed up to her doorstep covered in pig poop!"

I almost dropped the jar in my hand. Eligible bachelor? Caleb Stoltzfus? Sure, he was tall and handsome in a brooding, lumberjack kind of way, but Edna talking about that and poop in the same conversation? For a second, I found it hard to keep my composure.

"Edna," I said quickly, hoping to steer her away from whatever embarrassing turn this conversation was about to take, "how can we help you today? Need anything special?"

She waved me off, clearly more interested in stirring the pot. "Oh, nothing right now, dear. Just stopping by to see who's around. Always good to keep an ear to the ground, you know."

Caleb's hands clenched into fists at his sides, and I could tell he was two seconds away from bolting. Before he could, Edna leaned in closer, her voice conspiratorial. "And Sadie, dear, have you thought about who you might consider courting? You're not getting any younger."

I froze, my face burning the moment Edna turned the tables on me. Caleb stiffened beside me, and the air between us felt suddenly too heavy to breathe.

The older woman's question hung in the air, the awkwardness between Caleb and me growing thicker by the second. I couldn't even manage a polite laugh, my brain scrambling for a response that wouldn't dig this hole any deeper. Caleb's stoic expression didn't help—his jaw was tight, his eyes fixed somewhere above Edna's shoulder, as if staring hard enough might make her disappear.

Before either of us said something we'd regret, my *dat* stepped out from the back room, his presence as calming as a midday prayer. "Good afternoon, Edna," he said with his signature smile, his hands dusted with flour. "What brings you by today?"

"Just checking in." Edna's eyes darted between Caleb and me like a cat watching a bird. "You know, making sure everyone's keeping busy. Idle hands are the devil's workshop, you know."

Dat gave a small chuckle, his warm tone effectively smoothing the edges of her pointed words. "Busy, indeed. Sadie's been running the store like clockwork, and from what I overheard, Caleb here was kind enough to return something she left behind during deliveries the other day. Not much to see here."

"I heard about these two making *deliveries* together." Edna perked up at this, her eyebrows raised in a way that made me wish *Dat* had phrased that differently. "It's so thoughtful of Caleb to step in and help," she crooned, her gaze sharpening on him. "It's good to see young men taking responsibility these days."

Caleb shifted uncomfortably, his hand flexing at his side like he was itching to grab the buggy reins and leave. "It was nothing," he muttered, his voice low. "I would do the same for anyone I know."

"And yet," Edna began, her tone dripping with curiosity, but *Dat* didn't let her finish.

"Well, we're grateful all the same." He stepped forward as if to physically block Edna from any further questioning. "And I know you're busy yourself, Edna. Always so much to do in a town like ours."

Edna's mouth opened slightly, as if she wasn't sure whether to be flattered or dismissed. She straightened her *kapp* with a sniff, then glanced at me. "Sadie, dear, always a pleasure. And Caleb," she added, her tone taking on a coy edge, "don't let these chores keep you too long. A man should have time for himself now and then. And the young ladies would like to see more of you. Especially, that Esther King. You would do well to take my words to heart. You're not getting any younger either. Time to set an example for your five *bruders*."

Caleb gave a polite nod, and Edna finally swept out the door, her head held high as if she'd just accomplished some grand mission.

The silence she left behind felt like a balm, and *Dat* patted Caleb on the shoulder, his easy smile returning. "She can be… persistent. But it's always a wise idea to respect your elders whether they deserve it or not. *Gott* would approve of your restraint."

"I try my best," Caleb replied, his voice still gruff but tinged with the faintest hint of humor.

Dat turned to me, his eyes twinkling. "Sadie, you've got things handled here, right?"

"Of course, *Dat*."

Caleb cleared his throat, looking anywhere but at me. "Well. That was… something."

I nodded, not trusting myself to speak. My heart thumped louder than I would have liked as I reach for something—anything—to say that wouldn't make this moment feel as charged as it did.

Before I could say more, the door creaked open, and my best friend, Becca, strolled in, her ever-present basket swinging at her side. She paused mid-step, her gaze locking onto Caleb with the kind of glee that made me brace myself.

"Well, well," Becca said, her voice dripping with amusement. "What's this? Caleb Stoltzfus in the General Store on a social visit? Stop the presses."

"It's not a social visit," Caleb replied flatly, his tone as sharp as the edge of a shovel.

Becca's grin widened as she walked toward us. "Could've fooled me. You're standing still, talking to Sadie. That's more socializing than I've seen you do in a month."

"Then you're not paying attention," Caleb muttered, his ears already starting to redden again.

Becca leaned her elbows on the counter, her basket swinging lazily from her arm as she turned her attention to me. "Sadie, dear, has Caleb always been this charming, or is he saving his best for you?"

"Oh, he's just warming up," I replied, biting back a grin as I caught Caleb's narrowed glare. "Give him a minute, and he might even string more than one sentence together."

"I doubt it," Caleb deadpanned.

Becca's eyebrows shot up. "A bag? Caleb's bringing you bags now? My, my, things are getting serious."

Caleb's jaw tightened as I tied the drawstring and flopped it on the counter behind me, my cheeks warming at Becca's teasing. "It's just something I left in the buggy that I was supposed to deliver to Mrs. Schultz," I explained quickly, pulling out the jar of jam. "Caleb was helping me after *Dat's* buggy broke a wheel. No need to make a fuss."

"No fuss at all." Becca's tone dripped with mock innocence. "It's not every day Caleb goes out of his way to make a special delivery. You should be flattered, Sadie."

Caleb groaned, rubbing the back of his neck. "I didn't go out of my way. I was already passing by."

"Of course you were," Becca said, her grin as wide as ever. "And I'm sure the thought of seeing Sadie had nothing to do with it."

"Becca!" I hissed, mortified, but she just waved me off.

"Oh, don't 'Becca' me," she teased, her blue eyes twinkling. "I'm just saying what everyone's thinking."

"I highly doubt that," Caleb muttered, his gaze firmly fixed on the floorboards as if they might offer him an escape route.

Becca straightened, her basket swinging as she headed toward the shelves. "Well, don't let me interrupt. I'll just grab what I need and leave you two to... whatever this is."

"Nothing," Caleb said quickly. "This is *nothing*."

Becca threw a sly look over her shoulder. "If you say so, Caleb."

As Becca wandered off toward the shelves, I could finally feel my heartbeat slowing. Caleb stood there like a statue, his jaw tight and his hands shoved into his pockets. I had half a mind to apologize for Becca's teasing, but I wasn't sure how much more awkward I could make things before he bolted.

"*Ach*, wait!" Becca spun back around, her yellow dress twirling, and her basket swinging dangerously close to a display of pickled beets. "I nearly forgot. Mrs. Fisher from Hearthside Remedies sent me with something for you, Caleb. She spotted your buggy outside and figured she'd save you a trip."

His brows furrowed. "I was going there next," he grumbled.

"But why would you need to when I can hand-deliver it to you in person?" Becca chirped, clearly enjoying herself. She plucked a small package from her basket and extended it toward Caleb, her grin practically daring him to refuse.

Reluctantly, he took it, muttering a quiet "*denke*" before shoving it into the pocket of his pants.

And that's when it happened.

The bag tipped slightly in his haste, and out tumbled a small, very conspicuous tube.

I would know that label from Amish Origins anywhere. Caleb Stoltzfus had special ordered...

Hemorrhoid cream.

Time froze. My face went red-hot, and Caleb's turned a color that might've rivaled the jar of pickled beets Becca had just passed. The room was silent for all of two seconds before Becca doubled over in laughter.

"Oh, no," I whispered, crouching down to snatch up the tube before Caleb could. "Here, let me—"

"I've got it!" he snapped, his voice an octave lower than usual as he swiped it out of my hand, his movements frantic.

Becca gasped between laughs, barely managing to stand upright. "Well, Caleb Stoltzfus, if I didn't know better, I'd say you've been keeping secrets! Is this what you've been up to during your 'busy' days?"

"Enough, Becca," I said firmly, glaring at her while Caleb stood frozen, his mortification radiating off him in waves. "It's none of your business. Mrs. Fisher shouldn't have even given you Caleb's package."

Becca's honey-blonde hair bounced underneath her *kapp*. "Oh, but it's everyone's business now."

The door creaked open, and who else but Edna Zook strolled back in, her eagle eyes immediately zeroing in on the scene. "Sadie, I forgot that I needed a loaf of that Sourdough bread I like so much. Why is everyone being so quiet? Why does Caleb look like a Beefsteak Tomato?" With all the couth of an elephant stomping on peanuts, she leaned down to a giggling little boy near her and asked him what had happened. Then her sharp gasp echoed through the store. "What is this? Caleb Stoltzfus, don't tell me—oh, dear me. I didn't think young men needed such things. Are you ill? You, young man, must start to eat more fiber. Post haste!"

"*Nee*," Caleb ground out, clutching the cream to his chest like it held state secrets. "I'm fine."

"Fine? Well, this doesn't look fine to me!" Edna declared, her voice rising with every word. She tapped her pointer finger to her temple. "Did you strain yourself when you fell in the manure pile?"

"Edna, really—" I began, but she was already gesturing wildly toward the counter.

"Sadie, dear, have you been feeding this poor boy something that disagrees with him? Surely a man his age doesn't—"

"*Bitte*, stop!" Caleb barked, his face the deepest shade of crimson I'd ever seen.

Edna clucked her tongue, clearly unimpressed with his outburst, but Becca only howled louder, her laughter reaching new heights as she leaned against the counter for support.

I stepped forward, determined to salvage what was left of Caleb's dignity. "Becca, help Edna with her shopping. Caleb and I have things to finish here."

Becca wiped her eyes, smirking. "Sure thing, Sadie. But I'll be thinking of this all day. I'm so glad Mrs. Fisher sent me on this particular errand."

As Edna and Becca drifted toward the shelves, I turned back to Caleb. His shoulders were stiff, his expression one of pure misery.

"Here," I said softly, tugging on the sleeve of his shirt. "Let me walk you out to your buggy."

He hesitated, his grip tightening on the cream, but after a moment, he relented with a stiff nod and shoved it back into his pocket. Together, we walked toward the door, his silence heavy with unspoken words. I didn't press him, but I couldn't shake the ache in my chest at the thought of how deeply embarrassed he must feel. For all his grumpiness, Caleb didn't deserve this. Not any of it.

As we reached the buggy, I placed a hand on the seat, steadying myself. "For what it's worth, Caleb, I don't think anyone's going to remember this tomorrow."

He gave a short, humorless laugh, climbing into the buggy without looking at me. "You're wrong, Sadie. I can't ever catch a break. They'll remember."

And then, just as quickly as he'd arrived, he was gone, leaving me standing in the dust with a strange, hollow feeling I couldn't quite name.

Chapter Seven

CALEB

The laughter hit me first, a steady hum of voices blending with the clink of dishes and the soft humming of a hymn. The community gathering was already in full swing, and the whole of Grace Hollow had turned out for it. Long wooden tables stretched across the grassy clearing, laden with pies of every variety—apple, cherry, shoofly, you name it. The scents mingled with the crisp spring air, a mix of sweetness and earthiness that should've felt comforting. But instead, I stood on the sidelines, wishing I were anywhere else.

I leaned against the edge of one of the tables, scanning the crowd with what I assumed was my usual neutral expression—at least, that's what I told myself. I could vow and oath that everyone was staring at me. And laughing. But then they turned away before I could say anything. Truthfully, my jaw was tight, and my shoulders were stiff enough to make the bishop worry I was hiding some kind of ailment.

Sadie Miller's laugh rang out somewhere near the dessert tables, and my eyes betrayed me, seeking her out like I hadn't already seen enough of her this week. She was surrounded, of course—people drawn to her like moths to a flame. Her *kapp* was tied neatly under her chin, her smile brighter than the sun glinting off the plates of molasses cookies. She was in her element, wearing her pretty pink dress, and darting between neighbors like a hummingbird, greeting everyone with that warm, easy way of hers.

I looked away before she could catch me watching. It wasn't the first time I'd caught myself noticing her lately, and I didn't like the direction my thoughts had been taking.

Her kindness had been a simple thing—handing me back that blasted cream, her hands quick and steady, her voice soft enough to strip me bare. It wasn't the teasing or the laughter from Becca or Edna that had stuck with me; it was the way sweet Sadie had crouched beside me, eyes earnest, as if she could sense how much I hated the spotlight on my misstep. There was no judgment in her, no sharp edge to her humor when she realized how mortified I was. Just a quiet, grounding presence that felt like being seen without having to say a word.

Sadie was soft in a way I didn't think I deserved—like a patch of sunlight I'd wandered into by mistake. I'd spent years building walls around myself, locking everything away in a place no one could reach. It wasn't hard to do when people didn't bother to try. But she didn't knock on those walls; she slipped through the cracks, laughing as she went. And now, standing here with the sound of that laugh drifting over the crowd, I couldn't stop thinking about how her light had lingered in places I thought I'd sealed off for good.

And most importantly, I didn't want to *ruin* her with my grumpy ways.

"Still brooding, are you?"

Jonah's voice came from over my shoulder, easy and familiar. My best friend clapped me on the back as he joined me, his grin wide and teasing as always. Jonah had been my confidante since we were boys, though the two of us couldn't be more different if we tried. Where I was quiet and steady,

Jonah was the kind of man who could walk into a room and leave with ten new friends.

I shook my head, exhaling sharply. "I'm not brooding."

"Sure, you're not." He leaned against the table beside me, his grin turning sly. "Thinking about the cream incident, aren't you? *Jah*, I heard about that."

My stomach dropped. I shot him a warning glare. "Don't start."

Jonah just laughed, not even bothering to hide his amusement. "*Ach*, Caleb, it's not so bad. It's natural to have issues with your health. Half the town's forgotten already."

"Half's still too many," I muttered. My hand flexed at my side, the memory of Edna's smug smirk making my skin crawl. "And I don't need you reminding me."

He raised his hands in mock surrender, his grin never faltering. "Alright, alright. But you've got to admit, it was funny."

"It wasn't."

Jonah chuckled, his eyes scanning the crowd. "You know, maybe you'd feel better if you stopped lurking in the shadows and joined the fun. It wouldn't hurt you to socialize. If you weren't so stodgy, when things like that happened, people would just laugh with you instead of at you."

"I socialize plenty," I replied flatly.

"Sure you do. With me and your *bruders*."

His comment hit harder than it should have, but I didn't let it show. Instead, I crossed my arms and focused on the tables in front of me, wishing for once that Jonah would just let things be.

Jonah was still grinning like he'd just told the best joke of his life when his name was called from across the clearing. He straightened, throwing me a knowing look. "Duty calls. Don't brood yourself into the ground, Caleb. All the young ladies are here tonight. And they're watching."

"I don't brood," I muttered, but Jonah was already weaving through the crowd, his laughter trailing after him.

I shook my head, grateful for the reprieve. Jonah meant well, but sometimes his relentless cheerfulness was exhausting. I turned back to the table, my gaze wandering over the sea of familiar faces, wishing for a quiet corner where I could wait out this gathering in peace.

"*Ach*, there you are," came a familiar, gentle voice. I looked up to find my *grossmamm*, Eliza, approaching with a steady gait and her ever-present smile.

"*Grossmamm*," I greeted, standing a little straighter. Her presence always had that effect on me—like I was a boy again, caught with muddy boots in the house.

She came to my side, leaning lightly on the cane she refused to fully depend on. "Why are you hiding over here, *liebling*? You look like a storm cloud waiting to break."

I sighed, glancing around to make sure no one was listening. "Just trying to stay out of trouble."

Her sharp blue eyes narrowed, full of the wisdom that always made me feel like she could see right through me. "Trouble, or people?"

"Perhaps a bit of both," I admitted, though my tone had softened.

She chuckled, a sound as warm as fresh bread straight from the oven. "Caleb, you've been like this since you were a boy—so serious. Always taking everything on yourself, always trying to shoulder the world. But no one expects you to do that, you know. Not your *mamm* or your *dat*. And certainly not me."

I didn't respond right away, the weight of her words settling uncomfortably in my chest. She reached out, her hand lightly resting on my arm, her touch grounding me in a way few things could.

"I know you feel responsible for so much," she continued, her voice quieter now, meant only for me. "And that's not a bad thing. But you have to leave room for joy, *liebling*. You can't pour from an empty pitcher."

I looked away, her words hitting too close to home. "It's not that simple, *grossmamm*. Someone has to keep things steady. Our *haus* is so... chaotic."

"Steady doesn't mean joyless," she said, her tone firmer now. "And it doesn't mean shutting people out. You're a good man, Caleb, but don't let the weight you carry keep you from seeing what's right in front of you."

Her gaze flicked to something—or someone—behind me, and when I turned to look, my stomach tightened. Sadie was across the clearing, laughing with a group of neighbors as she balanced a plate of desserts in one hand. Her smile was like sunlight breaking through clouds, and for a moment, I couldn't look away.

When I turned back, *grossmamm* was watching me with a knowing glint in her eye.

"You don't have to do it all alone," she said softly. "And maybe it's time you stopped trying."

I nodded, swallowing against the lump in my throat. "As always, I will take your words to heart."

She patted my arm again, her smile tinged with a sadness that made my chest ache. "*Gut*. Now, go on and enjoy yourself. I'll be around if you need me."

As she moved away, I stayed rooted to the spot, her words echoing in my mind. Maybe it was time I stopped trying to carry everything on my own. But letting go? Letting someone in? That was easier said than done.

The brief calm my *grossmamm* brought me didn't last long. Just as I was about to make a beeline for the edge of the gathering, where a quiet bench promised some much-needed solitude, Sadie's laugh rang out over the hum of the crowd, followed closely by another familiar voice.

"Well, if it isn't Caleb Stoltzfus himself, looking as cheerful as a thundercloud."

I turned to find Sadie's best friend, Becca, striding toward me with her usual unshakable confidence. Her basket swung on her arm, and her teasing grin was already in full force.

"Becca," I greeted, bracing myself for the verbal sparring match she seemed to relish every time our paths crossed.

"Don't 'Becca' me with that stoic tone," she shot back, coming to a stop beside Sadie, who looked entirely too amused by my discomfort. "I heard you've been making waves around Grace Hollow. That little incident at the General Store? I think the story's already traveled three counties over."

I froze, my stomach dropping. "What?"

Sadie winced, though her lips twitched as if she was fighting back a grin. "Don't mind her, Caleb. She's just here to stir the pot."

"Oh, I'm not stirring," Becca said, her eyes sparkling with mischief. "I'm merely pointing out that Edna Zook has been quite chatty about a certain... medicinal discovery. She can't shut up about it. And you know what happens when she sinks her teeth into a particular topic."

Heat crept up my neck as I clenched my jaw. "Edna needs a new hobby."

Sadie stepped in, trying to defuse the situation. "Come on, Becca. Leave him be. It's not like Caleb's the first person to need... you know..."

Becca snorted. "Oh, you're defending him now? This just gets better."

Before I could muster a response that wouldn't dig me deeper into the hole Edna had apparently excavated for me, a hand clapped onto my shoulder.

"*Ach*, there he is! The man of the hour!" Levi's voice boomed, drawing attention from nearby groups. "How's the cream working for you, *bruder*? I haven't seen you sit down yet, so I'm still pretty concerned."

I turned, my glare sharp enough to cut wood. "Levi."

He grinned, completely unfazed. "What? I'm just checking in. It's important to support family in times of need."

Sadie made a strangled sound that might've been a laugh, while Becca outright cackled, her shoulders shaking with mirth.

"Levi, you are not helping," Sadie said, though the corners of her mouth betrayed her struggle to stay serious.

"Oh, I think I am," Levi replied, winking at her. "After all, we wouldn't want Caleb's... condition... to go untreated."

"That's enough," I growled, my voice low.

But my younger brother wasn't done. "Just let me know if you need another run to Hearthside Remedies. I can put it on my tab. Just don't ask me to apply it for you."

Sadie lost her battle then, her laughter spilling out as she clutched her sides. Becca was nearly doubled over, tears in her eyes.

And me? I stood there, face burning, plotting Levi's demise. The only solace was Sadie's attempt to defend me—even if she couldn't stop laughing.

By the time my most annoying family member wandered off, likely to spread his nonsense to another corner of the gathering, I was ready to disappear. But before I could make my escape, Sadie stepped into my path, her grin still lingering but softer now.

"You know," she said, tilting her head, "you could crack a smile just once. Laugh with me, Caleb. I know you can."

"I'm smiling on the inside," I muttered, though I knew the words lacked any real conviction.

Sadie's brow lifted. "Oh, really? Because your face doesn't seem to have gotten the message."

"Not everyone finds joy in these... social events," I replied, crossing my arms. The crowd buzzed around us, voices rising and falling like waves. "Or the humiliation of other people. Some of us have better things to do."

"Like what?" she asked, her eyes sparkling with challenge. "Sulking? Glowering at your *bruders*?"

"Farming," I said firmly. "Chores don't do themselves."

Sadie stepped closer, and I could feel the warmth of her presence, disarming in a way that made me itch to take a step back. But I didn't. She leaned in, lowering her voice like she was about to share some grand secret. "Well, Caleb Stoltzfus, I dare you to try something different today."

"What's that supposed to mean?" I asked, already regretting engaging her.

"Smile," she said simply, her lips curving into one of her own. "At me."

The need to give in was almost overwhelming, like a dam about to burst. She didn't just smile; she radiated. And I wanted to be the reason for it—wanted to see that light aimed squarely at me, to feel like I'd done something right for once. I wanted to indulge her, to give her the world if it meant keeping that look in her eyes. But how? How could I give her something I barely understood myself? My life was made of lines and rules, of responsibilities that didn't leave room for warmth or laughter. *Gott*, work, family. Sadie deserved more than a man who carried his burdens like a second skin. She deserved someone who could match her joy, not someone who might snuff it out without meaning to.

I blinked the urge away. "That's ridiculous."

"Oh, come on," she teased, hands on her hips. "What's the harm? I'll even make it worth your while."

"I'm not interested," I said quickly, but the curiosity in my tone betrayed me.

Sadie's grin widened. "If you manage to smile before the end of the gathering, I'll bake you a pie. Any kind you want. Apple, blueberry, shoofly... You name it. From my hands to your lips."

A pie? Of all the things to bet on, she'd chosen pie. I stared at her, trying to gauge whether she was serious, but the twinkle in her eyes left no doubt. "You're out of your mind."

"Maybe," she said cheerfully. "But I'm not backing down. What do you say?"

I hesitated, glancing around. People milled about, too caught up in their own conversations to notice ours, but that wouldn't last long if Sadie kept up her antics. And there was a small part of me—buried deep—that didn't want to disappoint her.

"I'm not making any promises," I muttered.

"That works for me," she said, clapping her hands together. "Now, let's see what you've got, Sherrif."

"Stop calling me that," I grumbled, turning away before she could see the heat rising to my cheeks. Because when it came down to it, I wish she would call me something else. Something more... personal.

Sadie just laughed, the sound light and easy, trailing after me like sunshine on my back. As much as I hated to admit it, I was already losing this ridiculous bet. Not because I wanted the pie, but because her laughter had a way of doing the impossible—making me feel like maybe I could smile after all.

"I'm going to get some lemonade," I told her, turning away.

I made it about three steps before Jonah caught up with me, his grin a mirror image of Sadie's. "So, she's asking you to smile at her? That's new. Most girls understand such a quest is really an exercise in futility."

"I didn't agree to it," I muttered, though my ears felt uncomfortably warm. "And don't you have anything better to do?"

"Not a chance." Jonah fell into step beside me, his stride annoyingly relaxed. "This is too good to miss. Sadie Miller betting you, the most serious man in Grace Hollow, to crack a smile? This'll be talked about for weeks. I should see if anyone is taking side bets. Not monetary, of course. Bishop Yoder wouldn't approve of that."

"Not if I have anything to say about it," I grumbled. The gathering had grown livelier, the hum of conversation mingling with the clinking of dishes and bursts of laughter. The scent of cinnamon and apples from the dessert table carried on the breeze, mingling with the faint lilt of a woman's voice in the distance.

Jonah elbowed me. "Come on, Caleb. You've got to admit, it's kind of funny."

"Nothing about this is funny," I said flatly, though the corner of my mouth twitched in betrayal. "I like to be a small fish in a large pond. Going unnoticed." But Jonah noticed, of course. He always noticed.

"*Ach*, there it is!" he crowed, pointing dramatically. "A smile. Barely there, but it counts."

"Stop it." I swatted his hand away. But my tone lacked the heat to make it stick. Jonah just chuckled, shaking his head.

"Unlike most people around here, I can remember what your true smile looks like. When we were boys, it never left your face. Sadie's good for you, you know," he said after a moment, his voice quieter. "Not many people can get under your skin like she does. I think she's making you grow into a better man."

"She doesn't—" I started, but Jonah's knowing look stopped me short.

"Relax," he said, his grin returning. "I'm not suggesting anything. Just... noticing."

I let out a breath, grateful when the sound of someone clearing their throat nearby saved me from further conversation. Becca stood a few feet away, a plate of cookies in her hand and a mischievous glint in her eye.

"Don't let me interrupt," she said sweetly. "I just wanted to make sure Caleb knows I'm rooting for him. A pie is a high-stakes prize, after all."

Jonah snorted, and I shot him a warning glance before turning back to Becca. "I don't need anyone rooting for me."

"Sure you don't," she said, her smile widening. "But you'd better start practicing. Sadie's not one to back down."

"Apparently not," I muttered, wishing I could disappear into the ground. But Sadie's laughter carried over to where we stood, drawing my gaze despite myself. She was talking with a group of women near the dessert table, her face bright and animated as she gestured.

"She really is something, isn't she?" Becca said, her tone softer now. "She's the best friend anyone could ask for. Kind, considerate, patient."

I didn't respond, my throat tightening. Becca didn't press, just handed Jonah the cookies and walked off, leaving me standing there, more aware than ever of the impossible challenge Sadie had set for me—and the way she made me feel like it wasn't so impossible after all.

Sadie's laughter rang out again, the kind that seemed to weave through the air and settle right under my skin. I gritted my teeth and turned away, determined to focus on anything else—the pies on the tables, the clouds overhead, Jonah stuffing a cookie into his mouth like he hadn't eaten in days.

But no matter where I looked, I couldn't shake the feeling that Sadie was everywhere. Her presence was like the sunlight at dawn—soft but insistent, seeping through cracks I didn't even know existed. And for the first time in what felt like forever, I wasn't entirely sure I wanted to block it out.

"I'll tell you one thing," Jonah said around a mouthful of cookie, his tone teasing. "If you lose this bet, I expect you to bake her a pie in return. And trust me, Caleb, no one in this town would let you live that down."

I glared at him, but his words planted a seed of dread in my chest. It wasn't about the pie, though. It was about the simple truth that I was losing ground where Sadie Miller was concerned—and fast. She was too much for me, too bright, too full of life. And yet, she made me want things I'd buried a long time ago. Things I didn't even have names for anymore.

"Jonah, go torment someone else," I muttered, shoving my hands into my pockets as I moved toward the edge of the gathering. I needed distance, a chance to breathe. But even as I tried to escape, my gaze betrayed me, flickering back to where she stood, her eyes alight with mischief as she crowned someone else with a flower from the pies. The sight shouldn't have bothered me, but it did. It left a strange ache in my chest, one I couldn't seem to ignore.

Sadie must've noticed me lingering near the dessert table, because before I knew it, she was beside me, holding a flower garnish from one of the pies. She waved it in front of my face like a victorious banner.

"Well?" she asked, her grin wide and expectant. "Don't think I didn't see that twitch earlier, Caleb Stoltzfus. It counts. A deal's a deal."

I frowned—or tried to. Her excitement made it impossible to muster a proper scowl. "It wasn't a smile," I argued, my voice lacking its usual sharp edge.

She rolled her eyes, undeterred. "Oh, it was close enough. But let's see if we can do better." With that, she placed the flower on my head like it was a crown, her giggle ringing out as she took a step back to inspect her work.

"Perfect," she declared, hands on her hips. "The King of Frowns has been dethroned."

I reached up to brush the flower away, but her laughter stopped me. It was warm, unrestrained, and... contagious. Before I knew it, my lips curved into something real, something genuine—a smile I hadn't felt in years. Sadie gasped, clapping her hands together like she'd just won a prize.

"There it is!" she exclaimed. "I knew you had it in you! And now," she added, her tone softer but no less triumphant, "I owe you that pie I promised. I will deliver it on Tuesday."

I shook my head, a mix of exasperation and something warmer curling in my chest. "You don't owe me anything, Sadie."

"Oh, but I do," she said, her smile softening into something more personal. "A promise is a promise, Caleb. And you earned this one fair and square. I know how hard that was for you."

Levi caught me then, his grin as sharp as a blade. "Don't think you're getting away that easily, big *bruder*. I totally saw you smile. With your whole face!"

I groaned. "Levi, not now."

"Not now?" he repeated, feigning shock. "*Ach*, Caleb, what could be more important than smiling for real? And winning a pie from a pretty girl, of course. Although," he added, his voice lowering conspiratorially, "you might want to make sure none of those flowers on your head are also ingredients in your holistic rear-end cream. I think I see some chamomile."

The laugh Jonah let out was loud enough to turn a few heads, and I shot Levi a look sharp enough to cut steel. "*Nee*, Levi. Just *nee*. Consider yourself disowned."

But even as I shook my head, a sliver of another smile threatened to break through. I hated it—how Sadie, Jonah, and even Levi could worm their way into my guarded thoughts, pushing and pulling me in ways I didn't know how to handle.

Tossing the flowers aside, I decided to walk home. And dream about a certain someone until Tuesday. Because that day couldn't come fast enough.

As I stalked toward the edge of the field, one thought echoed through my mind: I was in trouble. Deep trouble. Because no matter how much I tried to fight it, Sadie Miller was getting under my skin—and I wasn't sure I could stop her.

Chapter Eight

SADIE

The pie sat on the passenger seat of my buggy, wrapped neatly in a cloth napkin embroidered with tiny pink roses. The scent of cinnamon and butter filled the air, and I'd checked it three times to make sure it hadn't slid or smudged on the way over. It was perfect—golden, flaky, and fragrant. The kind of pie *Mamm* would say could win a blue ribbon at the county fair. And I'd made it just for Caleb Stoltzfus.

I let out a small sigh, gripping the reins tighter. Why did it matter so much? Why had I spent an extra half hour brushing flour off my *kapp* and apron before heading out? And why did my heart give a little flutter every time I thought about the way his face had softened when he'd smiled at me during the gathering?

That smile. It was like the sun breaking through storm clouds—unexpected, warm, and entirely too beautiful for a man who usually wore his frown like armor. I couldn't get it out of my head, no matter how hard I tried. Caleb Stoltzfus, smiling at me. The thought made my cheeks heat even now.

I pulled into the Stoltzfus farm, taking in the familiar sights. The barn stood tall and sturdy against the sky, with chickens clucking lazily around the yard. The fields stretched out beyond, a patchwork of green and gold, as if *Gott* Himself had painted the landscape. The solar panels that annoyed Edna Zook so much. It was a place that felt rooted, dependable—much like Caleb.

As I climbed down from the buggy, my stomach twisted with nerves. I shouldn't be this nervous. It was just a pie. Just Caleb. And yet, I found myself smoothing the wrinkles in my apron, taking an extra second to compose myself before heading toward the house.

The screen door creaked open, and Levi appeared, his grin as mischievous as ever. "Well, well, if it isn't Sadie Miller. Come to brighten Caleb's day again, have you?"

I shot him a look, though I couldn't help but smile. "I brought the pie. It's not for you, remember?"

"Not for me?" Levi clutched his chest dramatically. "*Ach*, Sadie, you wound me."

Even though Levi was closer to me in age, he didn't make my heart squeeze like Caleb did.

"Caleb earned it," I said, my voice light but firm. "And besides, you have plenty of your own admirers to bring you baked goods, don't you?"

Levi's laugh boomed as he held the door open. "Fair enough. He's in the barn. I'll let him know you're here. Don't let *Mamm* rope you into shelling peas—she's on the warpath today. Micah's helping her right now, and she's almost made him cry twice."

I stepped inside, my eyes adjusting to the cool dimness of the kitchen. Miriam Stoltzfus was at the counter, her hands busy kneading dough. She glanced up, her face lighting with a welcoming smile. "Sadie, dear. What a surprise! Are you here for Caleb?"

I nodded, holding up the pie. "Just keeping a promise."

"*Ach*, I heard about that." Her eyes twinkled as she waved me toward the porch. "He'll appreciate it more than he'll let on. Go on back out to the porch, dear. I'll fetch some lemonade for you both."

I settled into one of the rocking chairs, my heart racing as I heard Caleb's boots on the steps.

Caleb stepped onto the porch, his footfalls heavy on the wooden planks, and stopped short when he saw me sitting there. His gaze flicked to the pie in my lap, then back to my face. He looked like he'd rather wrestle a certain pig than deal with me at that moment.

"Um... it's Tuesday, isn't it?" Caleb's jaw tightened, and I caught the faintest twitch at the corner of his mouth, like he wasn't sure whether to frown or smile. "And you brought a pie."

"A pie," I confirmed, lifting it slightly. "Apple, as promised. Your favorite, if I remember correctly."

He hesitated, glancing back toward the barn as if he might find an escape route there. "You didn't have to go to all that trouble."

"It wasn't any trouble," I said quickly, feeling the heat rise in my cheeks. "I figured a man who smiles as rarely as you do deserves something sweet every now and then."

His eyes narrowed, though not in the usual irritated way. It was more like he was trying to figure me out, like I was some kind of puzzle he couldn't solve. "You're not going to let this go, are you?"

"Not a chance." I held out the pie. "Consider it a peace offering. Or a reward. Or both."

With a reluctant sigh, he took the pie from my hands, his calloused fingers brushing mine for just a second. The brief contact sent a jolt through me, and I quickly folded my hands in my lap to keep from fidgeting.

"It smells delicious." he offered after a moment, his tone awkward but genuine. "Would you like to stay for a glass of lemonade?"

"That would be lovely," I replied, surprised by the invitation. I half-expected him to take the pie, bolt back into the barn, and eat it like a caveman.

Caleb disappeared into the house, and I heard him exchange a few words with his *mamm* before returning with two glasses of lemonade. He handed one to me, then leaned against the porch railing, his posture stiff but his eyes softer than usual.

"So," he said, taking a sip, "what's your real reason for coming all this way?"

"Huh?" I tilted my head innocently. "Can't a woman bake a pie without some ulterior motive?"

"You could have just left it at the store for me," he said flatly, though there was a hint of humor in his voice. "Instead, you've got that look that you're up to something.."

I laughed, setting my glass on the table beside me. "Alright, you caught me. I do have something I want to talk to you about."

Caleb raised an eyebrow but said nothing, his silence urging me to continue.

"It's about a charity drive," I began, my voice softening. "I want to organize something for the less fortunate in the nearby towns—collecting goods, raising funds, that sort of thing. And I thought you might... want to help. Because of our partnership delivering things to our neighbors last week. We work well together."

His expression shifted immediately, the softness giving way to skepticism. "Me? Why?"

"Because you're reliable," I said simply. "And because I think you care more than you let on."

Caleb stared at me like I'd just asked him to hitch the buggy to the moon. "You've got the wrong person for this," he said, crossing his arms over his broad chest. "I'm not much for... community events. I'm afraid I'd only end up disappointing you."

I didn't falter, keeping my smile steady. "That's exactly why you're perfect for this role. No one would expect it."

"That's not a reason," he muttered, looking away as if the horizon might offer a better argument.

"It's a reason," I said brightly, leaning forward. "Besides, this isn't just a community event. It's a chance to help people who really need it. You care about that, don't you?"

His jaw tightened, and I could see the internal struggle playing out behind his eyes. Caleb Stoltzfus, the reluctant hero, never wanting to draw attention to himself but unable to completely ignore a plea for help. It was one of the things I admired about him, even if he'd deny it to the grave.

"You could ask anyone else," he said finally, his voice softer now. "Jonah, Levi—"

I cut him off with a shake of my head. "They don't have your organizational skills. Or your knack for getting things done. When you put your mind to something, Caleb, it happens. That's what this drive needs."

He shifted, his weight moving from one foot to the other as he considered my words. "You make it sound like I'm the only one who can do this."

"You might be," I said, my tone light but genuine. "Besides, you don't have to do it alone. I'll be there every step of the way, along with the other volunteers. It'll be fun—maybe even inspiring."

His lips twitched, but he didn't fully smile. "Fun isn't exactly my specialty."

"Well, then it's time you learned," I teased, taking a sip of my lemonade. "Think of it as an opportunity for personal growth."

Caleb huffed, his gaze dropping to the glass in his hand. "And what exactly am I supposed to do?"

I suppressed the triumphant grin threatening to break free. He might not have agreed yet, but he was close. "You'd be the logistics expert. Help figure out how we'll collect and distribute the donations, where to store them, how to spread the word."

"Logistics expert," he repeated, as if the words left a sour taste in his mouth. "That's just a fancy way of saying I'll be doing the heavy lifting, but not out front. Not the face of the effort."

"Right," I said quickly. "I'll handle the people. You'll handle the planning. A perfect partnership."

Caleb let out a long sigh, shaking his head. "You're not going to give up on this, are you?"

"*Nee*." I grinned. "And if you say *jah*, I'll even bake you another pie. Because after you have a slice of this one, you'll be begging me for more."

His eyes flicked to me, then away again, but not before I caught the faintest glimmer of something—amusement, maybe, or resignation. "Fine," he said at last. "But only because you won't leave me alone otherwise."

"Exactly." I raised my glass in mock celebration. "To teamwork."

He didn't raise his, but he didn't look away either.

The porch had grown quieter, the hum of the farm softening as the shadows stretched long across the yard. Caleb set his empty glass on the railing, his movements deliberate, as if stalling the inevitable.

"Alright," he said, his voice carrying a resigned weight. "If we're doing this, what's the first step?"

I tried not to beam too obviously. "Well, first, we'll need to figure out what we're collecting. Food, clothing, blankets—things that will make a real difference. Then we can start organizing drop-off points."

Caleb leaned against the railing, his brow furrowing as he considered my words. "Where do you plan to store everything? That much stuff will take up space."

I bit my lip, realizing I hadn't quite thought that part through. "The church basement, maybe? Or... well, I suppose that depends on how much we collect."

His frown deepened. "That's a detail you'll want to figure out before you start. It'll be chaos otherwise."

"Chaos?" I shot him a playful look. "You act like you've never seen me organize anything."

"I've seen you organize," he replied dryly. "And I've seen you... improvise."

I rolled my eyes but couldn't help smiling. "Fine. You're right. We'll nail down the logistics. That's why I need you."

Caleb shook his head, a reluctant chuckle escaping his lips. "You're relentless, Sadie."

"I prefer determined," I countered, jotting down notes in the small notebook I'd pulled from my apron pocket. "Now, what else? Oh, advertising! We'll need posters or maybe word-of-mouth at gatherings."

"Posters?" Caleb raised an eyebrow. "Are we running a charity drive or a political campaign?"

"Why not both?" I teased, nudging his arm lightly. "You'd make a great campaign manager."

He didn't laugh, but the corner of his mouth twitched again. Progress.

As we worked through the details, I couldn't help but notice how Caleb's focus shifted. The more we talked, the more engaged he became. He'd start with his usual gruff, pragmatic tone, pointing out potential issues, but then he'd offer solutions just as quickly. It was like watching gears turn in a well-oiled machine—steady, dependable, and, dare I say, inspiring.

I leaned forward, resting my elbows on the table between us. "See? You're a natural at this. I don't know why you always resist."

"Because it's easier," he said simply, not meeting my gaze. "Easier to keep things... uncomplicated."

I watched him, the way his shoulders carried an invisible weight, the way his jaw tightened as if bracing against something unseen. Caleb wasn't stoic out of strength—it was a shield designed to keep failure and embarrassment at bay. He was a perfectionist to the core, someone who would rather do nothing at all than risk doing something imperfectly. But life wasn't about staying in the safety of a well-ordered pen; it was about getting out in the world, facing the messy, unpredictable moments, and growing from the failures. Caleb didn't see that yet, but I wanted him to. I wanted him to understand that letting people in, letting himself stumble, didn't make him weak—it made him human. And maybe, it would make him happy, too.

"Well," I said softly, "this might be a little complicated, but it'll be worth it. You'll see."

He didn't reply, but the faintest flicker of something—hope, maybe—crossed his face. And that was enough for now.

Just as Caleb leaned back, clearly trying to draw our session to a close, the door creaked open, and a familiar voice drifted through the evening air.

"*Ach*, so this is where my *liebling* has been hiding," Eliza Stoltzfus said, stepping onto the porch with the grace only years of practice could give. She carried a basket of folded linens in one arm, her sharp eyes instantly taking in the scene. "Sadie, what a pleasant surprise."

I stood quickly, smoothing my apron. "Good evening, Eliza. I brought Caleb his pie, and we started discussing a charity drive for the community."

Her brows lifted with interest as she set the basket down on a nearby chair. “Charity drive? Now that sounds promising. And Caleb’s helping, is he?”

“He’s organizing,” I said, unable to resist the light jab as I shot Caleb a teasing look. “Turns out, he’s a natural at it.”

Caleb shifted, rubbing the back of his neck. “I wouldn’t go that far.”

“Nonsense,” Eliza said firmly, her smile warm but her tone leaving no room for argument. She crossed the porch to place a gentle hand on Caleb’s shoulder. “This community could use more young men like you, stepping up for something bigger than themselves.”

Caleb’s jaw tightened, but he didn’t pull away from her touch. “It was Sadie’s idea,” he muttered, his gaze falling to the floorboards.

“And you’re the one bringing her idea to life.” Elize glanced at me, her eyes twinkling. “The two of you make a fine team. Perhaps *Gott* had a hand in this, hm?”

Heat rushed to my cheeks, and I opened my mouth to reply, but Caleb beat me to it.

“We’re just planning a drive,” he said, his tone clipped but not unkind. “That’s all.”

Eliza chuckled softly, patting his arm. “Of course, *liebling*. But sometimes, *Gott’s* plans are bigger than our own. You’d do well to remember that.”

She turned her attention to me, her expression softening. “And you, Sadie—don’t let his grumpy ways fool you. He’s got a big heart under all that scowling.”

I nodded, unsure of what to say. Eliza had a way of making the simplest statements feel profound, and her words lingered in the air long after she stepped back inside, leaving Caleb and me alone again.

The silence stretched between us, heavy and charged. Caleb shifted in his seat, his hands resting on his knees as if preparing to stand.

"Well," he said finally, his voice low, "I suppose I should—"

"Let me get out of your way," I said quickly, standing and smoothing my dress.

"No, I meant—" Caleb started, but stopped, running a hand through his hair as he stood too.

"I mean, you've probably got chores," I added, trying to fill the awkward gap. "Lots of things to—"

"I wasn't saying—" he tried again, his brow furrowing.

We both stopped, staring at each other for a beat, the tension thick enough to choke on. Then, with a resigned sigh, Caleb gestured toward my buggy. "You should... uh... get going. Before it gets too late. I don't like the thought of you driving in the dark. *Denke* for the pie, Sadie."

"*Jah*, of course." I grabbed the notebook I'd brought as an excuse to stay longer. "I'll be in touch about the charity drive."

My heart thudded in my chest as I made my way to the buggy, acutely aware of his eyes on me. Caleb followed, his steps slow and deliberate, as if he were hesitating to see me off.

He opened the buggy door for me without a word, his hand brushing mine as I climbed in. The brief contact sent a little jolt through me, but I swallowed the feeling down, offering him a polite smile. "*Denke*."

Caleb nodded, his expression unreadable, and stepped back. "Drive safe."

"I always do," I replied, lifting the reins and clicking my tongue softly to signal my roan gelding.

The wheels creaked as the buggy pulled away, and I kept my gaze fixed on the road ahead, fighting the inexplicable urge to look back. But as the distance between us grew, I couldn't help myself. I glanced over my shoulder, half-expecting Caleb to have already gone inside.

Instead, he stood there, still and quiet, watching me leave. His face was softer than I'd ever seen it, the usual hardness of his features giving way to something unspoken. Something that made my chest tighten.

I didn't know what it was—sadness, regret, or maybe something else entirely. But for the first time, Caleb Stoltzfus looked like a man who didn't want to be left alone. And I couldn't shake the feeling that leaving him standing there was somehow the wrong choice.

Chapter Nine

CALEB

The community flower garden spread out before me, an explosion of color and order that somehow felt unnatural to me. Flowers weren't crops, and planting them didn't feel like work. But here I was, shovel in hand, standing on the edge of a freshly tilled patch of earth. *Mamm* had volunteered me and Levi for this "project," likely knowing full well I'd have preferred to be anywhere else. The sun was warm, the air thick with the mingling scents of soil and blossoms, but it didn't settle me the way the barn or fields did. This place hummed with a different kind of energy—one I wasn't sure how to handle.

I spotted Sadie almost immediately, of course. Her purple dress stood out against the greens and browns of the garden, her *kapp* starched perfectly as if she hadn't been sweating over marigolds all morning. She moved among the rows with an ease I couldn't even pretend to understand, a tray of seedlings balanced in one arm as she directed neighbors with her usual cheerfulness.

My grip on the shovel tightened as my thoughts drifted back to Tuesday, the day she'd brought me that apple pie. I'd watched her buggy drive away until it disappeared, wishing I'd had the guts to ask her to stay. Not just for another glass of lemonade or to sit a while longer on the porch. No, I'd wanted to ask her to stay in a way that was permanent, like the furniture in the sitting room. Like the trees lining the driveway. But what did I have to offer her besides this life of chores, obligations, and watching other people's happiness from the sidelines?

I shook the thought away and dug the tip of the shovel into the dirt, trying to focus on the task in front of me. But it was impossible to ignore her. The sunlight caught her hair every time she moved, sending little golden flashes that made my chest ache. She laughed at something someone said—one of her cousins, maybe—and it carried across the garden, light and warm, wrapping around me like a memory I didn't know I had.

"Caleb, over here!" *Mamm's* voice snapped me out of it. I turned to see her pointing to a spot where a gap in the flower beds disrupted the otherwise perfect symmetry. She gave me a little wave, then went back to her group of friends, leaving me alone with the most visible patch of dirt in the garden.

Great. Just what I needed.

I trudged over, planting the shovel with more force than necessary. My brothers would have laughed if they saw me now, muttering to myself as I prepared a space for the marigolds Sadie seemed so fond of. Maybe if I worked fast enough, I could finish and escape before she noticed me. But that thought didn't sit right either. Because as much as I didn't want to be here, I wasn't sure I wanted to leave either. Not if it meant leaving her.

Not again.

Sadie spotted me, of course. The moment I turned to grab the trowel from the wheelbarrow, her face lit up like the morning sun breaking through storm clouds. She handed a tray of seedlings off to someone else and made a beeline for me, her steps quick and determined. I stiffened, knowing there was no escaping her.

"Caleb," she greeted, her tone already teasing, "if you plant flowers the way you scowl, we're going to have the most intimidating garden in all of Grace Hollow."

I sighed, trying to busy myself with arranging the tools. "I wasn't aware flowers needed a mood to grow."

"They don't in theory." She grabbed a trowel from the wheelbarrow. "But they might appreciate not being glared at while they're getting settled."

I glanced at her out of the corner of my eye. Her cheeks were already flushed from working in the sun, and her sleeves were rolled up to her elbows, revealing dirt-smudged forearms. She looked... happy. Content in a way that made me feel like an alien in my own community. How did she make it all seem so effortless?

Sadie crouched down beside me, her movements graceful despite the clunky gardening boots she wore. A strand of hair escaped her *kapp* and fell across her cheek. I had to fist my hand to keep from touching her. From sweeping it away and out of her eyes. "Here." She handed me a marigold. "Start with this. They're easy. Even you can't mess it up. Marigolds are my favorite flower, especially the Queen Sophia variety."

I took the plant from her hand, our fingers brushing for the briefest moment. She didn't seem to notice, but I did. My grip on the marigold tightened slightly as I cleared my throat. "You've got quite the faith in me."

"Oh, I do," she replied, her grin widening. "You might surprise yourself. Gardening isn't all that different from farming, you know."

"Except I can't eat these when they're done growing," I muttered, kneeling to dig a small hole in the dirt.

Sadie laughed, a sound that warmed the chilly part of my chest I usually kept locked up tight. "Not everything has to be useful, Caleb. Sometimes things are worth doing just because they're beautiful. Like this garden. It's for everyone to enjoy."

I didn't respond. My hands worked the soil, but my thoughts wandered to her words. Beautiful things had their place, sure. But life wasn't about beauty—it was about responsibility. Making sure my family felt secure, my home stood strong, and my faith in *Gott* stayed steady. What could a patch of marigolds possibly add to that?

"You know," Sadie began, her voice softer now, "flowers remind me of faith. You plant them, tend them, and trust that they'll bloom. Even when the storms come or the soil's not perfect, they find a way."

I glanced at her, expecting to see her teasing grin, but her expression was thoughtful, her gaze focused on the tray of seedlings between us. The weight of her words hung in the air, settling in the same part of me that had been restless since Tuesday.

"I suppose," I said quietly, more to myself than to her. "But not everything blooms, no matter how much care you give it."

Like my smile.

Sadie's eyes flicked to mine, and I looked away, focusing on the marigold in my hand. Because if I kept looking at her, I'd have to admit how much I wanted her to be right.

Sadie didn't let my comment hang in the air for long. She brushed her hands off on her apron and planted herself squarely beside me, holding another marigold in her palm. "That's true," she said softly. "Sometimes you do everything right, and things still don't work out. But that doesn't mean you stop planting."

Her words settled over me, soft yet heavy, like the weight of the earth pressing down on the seeds we were burying. I turned the trowel over in my hand, staring at the neatly dug hole in front of me. I could feel her watching me, waiting for a response, but I wasn't sure I had one that wouldn't give away more than I wanted to.

"Not everyone's got your optimism," I said finally, lowering the marigold into the hole and covering its roots with soil.

"It's not about optimism." Her blue-gray gaze snapped to mine and held. "It's about faith. And stubbornness. You know, the good kind."

I snorted, shaking my head. "I think you've cornered the market on stubborn."

She laughed, nudging my shoulder with hers. "Takes one to know one, Stoltzfus."

Her touch was fleeting, casual, but it left a trail of warmth that lingered long after she turned back to her tray of seedlings. I found myself watching her hands as she worked, quick and efficient but careful, as if each flower deserved her full attention. It reminded me of the way *Mamm* used to tend to her garden when I was a boy, humming hymns under her breath and telling me to "handle the soil like you're handling a baby chick."

The memory made something tighten in my chest, and I shoved it down as quickly as it surfaced. "You really believe that?" I asked, my voice gruffer than I intended.

"Believe what?" She glanced up at me with a smudge of dirt on her cheek.

"That planting something... even when you don't know if it'll grow... is worth it?"

Sadie tilted her head, considering me with those bright, knowing eyes that made me feel like she could see right through me. "I do," she said simply. "It's worth it because you tried. And sometimes, things grow in ways you don't expect."

Her words hit deeper than they should have, stirring something I wasn't ready to name. I looked away, focusing on the marigold I'd just planted. It stood upright in its neat little patch of dirt, its golden petals bright against the dark soil. Something about it felt too fragile, too vulnerable, and yet... it stood tall anyway.

"Maybe," I muttered, unsure if I was agreeing with her or trying to convince myself.

Sadie just smiled, her eyes soft with understanding. "Maybe's a good start."

I shook my head, the corner of my mouth twitching despite myself. Sadie Miller had a way of turning everything into a lesson, but for once, I didn't mind. She made me want to believe her, even if it went against every practical instinct I had.

Sadie leaned closer, brushing her hands free of dirt as she eyed me with an expression that was half-teasing, half-sincere. "You know, Caleb, there's more to life than self-imposed responsibilities. Even you have to see that."

I gave her a sideways glance, unsure whether to take the bait or let her words roll off me. "Some of us don't have the luxury of chasing butterflies, Sadie. Things need to get done."

"And yet," she replied, not missing a beat, "here you are, planting marigolds instead of plowing a field. Seems to me even you can make room for something unexpected."

I wanted to argue. To tell her that this—this entire afternoon—was an obligation, nothing more. But the truth was harder to face. I'd stayed longer than I had to, worked slower than I normally would, just to be here. Just to see the way her hair caught the sunlight when she turned her head, or to hear her laugh, even when it was at my expense. That was what scared me most—how easy it was becoming to let her in.

She dug her trowel into the soil, her movements sure and purposeful, and tilted her head toward me. "Do you remember the parable of the mustard seed?"

"Of course." I brushed the dirt from my palms. "A tiny seed grows into a tree big enough for the birds to rest in its branches."

Sadie smiled, her eyes glinting with something deeper. "Exactly. Big things can come from small beginnings, Caleb. You just have to plant the seed and tend to it."

I stared at the marigold in my hand, its bright orange petals vivid against the backdrop of green. It felt like she was talking about more than flowers. "Not everything grows the way you want it to," I said, my voice quieter than I intended.

"No," she agreed, her tone softening. "But you won't know what could grow unless you plant it first. Even you have to admit that's true."

She had a way of turning simple truths into something much larger, something I couldn't ignore. I didn't want to admit how much her words were working their way into my head. I didn't want to admit how much she was working her way into my heart. But standing there, with the sun warming my back and the smell of freshly turned earth all around us, I couldn't escape it.

Before I could stop myself, I reached down and plucked a small cluster of wildflowers growing at the edge of the garden. They weren't much, just a mix of purple and white blooms, but they felt right. I held them out to her, feeling like a fool but unable to stop. "For you."

Sadie blinked, her cheeks flushing as she took the flowers from my hand. "Caleb, these are—"

"Don't make a big deal out of it," I muttered, turning back to the soil before she could see the heat creeping up my neck. "They were just... there."

Her laughter bubbled up, light and genuine. "*Denke*, Caleb."

I didn't respond, but the sound of her laughter lingered long after she turned back to her planting. And for the first time in a long while, I felt like maybe I'd done something right.

Sadie cradled the wildflowers in her hands like they were something precious, her fingers brushing the delicate petals as she studied them with a soft, thoughtful smile. It wasn't a grand gesture—not by any means—but it had felt monumental in a way I couldn't explain. The sight of her holding them stirred something I couldn't quite put a name to, something equal parts warmth and discomfort.

She looked up, her gaze meeting mine. "I think these are the most beautiful flowers I've ever been given."

I shifted awkwardly, gripping the trowel tighter than necessary. Who else had given her flowers? I wanted to sweep away the thoughts of anyone else. "Don't make it a thing. They're just flowers."

"*Ach*, Caleb." She laughed, but it was a quiet, tender sound, not the teasing one I'd grown used to. "You can try to downplay it all you want, but I'll remember this. Because these flowers came from you."

Her words struck a chord, making me wonder if maybe that wasn't such a bad thing. Still, I busied myself with patting down the soil around the last marigold, avoiding her gaze. "You should focus on planting instead of keeping track of sentimental nonsense."

Sadie tilted her head, her smile growing. "You're not as tough as you want people to think, you know."

That did it. I set the trowel down and gave her a hard look, trying to summon the gruffness I usually wore like armor. But the way her eyes sparkled, the way the late afternoon sun cast a golden hue across her face—it disarmed me in a way that left me raw and exposed.

"Maybe not," I admitted before I could stop myself. The words hung in the air, heavier than I'd intended.

Her smile faltered, just slightly, as if she wasn't sure what to do with my honesty. For a moment, neither of us spoke, the air between us charged with something neither of us seemed ready to name.

Then *Grossmamm's* voice called out from the other side of the garden. "Caleb, are you finished planting yet? I want to see those marigolds before the sun sets."

Sadie's gaze flicked toward the sound, then back to me. She smiled, a little softer now, and held up the flowers I'd given her. "I should get these home. They'll look lovely in a vase on my bedside table."

Ach, she said flowers and bed in the same sentence. The flowers I'd given her were going to be in her bedroom, right next to her while she slept. My chest ached so hard it stole my breath. I had to stop doing this!

I nodded, watching her rise to her feet and dust her hands off on her apron. "Take care of them."

"Oh, I will." She hesitated, her eyes searching mine for a moment longer than was comfortable. "And Caleb?"

I raised an eyebrow, bracing myself for whatever she was about to say.

"*Denke*. Just for being you," she said simply, turning away before I could even begin to process her words.

I stayed where I was, rooted to the spot, watching her walk away with the flowers tucked against her chest. For the second time in a week, I found myself wishing I could ask her to stay. Only this time, I wasn't sure I'd be able to stop myself from doing it next time.

And that thought caused my heart to twist right along with my lips.

Chapter Ten

SADIE

The faint light of dawn crept into my room, painting soft gold across the wooden floor. I sat on the edge of my bed for a moment, staring at the prayer stool in the corner. It had been my *grossmamm's*, passed down to me when I turned sixteen, and its worn edges held generations of whispered hopes and thanks. Pulling my *kapp* snugly over my hair, I knelt, letting the stillness settle over me like a comforting quilt.

"Dear, *Gott*," I whispered, folding my hands tightly, "*denke* for another day to do Your will. *Denke* for *Mamm* and *Dat* and my sisters and for the laughter they bring, even when it comes at my expense. *Denke* for our community, for strength in work, and for the flowers that bloom as reminders of Your grace."

I hesitated, my words catching somewhere between gratitude and the unspoken knot in my heart. I had no idea how to phrase what had been circling in my thoughts since yesterday at the garden—or, if I were honest, since the day Caleb Stoltzfus gave me that smile. It wasn't the smile itself, though that alone had been something rare and wonderful. It was the way it lingered in my mind, unbidden, each time I closed my eyes.

"*Gott*," I murmured, my voice softer now, "if it's Your will, please help me understand this pull I feel. You know the one I'm talking about. And if it's not, please take it from me. Because I don't know what to do with it."

My cheeks burned even in the solitude of the prayer. I shook my head, scolding myself. Caleb was Caleb—serious, stoic, and as predictable as the sunrise. He was the type of man who carried the weight of the world on his shoulders and barely left space for anyone else. And yet... when he smiled, it was like watching a storm cloud split apart to reveal the sun. For just a moment, I'd seen something in him that was softer, more vulnerable, and it had taken my breath away.

I thought about him way too much. More than that, I thought about being *his*.

Pushing myself up, I smoothed the wrinkles in my dress and ran a hand over the *kapp* ties at my chin, making sure they were neat. Dwelling on Caleb Stoltzfus wasn't going to help me get through the day. I had responsibilities—bread to bake, butter to churn, and two younger sisters who wouldn't stop pestering me if I wasn't downstairs soon.

But as I glanced toward the window, where the first blush of morning lit the horizon, I couldn't help but think of him again. His strong hands planting those marigolds, his brow furrowed in concentration, and the quiet way he'd listened when I talked about nurturing the earth like we nurture each other. He might not have said much, but I'd seen something in his eyes—a flicker of something he tried to hide.

"*Ach*, Sadie," I muttered to myself, shaking my head. "Get a hold of yourself."

Still, as I turned to start my day, the echo of that smile followed me like a shadow.

The smell of bread rising in the oven filled the kitchen, mixing with the faint aroma of coffee brewing on the stove. *Mamm* bustled around the room, humming a hymn under her breath as she stirred porridge in a heavy pot. My younger sister, Greta, sat at the table peeling apples, her brows furrowed in concentration as she tried to keep the slices even. At sixteen, she had the enthusiasm of youth, though her patience often ran thin.

"Those are for the pie," I reminded her gently, passing behind her to set a basket of eggs on the counter. "If you slice them too thin, it'll be mush by the time it's baked."

"I know," she huffed, but her tone lacked the bite it might've had if *Mamm* weren't in the room. "Why don't you peel them, then, if you're so particular?"

Mamm turned, fixing Greta with a look that spoke volumes without a word. Greta sighed dramatically but adjusted her slicing all the same.

"Sadie," Mamm said, her voice soft but firm, "the flowers Caleb gave you—are you going to put them in water? It'd be a shame if they wilted after he took the time to pick them."

The question caught me off guard, and I hesitated for a moment before nodding. "*Jah, Mamm*. I meant to do it earlier."

The truth was, I hadn't been able to decide what to do with them. They were just a small bundle of wildflowers, tied together with a bit of twine, but they felt heavier in my hands than they should have. Caleb wasn't the sort to hand out flowers lightly, and the gesture had stayed with me, looping through my thoughts long after I'd returned home.

I crossed to the counter where the flowers sat, their colors bright against the dull wood. Finding a small vase, I filled it with water and carefully arranged the blooms, letting my fingers linger on the delicate edges of the petals.

"Do you think he likes you?" Greta asked suddenly, her tone sly. "Caleb Stoltzfus, I mean. I thought he didn't like anybody."

"Greta!" *Mamm* scolded, but her eyes held a faint glimmer of curiosity as she turned back to the stove.

I felt heat rise to my cheeks. "Don't be ridiculous," I said quickly, though my voice wavered just enough to make Greta smirk. "He was being polite, that's all. We're going to be working together on the charity drive."

"Polite?" Greta snorted. "Since when does Caleb Stoltzfus do anything just to be polite? I think he liiiiiiikes you, Sadie."

"Enough," *Mamm* said, though the faintest twitch of her lips betrayed her amusement. "Sadie, set the table, and Greta, finish those apples. We've got a full day ahead, and there's no time for silliness."

I busied myself with plates and cups, my thoughts drifting as I worked. Caleb's gruff demeanor didn't lend itself to casual gestures, and I couldn't help but wonder if the flowers meant more than I wanted to admit. But if he liked me in that way as Greta was teasing, he would ask me if he could court me. And he'd not done anything that would make me think he had that in mind.

The morning rush always came and went in waves. Once breakfast was cleared and the dishes washed, I found myself back in the kitchen, kneading dough for the next day's loaves. The steady rhythm of my hands working the dough was a welcome distraction, but my thoughts refused to stay put. They kept wandering back to Caleb. His quiet intensity, the way he'd handed me those flowers like it was the most natural thing in the world, and the rare softness in his eyes whenever our hands touched—it all stuck with me in a way I couldn't shake.

"Sadie, are you daydreaming again?" Greta teased as she leaned in the doorway, a knowing smirk on her face. She had a knack for appearing whenever my thoughts were furthest from the task at hand.

"*Nee*," I said quickly, though the heat rising to my cheeks betrayed me. "I'm just thinking about the charity drive."

Greta rolled her eyes. "Uh-huh. Sure. If by 'charity drive' you mean Caleb Stoltzfus. I think you liiiiiike him too."

"Greta!" I threw a pinch of flour her way, but she ducked out of reach, her laughter trailing behind her as she disappeared into the other room. I shook my head, muttering under my breath. That girl had no sense of boundaries—or propriety. Was I like that at her age? *Ach*, I hoped not. She was close to being insufferable.

As I shaped the dough into neat rounds, I let my thoughts drift again, though this time I didn't try to fight them. Caleb wasn't just gruff or stubborn; he was... thoughtful, in his own way. The way he'd listened so intently as I talked about the drive, even when I could tell he thought it was a ridiculous idea, spoke volumes. And then there was the way he'd smiled at me—really smiled, not one of those half-hearted, reluctant things he usually gave.

That smile had undone me, more than I wanted to admit. It had lit up his entire face, softening the hard angles of his jaw and crinkling the corners of his eyes in the most endearing way. For just a moment, he'd looked like a man who could laugh, love, and let himself be free. And I couldn't help but wonder what it would take to bring that version of Caleb to the surface more often.

Mamm interrupted my musings as she entered the kitchen, her hands full of linens. "Sadie, I'll need your help with the mending this afternoon. Greta has already offered to finish the butter churning, and Emma has gone to the store with your *dat*."

"Of course, *Mamm*." I brushed the flour off my hands. But even as I answered, my gaze flickered to the vase of flowers on the windowsill. They seemed to catch the sunlight just so, their bright petals a reminder of the man who'd given them to me.

"Did Caleb say anything when he gave you those flowers?" *Mamm* asked casually, her eyes on the linens she was folding. But I knew what she was about. Unfortunately, I had no real answer for her curiosity. Caleb was a hard nut to crack.

"*Nee, Mamm,*" I replied, though my chest tightened with the memory. "He just... handed them to me. Then he told me not to read anything into it."

Mamm nodded thoughtfully. "Hmm... that's strange. But nevertheless, he's a solid man, that one. Stubborn, but *gut.*"

I didn't respond, but my heart thudded a little harder at her words.

After lunch, I found a rare moment of quiet in my bedroom. The sunlight filtered through the lace curtains, casting soft patterns on the wooden floor. I sat on the edge of my bed, my fingers tracing the worn fabric of the blanket my *mamm* had stitched years ago. My gaze drifted to the flowers, and for the hundredth time since he'd handed them to me, I wondered what they meant. Were they just a polite gesture? A way to soften his usual gruffness? Or did they mean something more?

I shook my head, laughing softly to myself. "*Ach*, Sadie," I muttered, "you're reading too much into a handful of pity blooms." But even as I said it, my chest tightened with the thought of Caleb's expression when he'd given them to me. He hadn't said much, just handed them over with that stoic air of his, but there had been something in his eyes—something unguarded and unsure, as if he wasn't quite used to doing such a thing.

A soft knock at the door pulled me from my thoughts. Greta poked her head in, her mischievous grin in place. "Sadie, what are you doing up here? Thinking about your not-so-secret admirer?"

"Greta!" I hissed, my face heating. "He's not my admirer."

"Oh, *bitte,*" she said, slipping into the room and plopping down on the bed beside me. "A man like Caleb doesn't just give flowers to anyone.

You should've seen the way he looked at you when you weren't paying attention. Like you hung the moon or something."

I rolled my eyes, but her words sent my heart racing. "You're imagining things."

Greta smirked, nudging my shoulder. "Am I? Or are you just too scared to admit that you like him back?"

I opened my mouth to protest, but the words caught in my throat. I'd spent so much time teasing Caleb, trying to crack through that tough exterior, but maybe it was more than that. Maybe I wanted to see the man beneath the scowls and the stubbornness—the man who'd carefully picked flowers just for me.

"It doesn't matter," I said finally, my voice quieter. "Caleb's... Caleb. He doesn't have time for someone like me."

Greta raised an eyebrow. "Someone like you? You mean someone who's kind, beautiful, and actually knows how to laugh? How to make life joyful in every moment? Who bakes perfect loaves of bread and the best apple pies I've ever tasted. Who quilts with uniform stitches and grows the biggest tomatoes on the county. Yeah, I'm sure he'd hate that."

"Greta," I muttered, shaking my head. "It's not that simple."

"Maybe not," she said, standing and heading for the door. "But you'll never know unless you find out, will you?"

As my younger sister left, I turned back to the window, a gentle breeze rifling through the simple white curtains. Greta's words lingered, unsettling and hopeful all at once.

The afternoon sunlight began to fade, casting long shadows across the yard as I worked on peeling apples at the kitchen table. *Mamm* was humming softly by the stove, the scent of cinnamon and nutmeg wafting through the air as a pie baked in the oven. Greta had gone back to her sewing, leaving me alone with my thoughts and the rhythmic motion of the knife against the fruit.

"Sadie?" *Mamm's* voice pulled me from my thoughts, and I looked up to find her watching me with a knowing smile. "You've been quiet today. Thinking about something—or someone?"

Heat crept up my neck, and I quickly shook my head, reaching for another apple. "Just tired, *Mamm*. That's all."

She didn't press further, but the warmth in her gaze lingered, making me feel both seen and exposed. *Mamm* had a way of noticing things I wasn't ready to admit to myself, and I wasn't sure how to feel about that.

After dinner, as the house settled into its evening quiet, I found myself drawn back to the vase on the counter. The flowers were starting to droop, their petals curling at the edges, but they still held a stubborn vibrancy that made me smile. Carefully, I plucked one of the blooms and pressed it between the pages of my Bible, letting it rest on Psalm 37:4—"Delight thyself also in the Lord; and He shall give thee the desires of thine heart."

I wasn't sure what my desires were just yet, but I couldn't deny that Caleb Stoltzfus was tangled up in them, no matter how much I tried to untangle him. He was frustrating and serious and far too guarded for his own good, but he was also kind in ways he probably didn't even realize. Like the flowers, quietly offered with no expectations, just because he could.

The thought stayed with me as I climbed into bed, the house quiet around me. I pulled the quilt up to my chin and stared at the ceiling, my mind replaying the way Caleb's hand had brushed mine at the garden, the way his eyes had softened when he'd looked at me—like maybe I wasn't the only one feeling this pull.

And as sleep finally claimed me, I made a quiet promise to myself: I wouldn't give up. Not on the charity drive, not on the hope for something more—and not on Caleb.

Chapter Eleven

CALEB

The moment dawn showed itself through my bedroom curtains, my eyes snapped open. After rising, I sat on the edge of my bed, my Bible open on my lap, fingers tracing over familiar verses. "Come to me, all you who are weary and burdened, and I will give you rest." The words felt heavier today, pressing into the quiet of my thoughts like a gentle rebuke. Rest? The idea seemed foreign, but still, I prayed for it—for the kind of peace that seemed to come so easily to others, and for the strength to keep going until it found me.

I closed my eyes and let the verse linger, trying to let its meaning sink past the shadows dancing through my mind. But my brain, restless as ever, wouldn't settle. It wasn't just the work or the weight of responsibility—it was the constant hum of doubt, the endless loop of questions and worries that chased me through every moment. Did I do enough? Did I say the right thing? Was I holding everything together, or was I just waiting for it all to fall apart? Sometimes, it felt like my own thoughts were the enemy, a tide that wouldn't let up, pulling me under when all I wanted was a moment to breathe. I envied the people who could let things go, who didn't live with their minds in overdrive, always bracing for what could go wrong. I envied Sadie most of all. How did she do it—carry so much light when the world felt so heavy?

The sound of boots scuffing against the floorboards pulled me from my thoughts. Levi, naturally. My *bruder* couldn't move through a room without announcing himself.

"Caleb, you coming, or are you planning to pray us into the next century?" His voice carried through the hall, thick with the teasing lilt that seemed to define his every word.

I sighed, closing the Bible and setting it on my nightstand. "Some of us actually take time for reflection."

"And some of us reflect while eating breakfast," Levi shot back, poking his head into my room. His grin was as wide as ever, dimples cutting into his cheeks. "*Mamm's* got cinnamon rolls on the table. You might want to hurry before the twins eat them all."

The twins—Ezra and Elias—were a whirlwind of energy and appetite, always in competition over something. If it wasn't chores or farm work, it was who could inhale the most food in one sitting. I followed Levi into the kitchen, bracing myself for the usual chaos.

Sure enough, the twins were already bickering, their voices rising over the clatter of dishes. Ezra had a streak of flour on his cheek, likely from sneaking a roll straight from the oven, while Elias was gesturing animatedly with a butter knife.

"*Nee*, you had the last one yesterday!" Ezra insisted, reaching for the plate.

Elias held it just out of reach. "That was yesterday. Today's a new day."

Mamm sighed from her place by the stove, shaking her head as she turned out another batch of rolls. "*Ach*, you two. Can't we have one morning of peace?"

"Not in this *haus*," Levi quipped, grabbing a roll and ducking out of *Mamm's* reach as she swatted at him with a dish towel.

I slid into a seat at the table, shaking my head. "Do you two ever think about anything besides food?"

Ezra grinned, unrepentant. "Sometimes. But not this early. My brain's not even awake yet."

Elias snorted. "At least we're not as boring as you, *bruder*. What's on your agenda today? More scowling at fields? Chasing escaped pigs? Falling into manure piles?"

Levi smirked as he dropped into the seat across from me. "*Nee*, he's probably got something more exciting planned. Planting flowers with Sadie Miller again."

I shot him a glare, but the heat in my face betrayed me. Levi laughed, leaning back in his chair. "Thought so. Caleb, you're too easy."

"Maybe if you all actually focused on your chores, you'd have less time for gossip," I muttered, reaching for a roll. "I could use some help with running some errands today."

Levi snorted. "I have to give you grief, *bruder*. You're so old, *Mamm* has been praying that you get married before your entire head of hair turns silver and no one but a blind woman would have you."

But even as I spoke, I couldn't shake the memory of Sadie's bright smile, lingering at the edge of my thoughts like a warm light I didn't quite know how to handle. Levi's jests hit a little too close to home. Was I too old? Was I too jaded to ever be the kind of *mann* that a woman like Sadie could make a life with? Truly, I didn't know. But I did know that I wanted her to be proud of me.

The morning sun was climbing higher by the time I finished tending to the horses. The rhythmic brush of their coats and the quiet hum of their breathing had always been steadying, but today, my mind felt anything but calm. Sadie's name kept circling in my thoughts, unbidden but persistent, like a hymn you couldn't stop humming once it took root.

Levi and the twins had taken off to help *Dat* with repairing the barn roof, leaving me to handle the errands. My *dat* had suffered a back injury when he'd fallen off a barn roof much like ours about ten years ago. That was when my life really changed. I had wanted to go into woodworking. I still made furniture in my spare time – little as it was. But being the eldest son, I had to commit myself to keeping the farm running smoothly and providing a livelihood for our large family when my *dat* couldn't. It might not have been the life I chose for myself, but it was an honest existence. Normally, I welcomed the solitude of taking care of the animals, but the quiet only gave my mind more room to wander.

I hitched up the buggy, stuffing the list *Mamm* had written into my pocket. It was mostly supplies for the house and a few things she wanted delivered to neighbors, but of course, she'd tacked on one last-minute request: dropping off a box of books to the schoolhouse for the children. I frowned at the thought of Sadie's teasing smile if she caught me hauling children's storybooks. The last thing I needed was more fodder for her amusement. She already made me feel so off kilter.

The General Store was bustling by the time I arrived, the familiar hum of conversation mixing with the clink of jars and the scent of fresh bread. As I stepped inside, the chaos of home seemed to follow me. Becca was by the counter, chatting animatedly with Simon while Sadie stacked a neat display of canned peaches nearby.

She looked up just as I entered, her face brightening like the first rays of sunlight after a storm. "*Hallo*, Caleb," she said, her tone already carrying that teasing edge. "What brings you here so early? Oh, I know! It's because you've missed me."

I snorted, pretending to ignore the way my heart skipped like an untrained colt at her words. Missed her? *Ach*, what nonsense. Still, I couldn't deny the faint jolt of anticipation when *Mamm* had handed me the list and shooed me toward the store this morning. "Don't forget to bring back flour," she'd said, but I knew what she really meant was, 'Get out of the house before you drive us all mad with your brooding.' And maybe—just maybe—I hadn't argued because some stubborn part of me liked the idea of seeing Sadie again. What was wrong with me? I didn't choose to be here, not exactly, but I wasn't in a hurry to leave, either. I truly had no idea what was coming over me lately.

Jah, you do. It's standing right in front of you.

I resisted the urge to smile at her which was becoming much more common than even I could have ever anticipated, instead holding up *Mamm's* list. "Errands."

Sadie smirked, her hands pausing mid-stack. "Errands? Or did your *mamm* send you out because she wanted to be around Levi instead?"

Behind me, Becca snorted. "If she did, she deserves a medal. I'd rather clean out the barn than spend an afternoon listening to Levi's endless jabbering. And you can bet on that."

I turned, leveling a look at her. "You shouldn't talk about betting. Bishop Yoder wouldn't approve."

"Oh, lighten up," Becca said, waving me off. "It's not betting when it's just a figure of speech. Besides, you're much more interesting when Sadie's around. She brings out your... softer side."

"*Nee*," I muttered, grabbing the nearest jar off the shelf just to have something to do. "I don't have a softer side."

Sadie's laugh was warm, almost musical. "Oh, I don't know about that. You were downright kind at the flower planting last week. Remember those marigolds you planted just so perfectly? They are currently growing strong, healthy, and reaching toward the sun."

"I was participating," I said, setting the jar down harder than I meant to. "And making my *mamm* happy. It was a win-win."

Becca's eyes about disappeared under her *kapp* and then she whispered, "I don't think it was your *mamm* you were trying to make happy, Sheriff."

Sadie leaned on the counter, her grin widening. "Practical or not, I think you're full of surprises, Caleb. And I kind of like it."

I opened my mouth to argue, excited to continue the dynamic of our banter, but Simon appeared with a box in hand, cutting me off. "Caleb, this one's for the schoolhouse. Miriam mentioned you'd be heading that way?"

I nodded, ignoring Sadie's knowing smile. Today was shaping up to be longer than I'd planned.

I left the General Store with the box of books balanced on one arm, feeling the weight of more than just paper and bindings. Sadie's laughter still echoed in my ears, light and warm, like she'd left some invisible mark on the air around me. It wasn't the first time she'd managed to rattle me, but it was starting to feel like I couldn't step foot in town without her finding a way to sneak into my day—and my thoughts.

When I was by myself later and had more time, I'd think about how much I actually liked it.

The twins were waiting near the buggy, leaning casually against the wheel. Ezra had a stalk of grass between his teeth, and Elias, ever the mirror image, was holding the reins with the same lazy ease. They straightened when they saw me, identical grins breaking across their faces.

"Got yourself a box of fairy tales there, *bruder*?" Ezra teased, jerking his chin at the stack in my hands.

"For the schoolhouse," I said curtly, hoisting the box onto the seat. "*Mamm's* orders."

Elias raised an eyebrow. "Don't suppose Sadie added anything to that list while you were inside? Maybe a note or a jar of peaches?"

"*Nee*," I snapped, though my face felt hotter than the sun overhead. "And even if she did, it's none of your concern."

Ezra let out a low whistle. "Hit a nerve, didn't we?"

"*Ach*, leave him alone," Levi said, stepping out from the shadow of the store. He had that easygoing smirk he always wore, but his eyes were sharp with amusement. "If Caleb's courting Sadie Miller, we ought to be helping him, not making sport of him. After all, he's practically an old man. I think I've seen a few grey hairs when he takes off his hat."

After handing Levi my most lethal glare, I said, "I'm not courting Sadie," I climbed aboard my buggy, "And I don't plan to. Mostly because she wouldn't have me. And where did you three come from anyway? I thought you were at home doing chores?"

The twins exchanged a look, their grins widening. "Plans change," Elias said. "We needed a break."

"Sometimes they shouldn't change," I shot back, giving the reins a sharp flick to get the horse moving. "You three should be back at home. I shouldn't be courting *anyone*. Because some leopards never change their spots."

The words sat bitter on my tongue, sharper than I intended, but the truth was, they felt truer than anything else. I was twenty-seven—practically ancient by Amish standards—and every time I looked at Sadie, so full of light and possibility, it hit me just how far behind I'd fallen. Six years stretched between us, and while they didn't seem like much when measured in numbers, they felt like a lifetime when measured in missed chances. Sadie deserved someone young, someone who could meet her where she stood instead of dragging her down with the weight of his own doubts and failures. What would I do if I risked my heart, only to have her look at me with pity—or worse, with nothing at all? The thought alone was enough to keep me in my place, pretending that the safest distance was the one I'd already convinced myself I preferred.

Far better that I take care of my family, live an honest life in the image of *Gott*, and die a lonely old man.

Levi jogged alongside for a few steps before hopping onto the back of the buggy. "You know, *bruder*," he said, settling in as if he owned the seat, "you can't fool everyone. Especially not us. If you thought about yourself for once—if you considered your own happiness, would that be so bad?"

"I'm not trying to fool anyone," I muttered, my jaw tight. "I'm just doing what needs doing. With *dat's* injury, I have to make sure the farm runs properly. That is *Gott's* will."

"*Gott's* will?" Levi chuckled, leaning back like he had all the time in the world. "And what needs doing is avoiding Sadie like she's carrying the plague? Being deliberately crabby to her when all she does is make your day brighter."

I glared at him out of the corner of my eye. "I'm not avoiding her."

"Sure you aren't," Levi said, his tone dripping with sarcasm. "That's why you look like you've swallowed a mouthful of vinegar every time her name comes up."

Elias and Ezra's laughter trailed behind us as the buggy pulled away, their voices carrying on the breeze. "Whatever, Caleb. You're so see-through, you could be wearing one of *Mamm's* lacy doilies."

I shook my head, gripping the reins tighter. My *bruders* were impossible, but it wasn't their teasing that got under my skin. It was the way Sadie's name lingered long after the laughter faded, leaving me with a hollow ache I couldn't quite shake.

For the first time in my life, I know knew what it felt like to want something you could never have.

I drove in blessed silence for a few more minutes until the schoolhouse came into view. The buggy creaked to a stop outside the structure, its wooden walls gleaming under the late morning sun. Children's laughter spilled out through the open windows, mingling with the faint rustle of the breeze. Ezra hopped off first, balancing the box of storybooks on his hip as he approached the door.

"I'll bet Mary Graber's already got these kids reciting their lessons like clockwork," Levi said, brushing off his trousers before following. "You coming, Caleb?"

I stayed seated, gripping the reins like they might anchor me in place. "You don't need me for this. Drop the books off and let's go. It's bad enough I have to weed *mamm's* flower beds."

Levi shot me a look over his shoulder. "Oh, come on. Don't be such a stick in the mud. Besides, you should see her face when she gets these. Mary's got a way of making gratitude feel like it's worth something."

"More than you deserve," Ezra muttered, shaking his head as he disappeared through the door.

I sighed, climbing down from the buggy. Better to keep an eye on them before they turned the delivery into another one of their schemes.

Inside, the schoolroom was a lively swirl of chatter and energy. Children sat at tidy wooden desks, their slates and chalk in hand, while Mary Graber stood at the front, her hands clasped as she guided them through a spelling exercise. She glanced up when we entered, her face breaking into a warm, open smile that could have disarmed even the most hardened soul.

"Levi, Ezra," she greeted, stepping forward with an air of calm authority that didn't diminish her liveliness. Her dark hair was swept into a modest bun, and her *kapp* framed a pretty face that, despite some signs of experience, radiated kindness. "And Caleb, too. Such an honor. What brings you here today?"

Ezra set the box on her desk with a flourish. "Delivery for the finest teacher in Grace Hollow."

"Storybooks," Levi added, leaning casually against the doorframe. "*Mamm* and Simon Miller thought the children might enjoy a little something extra for their reading."

Mary's eyes lit up as she peeked into the box, her hands gently lifting one of the books to inspect its worn cover. "Oh, this is wonderful. Please, thank your *Mamm* for me—and you, too, for bringing them here."

"She's the one who thought of it." I crossed my arms as the children craned their necks to see what treasures the box held. "We just follow orders."

"Don't let him fool you," Levi chimed in, a teasing lilt in his voice. "Caleb's always the first to step up when there's work to be done. Most day, I think his middle name might be work."

Mary's smile softened, her gaze resting on me for a moment longer than I was comfortable with. "Well, it's appreciated, Caleb. Truly."

I shifted my weight, nodding stiffly. "We should get going. Busy day ahead."

As we turned to leave, one of the children tugged on Mary's skirt, pointing to the books with wide eyes. "Miss Graber, can we read them today?"

Her laughter was light and melodic. "Patience, Jesse. All good things in time. You have to complete your lessons first."

Outside, Levi clapped me on the back, grinning. "See? That wasn't so bad."

I glared at him but couldn't find the words to argue. Instead, I climbed back into the buggy, my mind trailing behind as we headed for the garden.

By the time we arrived at the community garden, Levi had already hopped off the buggy, his energy spilling into the quiet space like a burst of morning sunlight. He gave the reins a quick tug and darted off toward a cluster of neighbors, no doubt hunting for someone to tease or charm. I stayed back, taking my time tying the horse to the post, hoping to keep my head down and escape notice. No such luck.

"Caleb!" Esther King's voice drifted over the garden, sweet and lilting, like a bird's call that carried just a little too much intention. She stood by the flower beds, her *kapp* perfectly tied, her skirts rustling as she walked toward me with purpose. "I didn't expect to see you here today."

Levi turned his head, catching the way Esther's eyes sparkled as she approached. "Oh, this is going to be entertaining," he murmured, just loud enough for me to hear before darting off again, no doubt to spread the news of my impending torture.

"*Hallo*, Esther," I said, keeping my tone polite as I tipped my hat. "Just here to help out with the weeding. My *mamm* is concerned about the flowers she planted."

Her smile widened as she clasped her hands in front of her. "It's nice to see you lending a hand. A man like you—so strong, so capable—could really make a difference in a place like this."

As her intense gaze swept my body from head to boot, I shifted uncomfortably, glancing toward the flower beds. "Just doing what *Mamm* asked. She really cares about the flowers."

"Well, it's nice to see you," she said, her tone dipping lower, softer. "Maybe we could work together on something? I've been needing help with the climbing roses over there. They're so stubborn." She tilted her head, the motion practiced and deliberate. "They could use a firm hand."

Before I could respond, Levi's voice boomed from across the garden. "*Ach*, Caleb! Don't let her work you too hard."

Ezra and Elias joined in, their laughter ringing out as they walked over. "Caleb's probably as stubborn as they are," Elias teased. "If anyone can make those roses behave, it's him."

"Maybe they'll even bloom extra bright for you, *bruder*," Ezra added, his grin sharp as he leaned against the buggy.

Esther giggled, her cheeks flushing delicately as she glanced at me. "Your *bruders* are so lively," she said. "I can see where you get it."

Me? Lively? What on earth is she talking about.

"I'm not anything like them," I muttered, brushing past them toward the tools piled near the beds. My face burned under their teasing, but what bothered me more was how empty it all felt. Esther was beautiful, the kind of woman any man would be proud to court, but her attention slid over me like oil on water. It didn't stick—not where it mattered. She didn't even come close to reaching my heart.

As I crouched by the marigolds that Sadie and I planted together, I couldn't stop the thought from creeping in: Why didn't Esther's presence stir anything in me? Why did the memory of Sadie's laughter, her dirt-smudged hands, and her determination linger instead? Esther might be perfect on paper, but it was Sadie who had carved a space in my chest I didn't know how to fill.

Levi nudged me as he passed, his voice low. "Don't let her get away, Caleb. Esther's as sweet as they come. Pretty, too. A woman any man would be proud to call his own. Maybe she'd even pluck out your gray hairs for you."

I just shook my head, gripping the trowel tighter. "She's not the one," I muttered under my breath, my thoughts drifting to Sadie once more. *Ach*, what is wrong with me? "Wait... scratch that. There is *nee* one. I am an old bachelor, and that is a fact."

"You're right about one thing." My younger *bruder* squatted down beside me. "You're old. Most likely as old as the dirt you have your fingers in right now."

I snorted. "Get out of here and leave me in peace."

Laughing more than I liked, Levi rose to his feet and trotted away. I went to work weeding Sadie's marigolds. Just when the sun was beating down across my back enough that beads of sweat were starting to form between my shoulder blades, a pair of women's boots appeared. I shaded my eyes with my hand and glanced up.

Esther shifted her basket, her smile faltering slightly. "How is the weeding going?"

"*Gut.*" *Ach*, that wasn't much better than a grunt. Just because I had no interest in this woman didn't mean I got be rude to her.

Her tragic expression almost broke me. "Well, Caleb, maybe next time we can..." Her voice trailed off, as if searching for a reason to linger. "Maybe you can show me the best way to plant marigolds. Yours look so neat."

I paused, trowel in hand, feeling the weight of her words. Levi was still grinning from *mamm's* beds a few yards away, clearly enjoying my discomfort. Esther was trying, and any other man would have leapt at the opportunity to court her. But instead of leaping, I felt like running—straight into the flower bed where I could bury myself and this awkwardness.

"Marigolds are straightforward." I forced my tone to stay smooth and polite. "Just need good soil, water, and sunlight. Nothing more to it." I crouched down, stabbing the trowel into the dirt with a bit more force than necessary.

Esther hesitated, her smile flickering, but she nodded gracefully. "Of course. It's just that... you make it look so effortless."

"Hardly," I muttered, keeping my eyes fixed on the soil. "I've got chores waiting back home. Need to get these weeds pulled before I can get to them. Best not to linger."

Her soft laugh followed me, but it carried a fragile edge this time, like glass threatening to shatter. When I glanced up, she was shifting her basket higher on her hip, her smile trembling at the corners. Esther hesitated, her gaze flickering between me and the path back to the gathering, as though she was waiting for something—a word, a gesture, anything to make her stay feel less futile.

"Well, Caleb," she said quietly, her voice softer now, "I should let you get back to your work. I didn't mean to interrupt."

I opened my mouth to respond, but no words came. What could I say? That her interruption didn't bother me, even though it did? That I appreciated her kindness when, truthfully, it slipped right past me like a breeze I barely felt?

She turned slowly, her steps measured, as if giving me one last chance to call her back. But I didn't. Couldn't.

Levi nudged me hard with his elbow, his grin gone. "You could at least say *denke*," he muttered. "You're going to make the name Stoltzfus synonymous with being ill-mannered."

But by the time the thought registered, Esther had already walked away, her head bowed slightly. The weight of her disappointment hung in the air long after her footsteps faded, and for the first time, guilt tugged at me—not because I hadn't returned her interest, but because I knew how deeply rejection could cut in a community where every glance and word carried so much meaning.

I sighed, dragging a hand down my face as Levi crouched beside me, his expression somewhere between pity and exasperation.

"What's wrong with you, *bruder*?" he asked quietly. "Esther's a peach. She likes you, Caleb. She sees something in you worth noticing. I don't know what that is, but she obviously does."

"I know," I said, my voice low. And I did know. Esther deserved a man who would meet her kindness with his own, who would cherish her the way she wanted to be cherished. But that man wasn't me.

Because every time I even considered giving Esther more of my attention, it felt like I was betraying something—or someone. Sadie's name pressed unspoken against my lips, a truth I wasn't ready to face but couldn't ignore.

Levi shook his head, his trowel sinking into the dirt beside mine. "You can't spend your whole life waiting for... whatever it is you're waiting for. Sometimes you have to take a risk. You say you don't like Sadie. You say you don't like Esther. You're going to run out of chances."

"It's not that I don't like them," I snapped, more harshly than I meant to. "I just... I have other priorities."

Levi arched an eyebrow, clearly unconvinced, but he let it drop. "If you say so," he muttered, turning back to the flower beds. "But you might want to figure it out before you end up alone."

I bent my head over the soil, gripping the trowel like it might anchor me, but the memory of Esther's retreating figure lingered in my mind, tangled up with the thought of Sadie's bright laughter and dirt-smudged hands.

Whatever this ache in my chest was, I didn't have the time—or the courage—to name it.

Levi leaned in closer, his grin sharp. "You know, Caleb, for a man who claims he has *nee* interest in courting, you're sure making some strong impressions. Too bad you're picking the wrong flowers."

"I'm not picking anything," I grumbled, glancing briefly toward the marigolds Sadie and I had planted. My chest tightened at the memory of her laughter, her hands working beside mine as if we'd been a team all along. It had felt so right that day. Just being with her working on a mundane task.

Levi caught the look and let out a low whistle. "*Ach*, Caleb. If you don't figure out what you want soon, you're going to end up like one of those weeds—rooted in place while everything else grows around you."

I didn't answer, just pressed the trowel harder into the soil. The sun dipped lower, casting long shadows across the garden. As much as I wanted to argue, Levi's words struck a nerve I didn't care to acknowledge.

By the time we finished pulling the last of the weeds, Esther had disappeared from the garden, her absence barely registering as I climbed back onto the buggy. My *bruders* clambered in behind me, their teasing quieter now but still present in their knowing glances.

The ride home was silent, save for the creak of the wheels and the rhythmic clip-clop of the horse's hooves. But in the quiet, Sadie's voice lingered, uninvited but welcome all the same.

What was wrong with me?

Whatever it was, I couldn't shake the feeling that this ache in my chest wasn't something I could pull out like a weed. It was deeper—rooted in something I wasn't sure I wanted to name.

Chapter Twelve

SADIE

The quilting circle buzzed with the hum of conversation as I slipped into Grace Hall, my basket of scraps bumping against my hip. The air inside was warm, a mix of lavender sachets and the faint sweetness of molasses cookies from the kitchen. Women bent over the long quilting frame, fingers busy stitching intricate patterns into the fabric. My *mamm* was already at her usual spot near the head of the frame, guiding a younger girl on her stitches with the patience of a saint.

"*Ach*, Sadie, there you are," *Mamm* said, looking up with a smile. "I thought you might not make it today."

I offered her a quick grin and slid into the empty seat beside Becca, who raised a knowing brow as she watched me settle in. "I told *Dat* I'd finish tidying the store first." I pulled my needle and thread from the basket. "Besides, someone has to keep up with these projects."

"Not all projects," Becca murmured under her breath, just low enough for me to hear. Her eyes sparkled with mischief as she leaned closer. "Speaking of which, any new sightings of our favorite brooding farmer?"

I glared at her, trying to hide the heat creeping up my cheeks. "*Nee*."

Before Becca could push further, Edna Zook's voice rose above the gentle murmurs. "Esther! What a delight to see you, dear." Heads turned as Esther King entered, her *kapp* pristine, her platinum blonde hair framing her face, and her cheeks flushed like ripe apples. She carried herself with the practiced grace of someone who always knew eyes were on her, and she met them with a soft, demure smile.

My back stiffened. But then I chastised myself. I could be as kind and sweet to Esther as I was to everyone else. I could.

"*Hallo*, everyone," Esther said, her voice lilting as she moved toward the quilting frame. "I've been so busy at the garden this week. You wouldn't believe how much work there is to do."

"Oh, do tell," Edna prompted, her tone eager. "The community garden has been the talk of the town. I hear Caleb Stoltzfus has been lending a hand quite often. Such a hard worker, that one."

I nearly pricked my finger with the needle. Across the table, Becca's smirk faded, replaced with a look that screamed don't react. But it was too late. My ears burned as Esther settled into a seat and began unraveling her tale. The only saving grace was that my *mamm* was so engrossed in teaching the younger girls, she wasn't paying any attention to Edna or the conversation.

"Oh, Caleb," she said, her tone turning syrupy. "He's been such a help. Why, just the other day, he carried the heaviest bags for me and insisted I take a rest while he finished the work himself. Such a considerate man. And so strong."

I gritted my teeth, forcing my stitches into neat, even rows. Becca shifted beside me, her hands still, as though weighing whether to jump in or let Esther's story run its course. I felt like I was balancing on the edge of a blade, the tension thickening with each word.

Esther's voice carried over the quiet murmurs of the quilting circle like the tinkling of wind chimes, sweet and light. "He's always so serious, you know," she said, glancing around the group with a shy smile, "but with me... well, he seems softer. Kinder."

The needle slipped from my fingers, clattering against the edge of the quilting frame. I scrambled to pick it up, avoiding Becca's sharp glance. My chest felt tight, each breath harder to draw as Esther continued, oblivious to the storm she was stirring.

"I suppose it's because he trusts me," she went on, her cheeks turning even rosier. "He doesn't put up that wall with me like he does with most people. Just the other day, he asked for my thoughts on the marigolds he planted. Can you imagine? Caleb Stoltzfus, asking for advice! It was like... well, like he valued my opinion."

Those were *my* marigolds. The thought slammed into me, sharp and unexpected, like stepping on a nail hidden in soft earth. My marigolds. The ones Caleb and I had planted together, side by side in the sun. I could still feel the warmth of that afternoon, the way the dirt crumbled between my fingers, the way he'd grumbled about straight lines but let a tiny smile slip when I teased him about it. And now, Esther was claiming them—claiming him—as though the flowers meant something special between them. As though she had any right to that moment.

It wasn't just jealousy twisting in my chest; it was something deeper, something raw and jagged that I didn't know how to name. The marigolds had been a connection, a small, fragile thread tying me to the man I was starting to care for more than I should. And hearing Esther spin her story felt like watching that thread fray, unraveling one stitch at a time.

Becca whispered next to me, "I can't believe she just said that. She's not telling the whole story! I know it!"

I forced my gaze down, blinking rapidly as my vision blurred. Keep stitching, I told myself. Keep your hands moving. Don't let them see. But each pull of the needle felt heavier, slower, as though the weight of Esther's words had seeped into my bones.

A chorus of murmurs and approving nods rippled through the room. "That's no small thing," Edna chimed in, her eyes gleaming with satisfaction. "He's always been so stubborn and set in his ways. If he's letting you in, Esther, that says something. Oh, I knew this day would come."

"It must mean something," Esther agreed, her tone modest but her expression anything but. "And the way he smiled when I told him how beautiful the garden looked. *Ach*, it was like seeing a whole new side of him."

My hands trembled as I pulled the thread through the fabric, the stitches uneven despite my best efforts to keep calm. Caleb, smiling at her? Asking for her opinion? It was like she was describing a stranger, not the man who grumbled and scowled his way through every conversation with me.

"Do you think..." Esther's voice dropped slightly, taking on a dreamy quality. "Do you think he might be considering me for courtship? I mean, we've spent so much time together lately. And he seems so... comfortable with me. Like we understand each other."

Becca's head snapped up, her needle poised mid-air. "Caleb? Comfortable?" she repeated, her voice tinged with disbelief. "Are we talking about the same Caleb Stoltzfus?"

Esther tilted her head, her smile faltering just slightly. "Well, I don't expect everyone to see that side of him. He's different with me. I'm starting to think I might have a touch with him. That I'm special."

I bit the inside of my cheek so hard I tasted copper. The image of Caleb crouching by the marigolds flashed through my mind, his quiet strength and focus etched into every movement. I thought of the rare moments he'd softened, like when I'd teased him into smiling, or when he'd helped me carry that bag in the garden. Had I been imagining it all? Had those moments meant nothing to him while he'd been offering something real to Esther?

"Well," Edna's shrill voice cut through my spiraling thoughts, "Esther, you'd be the perfect match for him. A fine woman like you is exactly what Caleb needs to soften that gruff demeanor of his."

Becca's sharp intake of breath was the only sound that broke through the roaring in my ears. My friend reached over and put a palm of support on my forearm. But I couldn't feel anything over the prickling of my skin.

Becca wasn't having it. She leaned forward, her needle poised like a weapon, her eyes narrowing at Esther. "You mean Caleb smiled at you, Esther? Caleb? Are you sure it wasn't a grimace? Maybe he was choking on the dust from those marigolds."

A ripple of laughter broke out, light and harmless, but it did little to ease the ache in my chest. Esther, however, didn't seem fazed. She merely smiled, tilting her head as if amused. "Oh, I know what I saw, Becca. It wasn't just a smile—it was genuine. A real, warm smile, just for me. It totally transformed his face into something magical."

Warm. Genuine. Just for her. The words hit me like a hammer, each one a nail driven deeper into the quiet hope I hadn't even realized I was clinging to.

"And why wouldn't he?" Edna chimed in, her voice sharp as ever. "Esther is exactly the kind of woman Caleb needs. Pretty, demure, kind—she's practically a blessing wrapped in an apron."

Becca rolled her eyes so hard I thought she might topple over. "Oh, come on, Edna. It's not like Caleb's out there drawing hearts in the dirt with her name in them. He's probably just being polite. Do you really think a surly man like him would completely change his entire personality overnight?"

"Polite?" Esther laughed softly, her cheeks coloring. "Caleb doesn't do polite for no reason. That's why it's so special when he does open up. He told me himself—he doesn't trust easily."

Becca's lips pressed into a thin line, her gaze flicking to me briefly before she focused on her stitching. "Well, I suppose if Caleb's suddenly turning over a new leaf, we'll all just have to watch and see. Maybe he'll plant you in the garden next, Esther."

The group chuckled, but I couldn't join in. My hands felt clammy as I fumbled with the fabric, the stitches blurring before my eyes. Caleb, opening up to Esther? Confiding in her? Smiling at her in a way he never smiled at me?

It felt like a betrayal, even though I knew it wasn't. Caleb wasn't mine. He'd never been mine. But that didn't stop the sting of it, the sharp twist in my chest as Esther continued to paint a picture of a man I thought I understood, a man who was beginning to feel as far out of reach as the stars.

I didn't realize my hands had stilled until Becca nudged me gently under the table. "You all right?" she murmured, her voice low enough that only I could hear. "I know. This is insufferable."

I nodded quickly, forcing a tight smile. "Fine."

But I wasn't fine. My thoughts were a tangled mess, and I couldn't shake the image of Caleb standing in the garden, his face soft and open, looking at Esther like she was the center of his world. Had I been wrong about him? Had I misread every glance, every grumble, every stolen moment?

"Sadie Miller, you're so quiet today," Edna remarked, her sharp eyes catching mine. "Cat got your tongue?"

"*Nee*," I said too quickly, my voice catching. "Just concentrating."

"Well, don't think too hard," Edna teased. "I wouldn't want your stitches to be uneven."

More laughter, more smiles. All I could do was keep stitching, pretending that my heart wasn't unraveling thread by thread.

The quilting circle carried on, the hum of conversation a soft backdrop to the rhythmic pull of needles through fabric. Esther had finally gone quiet, her smug expression firmly in place as if she'd won some unspoken competition. I focused on my stitches, willing my thoughts to settle, but they swirled like a storm cloud I couldn't escape.

Becca nudged me again, this time harder. "Don't let her get to you," she whispered, her voice low enough to avoid the others' notice. "Esther's just trying to spin a tale to make herself look good."

I kept my eyes on the fabric, my fingers moving automatically. "Maybe it's not a tale," I murmured. "Maybe Caleb does like her. Maybe she's exactly what he's looking for. I mean... what man wouldn't want someone like her. She's practically perfect."

Becca snorted softly. "*Nee*, not a chance. Esther's sweet and all, but Caleb's... complicated. She's too much sugar and not enough spice for a man like him."

The corner of my mouth twitched despite myself, but I quickly smoothed my expression. "It doesn't matter, Becca. He's not mine. Who am I to judge what he's doing or who he's seeing? It's truly none of my business."

"Not yet, but he could be," she said, her voice softening. "You know as well as I do that Caleb doesn't smile for anyone. Except you."

"That's not true," I said quickly, but the words rang hollow even to my own ears.

"*Ach*, Sadie, come on. The man practically scowls for a living, but when you're around, he almost-smiles. And don't even get me started on your banter—it's practically flirting. Or as much flirting as Caleb Stoltzfus is capable of."

Heat crept up my neck, and I glanced around the circle, relieved to see the others were still lost in their own conversations. "Right. Caleb doesn't flirt," I said, keeping my voice low. "He grumbles."

Becca grinned, her needle pausing mid-stitch. "Grumbles at you, maybe. But there's a difference between annoyed grumbling and 'I'm pretending not to like you' grumbling. You, my friend, get the second kind."

I shook my head, focusing harder on the fabric in my lap. "You're imagining things."

"Am I?" Becca's voice took on a teasing lilt. "Then why does he only argue with you? Why does he let you poke fun at him when he glares daggers at anyone else who tries? Why is he always showing up where you are as if he's a glutton for that kind of punishment?"

I opened my mouth to respond, but the words wouldn't come. Because Becca wasn't wrong. Caleb didn't have the same walls with me that he had with others. But did that mean anything? Or was it just because he thought of me as a friend—a safe person to let his guard down with?

"Listen," Becca said, her tone turning serious. "I know you've got this picture in your head now, thanks to Esther's little fairy tale. But don't let it cloud what's real. Caleb might not be shouting it from the rooftops, but he notices you. He cares. And trust me, Esther doesn't have what it takes to make him happy."

The words warmed me, but they also brought a fresh ache. If Becca was right, and Caleb did feel something for me, then why was he holding back? Why did he act like he couldn't see what was right in front of him?

The quilting circle was winding down, the final stitches being made as the women began gathering their things. The air had grown heavier, the earlier lighthearted chatter now replaced by a lingering tension I couldn't shake. Esther's words echoed in my head, each one twisting like a thorn in my chest.

Becca stayed close as we folded the quilt, her presence a quiet anchor, but even her teasing couldn't fully pull me out of the storm brewing inside. My thoughts kept circling back to Caleb—his surly demeanor, the rare almost-smiles he reserved just for me, the way his quiet strength felt like a shelter I hadn't realized I'd been seeking. And now, all I could see was Esther's radiant face, recounting her fantasy version of the garden scene. Maybe she was right. Maybe Caleb saw her in a way he'd never see me.

I bit the inside of my cheek, trying to steady myself, but the doubt refused to leave. Why had I asked him to help with the charity drive? What had I been thinking? The Caleb I thought I knew—the one who might enjoy teasing banter and secretly appreciate my cheerfulness—felt like a figment of my imagination. He wasn't that man. He was serious, practical, uninterested in frivolity. Uninterested in me.

And now I'd backed him into a corner.

Becca nudged me gently as we walked to the door. "Stop overthinking it, Sadie. You've always had a way of bringing out the best in people. Caleb's no different."

I gave her a weak smile, grateful for her optimism but unable to share it. "Maybe I've just been fooling myself," I said quietly. "Maybe he's just... tolerating me."

Becca rolled her eyes. "*Ach*, don't be *deerich*. You're the only one who gets under his skin in a good way. If Esther thinks she's got a chance with him, she's the one fooling herself."

Her words were meant to reassure, but they only added to the knot tightening in my chest. Because what if Becca was wrong? What if I'd misread every moment with Caleb, every glance, every subtle nuance of his expression? What if working with him on the charity drive only confirmed that he saw me as nothing more than a cheerful nuisance?

I couldn't bear the thought. The drive had been my idea, my bright, hopeful plan to bring the community together and help those in need. But now it felt like a burden—one I'd placed on Caleb without considering how much harder it would be for me to see him every day, knowing he'd never feel the same.

I stepped outside into the cool evening air, the sky painted in shades of lavender and gold. The sight should have calmed me, but my heart was too heavy. As I climbed into the buggy, I whispered a silent prayer for strength, for clarity, for the courage to face whatever this was between Caleb and me. Because no matter how much it hurt, I couldn't back out now.

And on the entire drive home with my *mamm* beside me, driving the buggy, I thought about how I would ever handle seeing Caleb courting Esther right in front of me while my heart shattered.

Chapter Thirteen

Caleb

The bell over the door chimed as I stepped into The Baker's Nook, the warmth of the bakery wrapping around me like a blanket. The air smelled of cinnamon and fresh bread, but the knot in my stomach refused to loosen. I spotted Sadie right away, seated by the window with her notebook open in front of her. She didn't look up, didn't smile. That knot pulled tighter.

I'd asked her to meet me here under the pretense of going over the charity drive, but the truth was, I had a different agenda. I needed to feel her out, to see if there was any chance she'd entertain the idea of courting me. The thought had been gnawing at me for days, ever since my conversation with Levi at the community garden. I'd decided this was the best way to ease into it—casual, no pressure. But now, standing in the doorway with her quiet, distant demeanor staring back at me, I wondered if I'd already lost whatever fragile chance I'd been hoping for.

"*Hallo*, Caleb," Hannah King, the owner, called out from behind the counter, her voice as cheery as always. "You're here bright and early. Let me guess—coffee and a cinnamon roll? Or perhaps a pie to bring home to your *bruders*?"

I gave her a polite nod and muttered, "Just here to meet Sadie."

Hannah's eyebrows shot up, but she didn't say anything. She handed me a menu, though I already knew I wouldn't need it. The closer I got to Sadie's table, the more I noticed how different she seemed. Her back was stiff, her shoulders tense. When I finally slid into the chair across from her, she didn't even glance up.

"Sadie," I said, testing the waters. "*Denke* for meeting me."

She finally looked up, her eyes sharper than I'd expected. "Of course. We have work to do."

There it was again, that coolness that had replaced her usual warmth. No smile. No gentle teasing. My mind scrambled for answers. Had I said something wrong the last time we talked? Had I done something to upset her? The last time we were together she was totally normal.

I took a steadying breath. "I thought we could start by going over the logistics," I said, nodding toward her notebook. "Figure out how to delegate tasks for the charity drive."

Sadie didn't respond right away. Instead, she flipped through her notebook, her fingers moving with precision, her expression unreadable. "I've already put together a list," she said finally, sliding the notebook toward me. "Everything's broken down by category. I'll take care of the outreach and organizing volunteers. You can handle the heavy lifting."

Her tone was clipped, her words like tiny hammers chipping away at my confidence. "Sadie, are you alright?"

"I'm fine," she said quickly, her eyes darting away. "Just busy at the store when I left."

It wasn't like her to be this closed off, and the realization unsettled me more than I wanted to admit. "If something's wrong, you can tell me. I'd like to help."

Sadie's lips pressed into a thin line, and for a moment, I thought she might actually open up. But then Hannah appeared at our table, two mugs of coffee in hand and a smile that could rival the morning sun.

"Here you go." She set the mugs down with a flourish. "And Caleb, Esther wanted me to thank you again for helping her at the garden the other day. She couldn't stop talking about how kind you were."

Sadie's jaw tightened, and I swore I saw her knuckles whiten as she gripped her pen. "How nice," she said, her voice brittle.

Hannah didn't notice the tension—or maybe she did and just didn't care. "Esther's such a sweet girl, isn't she?" she added with a knowing smile. "I'm so blessed to call her my *schweschder*."

I glanced at Sadie, hoping to catch her eye, but she was already looking down at her notebook, her expression unreadable. *Ach*, what had I gotten myself into? The last thing I wanted to be doing right now was talking about Esther.

I stirred my coffee, watching the spoon clink against the ceramic cup as if it held answers. Sadie hadn't looked at me once since Hannah's little speech about Esther. The weight of whatever was between us pressed down harder than any chore back on the farm. I needed to fix this, but I didn't even know what this was.

"So," I said, trying to sound casual, "about the charity drive..."

Sadie didn't look up. She flipped another page in her notebook, her movements sharp, like she was slicing through paper instead of just turning it. "I already said you'll handle logistics. There's not much to discuss."

"Not much to discuss?" I repeated, incredulous. "Sadie, this whole thing was your idea."

"Exactly." Her tone was as clipped as her handwriting was neat. "I've already done most of the work, so you wouldn't have to be bothered. Now it's just a matter of execution."

My chest tightened. She was shutting me out, and I had no idea why. "Did I do something to upset you?"

Her pen froze mid-word, the silence between us stretching long enough for Hannah to swoop back in, carrying a wicker basket containing a loaf of freshly baked bread. "Lunch is on its way," she chirped. "I thought you'd both enjoy a little something to start."

"Hannah, this looks like enough to feed the entire community," I said, forcing a smile. "We don't need an entire loaf of bread."

"Consider it a little extra from Esther," she replied, winking. "She wanted to make sure you were well taken care of, Caleb. You know how thoughtful she is."

I almost choked on my coffee. Sadie's hand twitched, her pen pressing too hard against the page. "That's very... generous of her," she said, her voice flat.

Hannah beamed, clearly pleased with herself. "She's such a dear, isn't she? Always thinking of others. You'd be hard-pressed to find a better woman in the entire state of Minnesota."

"Hannah," I said firmly, the warmth in my tone cooling by several degrees, "*denke* for the bread."

She blinked at me, her smile faltering just slightly before she bustled away. I looked back at Sadie, who had resumed writing in her notebook as if she were drafting a constitution.

"Sadie," I tried again, my voice lower, softer. "Talk to me. *Bitte*."

She slammed the notebook shut, the sound loud enough to turn a few heads in the bakery. "What is there to talk about, Caleb?" she snapped, her eyes finally meeting mine. They were bright with something that looked suspiciously like tears. "You've got Esther looking after you now, so you hardly need my help."

Her words hit me like a bucket of ice water. "Esther?" I repeated, stunned. "Sadie, I don't—"

Before I could finish, Edna Zook swept into the bakery like she owned the place, her black bonnet barely containing the silver wisps escaping at the edges. She moved with purpose, her sharp eyes scanning the room until they landed squarely on us. I tensed instinctively.

"Oh, Caleb! Sadie!" Edna's voice rang out, carrying across the bakery like she owned the place. Before I could do anything to avoid the incoming storm, she beelined straight for our table, her shawl swinging with authority. She didn't wait for an invitation before lowering herself into the third chair, smoothing her skirt as if she were the guest of honor. "Well, isn't this a charming little meeting?"

Sadie stiffened beside me, her posture too rigid to be natural. She stared at her notebook as if it held all the answers to life's problems, but I caught the faintest quiver in her hand. My heart sank.

"*Hallo*, Edna," I said, managing a tight smile. "What brings you here today?"

"Oh, just picking up some fresh bread for the bishop's wife," Edna replied with a wave of her hand, her tone casual but her sharp gaze flicking between Sadie and me. "But imagine my surprise seeing you two here, so cozily tucked away. What a lovely sight for a chilly day."

Sadie's voice was clipped when she spoke. "We're just discussing the charity drive."

Edna clucked her tongue, clearly unimpressed. "*Ach*, charity is a fine thing, of course. But, Sadie, it's not good to bury yourself in work all the time. A young woman like you should be thinking about other matters as well. Aren't you one and twenty this year?"

At that moment, Hannah decided to deliver our beef stew. Sadie just stared at it for a solid minute without taking a single bite. Then she finally looked up, her expression carefully blank. "I'm not sure what you mean."

"Oh, you know," Edna said, leaning forward conspiratorially. "There's a young man who's been asking about you—Jacob Lapp. He's a fine match, don't you think?"

Sadie's knuckles went white as she gripped her pencil. "Jacob Lapp?" Her tone was polite, but barely.

"Jacob Lapp?" The words fell out of my mouth before I could stop them, heavy with disbelief.

My mind reeled, conjuring the image of the man in question—a lumbering figure with mismatched suspenders that barely held up his trousers. His face always looked a shade too flushed, his round cheeks perpetually shiny, as if he'd been working in the hog pens all day. And maybe he had, considering the lingering smell that clung to him like an unwanted companion. Jacob wasn't all there, either—he'd never been. Dropped on the head as a babe, they said, and the years hadn't improved matters.

He spoke in grunts and half-sentences, more likely to scratch his head than offer a coherent thought. And now, with his parents gone, the community had to take turns keeping an eye on him. The idea of Sadie—bright, clever, beautiful Sadie—being paired with him? It was appalling. Distressing. "Are you out of your mind?" I wanted to ask Edna, but my mouth snapped shut instead, the words choking in my throat. This was beyond absurd. It was an insult. Did Edna even know Sadie at all?

Sadie looked tragic—like she might toss her bite of bread back up.

Edna beamed.

"*Jah*, Jacob Lapp," Edna repeated, as if savoring the sound of his name. "He's been asking about you quite a bit. A hard worker, that one, and he's got his own place—well, mostly. Sure, his barn leans a little, but it's nothing a good coat of paint and some sturdy hands couldn't fix. You could help him, I'm sure."

Sadie's pencil snapped in her hand, the sound sharp enough to make me flinch. "That's... kind of him to ask," she said evenly, though her voice had a strained edge to it.

"Kind? It's more than kind! It's an opportunity," Edna pressed on, either oblivious to or purposefully ignoring the tension in the air. "Not every man would be so bold as to ask about a girl directly. Shows initiative, you know. And he's got a... practical charm. A man of few words never becomes a nag."

Practical charm? I bit back a groan, wondering if Edna was talking about the same Jacob Lapp who couldn't manage to keep his pigs penned properly. The man smelled more like his hogs than a decent farmer should.

Sadie forced a tight smile, her face pale except for the red creeping up her cheeks. "That's... something to consider, I suppose."

Edna leaned back in her chair, clearly satisfied with herself. "I just think it would be a shame to see a fine girl like you waiting too long, Sadie. You never know when someone better might come along—or when they might not."

Her gaze flicked to me then, pointed and knowing, and my stomach twisted. Sadie's shoulders went rigid, and she stood abruptly, gathering her notebook and pencil shards. "If you'll excuse me," she said, her voice trembling just enough for me to notice. "I need to use the restroom."

"*Ach*, Sadie," Edna called after her, oblivious—or perhaps thrilled—at the impact of her words. "Don't take it to heart! I'm just looking out for your best interests."

Sadie didn't look back as she walked to the back of the restaurant, her chin held high, though her steps seemed a touch unsteady.

Edna sighed, shaking her head as she turned back to me. "Such a sensitive girl, isn't she? She'll come around, though. Jacob is a fine match, and she'll see that in time."

I stared at her retreating back, my jaw clenched so tightly it ached. "She's perfectly capable of deciding for herself."

Edna arched a brow but said nothing, her smile lingering as she rose from her chair. "Well, I'll leave you to it then. Do give my regards to your *mamm*, Caleb. And think about what I said—you'd do well to take more initiative yourself."

I didn't answer, too busy replaying the moment Sadie had stood up, her face a mask of composure that didn't hide the hurt in her eyes. Whatever just happened, I'd played a part in it, and the weight of that realization settled heavily on my chest.

After a few tense minutes of wondering if she'd escaped out the bathroom window, I saw her walk toward me. I stood as Sadie returned to the table, her chin high and her movements brisk. It was a mask, and I could see it cracking at the edges, but I couldn't figure out why. All I knew was that something was deeply wrong, and it felt like every move I made was just making it worse.

Hannah approached with the bill tucked neatly in her hand. I reached for it immediately. "I'll take care of this."

"*Nee*," Sadie said firmly, her voice low but sharp. She reached for her wrist satchel, fumbling with the clasp. "I can pay my own way."

"Sadie, that's not necessary." I tried to keep my tone even, but it came out more insistent than I intended. "I asked you to lunch. I'll take care of it."

"You didn't ask me," she shot back, her hands trembling as she wrestled with the stubborn clasp. "This was for the charity drive. A working meeting. Not... whatever this is."

I flinched, her words cutting deeper than they should have. "Sadie, please. It's just lunch."

"To you, maybe." Her voice cracked on the last word, and her hands stilled, the satchel slipping from her fingers. She looked up at me, her eyes shining with unshed tears. "I don't need you to pay for me, Caleb. I don't need you to do anything for me. In fact, I don't even need your help with the drive. I'll find someone else. Anyone else."

Anyone else? My chest tightened, the weight of her words sinking in like stones. "Sadie, wait—"

But she was already turning, her skirts swishing as she hurried toward the door. "Forget it, Caleb. Just forget everything."

The bakery door closed behind her with a soft chime, and I was left staring at the empty space where she'd stood, my heart pounding in my chest. I wanted to go after her, to tell her I didn't know what I'd done wrong but that I would do anything to fix it. But my feet wouldn't move. My head was too full of questions and doubts and the sinking realization that I'd hurt her somehow—badly.

"Caleb," Hannah's voice pulled me back to the moment, her tone sweet but firm. "Before you go, I thought you might like to know that Esther mentioned she's thinking of baking some special cinnamon rolls for the next market day. She said they're your favorite."

I turned to her slowly, the words barely registering over the roar of frustration in my ears. "*Denke*, Hannah," I said tightly, though my jaw ached with the effort of forcing the words out. Levi's voice boomeranged around inside my head about being nice and not ruining our family name by my rudeness.

She smiled, oblivious to the storm brewing inside me, and I nodded once before walking to the counter to pay the bill, leaving our uneaten bowls of stew and the entire loaf of bread behind. The coins felt heavy in my hand as I placed them down, the thought of Sadie's trembling voice echoing in my mind.

As I stepped outside, the sunlight felt harsh, and for the first time in a long time, I felt truly lost.

I leaned against the side of the buggy, staring down the road where Sadie had disappeared moments ago. The sound of the bakery door closing behind me felt louder than it should have, like it was hammering the final nail in some invisible coffin. She was gone, and so was any hope of finding out what had gone so wrong between us.

My hands gripped the edge of the buggy, the worn wood biting into my palms. Sadie had always been sunshine, full of warmth and light that seeped into even the coldest corners. But today? Today, she'd been storm clouds—distant, cold, and impossible to reach. It was like I'd shattered something delicate, and no amount of careful handling would ever put it back together.

I replayed every word she'd said, every glance she'd thrown my way. *Ach*, I'd been polite to Hannah about Esther, but that was only to avoid making a scene. What else was I supposed to do? Yet, somehow, it had all landed wrong, twisting into something that had hurt Sadie enough to bring tears to her eyes. The way she'd looked at me—like I'd let her down in a way I couldn't fix—cut deeper than I wanted to admit.

"Why?" I muttered under my breath, the question burning in my chest. Why did everything feel so out of control when it came to her? I'd spent my whole life keeping things steady, predictable. And now, one woman—one maddening, wonderful woman—had turned it all on its head.

A laugh drifted from inside the bakery, pulling me back to reality. It was Hannah, no doubt chatting with a customer or humming to herself as she bustled around. I couldn't bring myself to go back inside. Not now.

Not with her voice still echoing in my head: Esther's cinnamon rolls, your favorite.

The problem wasn't Esther. It never had been. I'd made that clear, or at least I thought I had. But what if Sadie didn't see it that way? What if every polite smile, every courteous word to Hannah about her sister, had only convinced Sadie that I didn't see her—that I didn't care?

I gritted my teeth, the thought lodging in my chest like a splinter. The truth was, Sadie had been the one filling my thoughts—her laughter, her determination, the way she lit up a room just by being in it. I'd come here today hoping to feel her out, maybe even ask her if she'd consider courting me. But now? Now it felt like I'd missed my chance entirely.

As I climbed into the buggy and took the reins, the ache in my chest only grew. I wanted to fix it, to make her see that she wasn't just some fleeting thought or passing interest. But how could I do that when I didn't even know what had broken her? Worse, when I had the sinking feeling that I was the one who'd done it?

I clicked my tongue to the horse, the buggy lurching forward. Each turn of the wheels carried me further from the bakery, but the weight in my chest stayed firmly in place. I'd come here hoping for clarity, maybe even a new beginning. Instead, I was leaving with nothing but questions and the bitter taste of regret.

Chapter Fourteen

SADIE

The General Store was in chaos, and I was the eye of the storm. Piles of boxes filled the space behind the counter, and my notebook sat open to a scrawled list of names and items yet to be collected. The charity drive felt like it was getting away from me, each unchecked box on the list a reminder of how much still needed to be done. Caleb's absence weighed heavier than I wanted to admit. I should've been used to handling things on my own, but this time, it felt different—emptier.

The bell above the door jingled, and I didn't even look up. "We're closed for new donations until this afternoon," I called, brushing a stray curl out of my face and squinting at the page. "Just leave it by the barrel, please."

"Well, that's not very welcoming," a familiar voice drawled, rich with amusement. I froze, my pencil hovering mid-air. Levi Stoltzfus.

He leaned against the counter, his usual smirk firmly in place, the sunlight behind him catching the dust motes swirling in the air. "Looks like you're running a one-woman show here. Need a hand?"

I narrowed my eyes. "And why would you offer? Don't you have a farm to run?"

He shrugged, glancing around at the organized chaos like it was a personal challenge. "Caleb told me about the charity drive, and I figured you could use someone with two strong arms and a bit of charm."

I snorted, resuming my scribbling. "I can do without the charm, denke."

"Aw, come on, Sadie," he said, dropping his voice to a mock-serious tone. "You don't really want to turn away free labor, do you? Especially not someone as strapping as me?"

I rolled my eyes but felt a reluctant smile tug at my lips. Levi Stoltzfus could charm the bark off a tree, and he knew it. "Fine," I relented, closing the notebook with a snap. "But if you're going to help, you'd better actually work. No doing one thing and then running off to flirt with the first pretty girl you see."

His grin widened as he pushed off the counter, already rolling up his sleeves. "Ach, you wound me, Sadie. I'm the very picture of hard work."

"We'll see about that," I muttered, handing him a list of names and tasks. "Here's what still needs doing."

He glanced at it, then at the stack of boxes. "This is it? Sadie Miller, you're making a mountain out of a molehill. We'll have this wrapped up in no time."

I watched as he started moving boxes with ease, his natural confidence reducing some of the tension that had been building in my chest all morning. As much as I hated to admit it, his presence did make things feel a little less overwhelming. Still, I couldn't shake the nagging thought that I shouldn't have needed his help at all.

"So," Levi said, glancing at me as he hefted a crate onto the counter, "what's the plan, boss?"

"The plan," I said with a sigh, "is to get through this without losing my mind."

Levi had a way of making himself at home, even in the middle of my carefully curated chaos. Within minutes, he was sorting boxes like he'd been born to it, flashing a grin at every small success. Watching him toss bags of donated quilts onto a pile with the casual ease of someone who didn't have a worry in the world, I felt an unfamiliar lightness creep into the room.

"So," Levi said, leaning against the counter after stacking the last of the heavier boxes, "who's next on the list? Or is this where we take a coffee break and I let you tell me how grateful you are for my help?"

I couldn't help but roll my eyes, though his teasing tugged at a smile. "Don't get ahead of yourself. There's still a wagonload of donations at the Yoder farm that needs picking up. And someone needs to organize all of this by tonight."

Levi rubbed his chin thoughtfully. "Picking up donations, checking off lists... sounds like work for a capable team. Lucky for you, I'm available."

I crossed my arms, giving him a skeptical look. "You sure you're not just bored?"

"Maybe," he admitted with a wink. "But seriously, Sadie, you've got a lot going on here. I know Caleb was supposed to help. But he... well..."

"He what?" I asked, narrowing my eyes.

Levi hesitated, his smirk softening. "He's complicated, you know? He doesn't always say what he means, and half the time, he doesn't know what he's feeling until it's too late."

I looked away, focusing on straightening a pile of papers that didn't need straightening. "This isn't about Caleb. The drive is for the community. And it's my fault he's not here. I told him I didn't need his help anymore."

"Right," Levi said, though his tone held a hint of disbelief. "But you're doing a lot of this on your own, and that's not fair, either. So, here I am. Your replacement Stoltzfus. Your savior in suspenders."

I sighed, unable to argue with his logic—or his charm. "Fine. If you're so insistent on helping, start loading those boxes onto the buggy. We can drop them off on our way to the Yoder farm."

He gave a mock salute, already moving toward the pile. "At your service, boss."

As Levi worked, I busied myself with tying up loose ends, though my mind kept drifting. His offer of help was unexpected, and I couldn't deny that having him around made the burden feel lighter. But there was a small, nagging voice in the back of my mind—the one that wondered if this sudden attention was more about Caleb than about me.

I shook off the thought, focusing on the task at hand. It didn't matter why Levi was here reminding me of his broody brother. What mattered was that the work was getting done, and for the first time in days, it felt like progress.

"Ready when you are," Levi called, his grin as bright as ever.

I nodded, grabbing my notebook and stepping toward the door. "Let's get to it, then."

If Levi noticed the way my smile didn't quite reach my eyes, he didn't say a word.

The wagon creaked and groaned as Levi and I made our way down the dirt road toward the Yoder farm. The late afternoon sun cast a golden glow over the fields, and for the first time in days, I felt a sliver of calm settle over me. Levi, of course, seemed as at ease as ever, humming a cheerful tune as he guided the horse along.

"You know," he said, glancing at me with that ever-present grin, "you're a lot more fun to work with than Caleb."

I raised an eyebrow. "Is that supposed to be a compliment?"

He laughed, the sound rich and genuine. "Absolutely. Caleb's all about straight lines and stern looks. You actually laugh and smile more than you don't. It's refreshing."

I rolled my eyes, but I couldn't stop the smile tugging at my lips. "Well, don't get too comfortable. There's still plenty of work to be done."

Levi waved a hand dismissively. "Work's not so bad when you're doing it for a good cause. And besides, I'm pretty sure I'm the reason this whole operation is running so smoothly now."

"Is that so?" I asked, my tone dry.

"*Jah*," he said, nodding solemnly. "You're the brains, obviously, but I'm the charm. Together, we're unstoppable."

I shook my head, laughing despite myself. "Whatever helps you sleep at night, Levi."

When we arrived at the Yoder farm, Mrs. Yoder greeted us warmly, her apron dusted with flour and her cheeks pink from the heat of the kitchen. "Sadie! Levi! Such a blessing to see you both. The boxes are all ready in the barn. I'll fetch Amos to help load them."

"Oh, there's no need for that," Levi said quickly, hopping down from the wagon. "I'll take care of it."

Mrs. Yoder beamed. "Such a fine young man. If only all the boys in Grace Hollow were as helpful as you, Levi."

I stifled a laugh as Levi puffed up like a rooster, tipping his hat with exaggerated charm. "Just doing my part."

As Levi disappeared into the barn, Mrs. Yoder turned to me, her expression softening. "You're doing a wonderful thing, Sadie. This charity drive is going to make a real difference."

"*Denke*, Mrs. Yoder," I said, feeling a flush of warmth at her words. "But it's not just me. The whole community has come together to make this happen."

She patted my arm. "Still, it takes a special kind of heart to bring people together like this. Don't sell yourself short."

I nodded, her words sinking in as I watched Levi emerge from the barn, a box balanced effortlessly in each hand. He caught my eye and winked, his grin as infectious as ever.

For a moment, I let myself believe that things were falling into place. But then the thought of Caleb crept in, and the calm I'd felt earlier wavered.

Levi loaded the last box onto the wagon and clapped his hands together. "That's everything. Ready to head back?"

I nodded, forcing a smile. "Ready."

But as we set off down the road, I couldn't shake the feeling that the path ahead was more complicated than it seemed.

By the time we returned to the General Store, the sun was beginning to dip below the horizon, casting the sky in soft hues of pink and gold. The wagon rattled to a stop, and Levi hopped down first, offering me a hand like the picture of a gentleman.

"Careful now," he said with a teasing grin. "Wouldn't want the brains of this operation twisting an ankle."

"*Denke*, Levi," I replied dryly, ignoring the warmth creeping into my cheeks. His antics were harmless, but they had a way of keeping me off balance.

The front of the store was bustling with neighbors, all dropping off donations or picking up supplies. Word of the charity drive had spread faster than I anticipated, and the sheer volume of goods was overwhelming in the best way.

"Sadie!" Becca's voice cut through the din as she made her way over, her eyes alight with excitement. "It's looking incredible in there. The shelves are already full, and there's more coming in by the hour. I heard Mrs. Fisher even brought over some quilts to auction off!"

"That's *wunderbaar*," I said, though my voice lacked the enthusiasm it should have had. My mind was too full—of lists, of tasks, and of thoughts I didn't want to entertain.

Levi, oblivious to my inner turmoil, clapped his hands together. "See? What did I tell you? The Sadie-Levi dream team strikes again!"

Becca raised an eyebrow, her lips twitching. "Oh, is that what we're calling it now?"

"*Jah*," Levi said, crossing his arms with mock seriousness. "And don't be surprised if people start calling us that around town."

I laughed lightly, shaking my head. "Let's just focus on getting everything organized before the auction tomorrow."

Becca's gaze lingered on me for a moment, her smile fading slightly. Before I could ask what was on her mind, she turned to Levi. "You know, Levi, a lot of people are saying how well you and Sadie work together. Someone even mentioned it might be more than just work. Of course, I don't think that because Sadie is perfect and you are as annoying as a hornet's nest buzzing in my ears."

Levi's grin widened, and he leaned against the wagon with exaggerated nonchalance. "Well, I can't say I'm surprised. Sadie's got excellent taste, after all."

"Levi!" I said, my voice sharper than I intended. "Don't start."

But Becca wasn't done. "I heard Mrs. Yoder saying she hasn't seen a pair work so well together since her youngest son and his wife started courting. Frankly, I can't understand why. Levi can't take anything seriously."

The words hit me like a stone, and I could feel the blood drain from my face. Levi, always quick with a retort, held up his hands in mock surrender. "Hey, don't look at me. I'm just the charming sidekick here."

"Right," I muttered, my chest tightening. "Let's just focus on the drive."

But as I moved toward the store, the chatter of voices behind me seemed louder than ever, each one carrying the same, unshakable thread: Sadie and Levi working so well together. The very idea left a knot in my stomach—and not for the reasons everyone assumed.

By the time the last of the donations were neatly stacked in the back of the General Store, the stars had begun to peek out from the darkening sky. Levi stood beside me, dusting off his hands with a satisfied grin. "Well, I'd say we've done our good deed for the day. You've got yourself a mighty fine operation here, Sadie. Glad I could be a part of it."

I smiled politely, but the weight in my chest made it hard to feel any real pride. Levi was wonderful—easygoing, kind, and endlessly helpful. He didn't complain, didn't frown. He treated me like I mattered. But as his words washed over me, my thoughts betrayed me, drifting toward the one man who could barely look at me lately without seeming to wrestle some invisible demon.

"*Denke*, Levi," I said, tucking a stray hair back under my kapp. "I couldn't have done it without you."

"Oh, I know," he teased, nudging me gently with his elbow. "But let's not tell Caleb, eh? Don't want to bruise the old *bruder's* ego."

The mention of Caleb's name sent a pang straight to my chest. I turned toward the doorway, not expecting to see him but unable to stop myself from looking. And there he was, standing just outside with his hands shoved deep into his pockets, his face shadowed but unmistakably Caleb.

He looked like a man torn in two, his eyes fixed on the bustling scene inside but his feet rooted firmly outside. I caught the way his jaw clenched, the way his shoulders tensed as if he were holding himself back from crossing the threshold. What was he doing here? Had he come to help? To check on me? Or was he just passing by?

The knot in my stomach tightened. Why did he have to be so difficult? Why couldn't we get along as easily as Levi and I did? With Levi, everything felt light, natural, and uncomplicated. But with Caleb, every glance, every word felt like stepping into a storm—wild, unpredictable, and completely overwhelming. And yet, Levi's easy charm didn't linger in my thoughts late at night. It didn't make my heart race or leave me questioning every word I'd said. That was Caleb.

Always Caleb.

I tore my gaze away from him, focusing instead on arranging a stack of canned goods on the counter. But my hands trembled, betraying the whirlwind of emotions churning inside me. Was Gott testing me? Why else would He put Caleb in my path over and over again, only for him to remain so closed off, so guarded? It was like being a toddler and having the piece of candy dangled in front of you only to have it snatched away. It felt cruel, this constant tug between hope and heartbreak.

Levi leaned against the counter, his grin unwavering. "What do you say, Sadie? Shall we call it a night and celebrate this big success?"

I forced a smile, nodding. "Jah, sounds like a plan." But as I stepped out into the cool night air, my heart betrayed me again, my eyes darting toward Caleb. He was still there, watching, and for a brief, unbearable moment, our eyes met. His expression was unreadable, but the ache in my chest told me everything I needed to know.

And then without saying one word, he walked away, got in his buggy, and drove off.

Levi tilted his head to the side. "That was odd. Or maybe not, depending on how you look at it."

"*Jah*, odd."

Gott, I prayed silently as I turned away, why does this have to hurt so much? Why did You let me fall for a man who can't seem to let me in?

Chapter Fifteen

Caleb

The morning sun had barely stretched over the horizon, and I was already wishing the day was over. Levi and I worked in silence—or at least, I worked in silence. Levi never could leave well enough alone. He lounged against the fence post I was trying to fix, his hat tipped back and that infuriating smirk tugging at his lips.

"So," Levi began, his tone light but laced with something sharper, "Sadie seemed mighty pleased yesterday. Said the charity drive's shaping up to be quite the success."

I gritted my teeth, my hammer pausing mid-swing. "Did she now?"

"Oh, *jah*," he continued, clearly enjoying himself. "Said it was all the donations—what was it she called me? *Ach, jah*, 'the unsung hero.'"

I slammed the hammer down harder than necessary, the nails groaning under the force. "If you're not going to help, at least stay out of the way."

Levi chuckled, pushing off the post to grab a bundle of fresh planks. "Touchy, touchy. I'd think you'd be grateful I stepped in to lend a hand. After all, you seemed busy enough sulking to leave Sadie high and dry.

Then you actually have the audacity to drive into town and leave without saying a word."

I dropped the hammer, turning to glare at him. "Sulking? You think I've been sulking?"

"Don't get your suspenders in a twist." Levi leaned the planks against the fence, crossing his arms. "I only meant that you're usually so... reliable. But you've been acting like a man trying to outrun his own shadow."

My jaw tightened, the accusation landing harder than I wanted to admit. "She's the one who told me she didn't need my help," I muttered. "And Sadie didn't need you meddling in her business."

"Meddling?" Levi repeated, his grin widening. "Is that what you call helping? Because from where I'm standing, you're the one doing nothing while the rest of us pitch in."

Heat rose in my chest, the words spilling out before I could stop them. "She didn't ask for your help, Levi. She asked for mine."

Levi blinked, his smirk fading for a moment. Then, to my frustration, he laughed. "Oh, now I get it. You're mad because you think I'm moving in on your girl."

"She's not my—" I snapped, but the words caught in my throat.

Levi stepped closer, his expression softening just slightly. "You're right, Caleb. She's not. But you want her to be, don't you?"

I turned away, grabbing another nail and forcing it into the wood. "I don't know what you're talking about."

"Don't you, though?" Levi asked, his tone low but insistent. "Because if you keep this up—standing on the sidelines, watching while she smiles at someone else—you're going to lose her. And it'll be no one's fault but your own. And I'll be right here to shove your face in the mess you made."

The hammer shook in my grip as Levi's words settled like stones in my gut. I didn't respond, but the silence between us was louder than anything he could've said.

Levi leaned against the fence, a stalk of hay between his teeth, looking entirely too pleased with himself. It set my teeth on edge. The rhythmic clinking of tools as we worked didn't do much to soften my mood, either. Every once in a while, Levi would glance at me, a grin twitching at his lips like he was waiting for me to snap.

"Go ahead," I finally bit out, throwing down the tool in my hand. "Say whatever it is you're dying to say. You've been grinning like a fool all morning."

Levi straightened, brushing off his hands with exaggerated care. "I'm just wondering, bruder, how it feels knowing Sadie and I make such a good team. Folks are already talking."

I froze, my pulse pounding in my ears. "Talking about what?"

"Oh, you know," he said with a shrug, his tone casual but his eyes sharp. "How we work so well together. How we'd make such a fine couple. It's funny, really. I'm not even trying, and yet..." He let the words hang, smirking when I took a step closer.

"You're trying to get under my skin," I growled, my hands curling into fists. "You have no interest in Sadie. You never have."

Levi's grin widened, and then, to my utter disbelief, he started laughing. Full-on laughing, doubling over like I'd told the funniest joke he'd ever heard.

"What's so funny?" I demanded, my voice rising.

"You!" he choked out, wiping his eyes. "*Ach*, Caleb, you're so blind it's painful. You're right—I have no interest in Sadie. Never have. But someone had to light a fire under you, and apparently, I'm the only one willing to do it."

His words hit me like a punch to the gut. "What are you talking about?"

Levi straightened, his expression sobering. "You're in love with her, Caleb. Don't bother denying it—I've seen the way you look at her. But you're too stubborn, or scared, or maybe both, to admit it. So yeah, I helped her. Not because I'm interested in her, but because I knew it'd drive you crazy enough to finally do something about it."

Heat surged in my chest, anger and something else—something rawer—mixing until I couldn't tell where one ended and the other began. "You think this is funny?" I said through clenched teeth.

Levi shrugged again, his smirk returning. "Not funny. Necessary. You're my bruder, Caleb. I'm not going to stand by and watch you ruin your life because you're too proud to take a risk."

I lunged at him before I even realized what I was doing. Levi ducked, laughing as we tumbled into the pile of hay behind him. "There he is!" he crowed, struggling to fend me off as I pinned him down. "There's the passion I was looking for!"

"You're impossible," I growled, but my grip loosened, and before I could stop myself, I was laughing too. It was bitter and rough around the edges, but it was real.

"You'll owe me later," Levi said, grinning up at me from the hay.

I doubted it, but his words stayed with me as I stood, brushing off my clothes and heading toward home. Levi's laughter followed me, but it couldn't drown out the truth in his words. I was in love with Sadie, and it was time to do something about it.

My boots kicked up little puffs of dirt with each heavy step. My hands were clenched at my sides, and my chest burned like I'd just run halfway to the bishop's house and back. Levi's laughter still echoed in my ears, and the worst part? He wasn't wrong.

I'd wanted to fight him. My own brother. Over Sadie.

The realization hit me like a bucket of cold water. What kind of fool was I? Levi wasn't interested in Sadie—he'd all but said so outright—but that hadn't stopped the jealousy from surging like a wildfire the second he so much as hinted at it. And why? Because the thought of her with someone else—anyone else—was unbearable.

I ran a hand through my hair, the muscles in my jaw aching from how tightly I'd been clenching it. Sadie deserved someone who would make her laugh, someone who wouldn't push her away or scowl through every conversation. And yet, the thought of her walking down the aisle toward another man made my stomach churn like sour milk.

I stopped at the edge of the field, the open sky stretching endlessly above me. The wind tugged at my shirt, the cool air doing little to calm the storm raging inside. Levi's words replayed in my head, each one cutting deeper than the last.

"You're in love with her, Caleb."

Could it be that simple? The answer sat heavy in my chest, and I hated how much truth there was in it. I thought back to the way Sadie's eyes sparkled when she teased me, the way her voice softened when she spoke about the charity drive. I thought about the way she'd stormed out of the Baker's Nook, her shoulders stiff and her voice trembling with unshed tears.

And I thought about how I'd wanted to chase after her, to tell her... what? That she mattered? That I wasn't as indifferent as I pretended to be? That I couldn't get her out of my mind no matter how hard I tried?

I let out a shaky breath, my fists clenching and unclenching at my sides. Levi was right—I'd been too proud, too scared to take a risk. But no more. If I had any hope of making things right with Sadie, of seeing if this ache in my chest could be something more, I had to act.

But first, I had to clear the path. Esther's name had been tossed around too much lately, and the last thing I wanted was for Sadie to think there was anything between us. If I wanted to court Sadie, I needed to make it clear to the community—and to her—that my intentions were true.

Without another thought, I turned toward the house, grabbing my hat as I passed through the doorway. My heart pounded with each step toward the buggy. If Simon was at the General Store, I'd find him. It was time to do what I should have done weeks ago.

The buggy rattled over the dirt road, the familiar sights of Grace Hollow passing in a blur. My hands gripped the reins tighter than they needed to, the leather digging into my palms. My gelding, sensing my tension, tossed its head, its hooves stamping against the ground in protest.

"Easy there, Duke," I muttered, though I knew the words were more for me than for him.

The General Store loomed ahead, its windows gleaming in the afternoon sun. It was a place of comfort and routine for the people of Grace Hollow, but right now, it felt like a battleground. My gut twisted as I pulled up, Duke slowing to a stop. I climbed down, tying the reins with hands that felt steadier than they should.

Inside, the store smelled of sawdust and spices, the kind of scent that clung to the walls no matter the season. A few neighbors milled about, chatting and inspecting shelves of canned goods and fabric bolts. But my focus was on Simon. He stood behind the counter, his broad shoulders hunched as he counted coins into the till.

He looked up when the bell jingled over the door, his expression shifting from surprise to curiosity. "Caleb," he said, nodding in greeting. "What brings you here?"

I cleared my throat, suddenly aware of the eyes around us. This wasn't a conversation I wanted overheard. "I need a word with you. Privately."

Simon raised an eyebrow but didn't question it. He gestured toward the storeroom door, and I followed him through, the murmurs of the customers fading as the door swung shut behind us. The room was small, lined with shelves of supplies and sacks of flour. It smelled of burlap and soap.

Simon leaned against a crate, his arms crossed. "What's this about?"

"Your *dauchtah*." I didn't waste time. "I'd like your blessing to court Sadie."

The words hung in the air between us, heavier than I'd anticipated. Simon's eyebrows shot up, and for a moment, he said nothing. The silence pressed against my chest, each second stretching like an eternity.

"You want to court Sadie?" he said finally, his tone a mix of disbelief and something I couldn't quite place. "You sure about that, Caleb?"

"*Jah*," I said, my voice firm even though my heart felt like it was trying to escape my ribcage. "I admire her. I care for her. And I think... I think I could make her happy."

Simon's gaze was sharp, scrutinizing me like he could see past the words to the truth underneath. "You've been grumpier than usual lately," he said, his tone almost teasing. "Guess now I know why."

Simon rubbed the back of his neck, his expression shifting from scrutiny to something softer—almost apologetic. The silence between us stretched, broken only by the faint creak of a floorboard under my boots. I was painfully aware of the state I was in, my shirt dusted with hay and stray pieces clinging stubbornly to my hair and sleeves after my tussle with Levi. A few errant stalks fell to the floor as I shifted my weight, but I didn't bother brushing them off. I'd come straight from the farm, and that in itself said more than any words could.

"Look," Simon said finally, his voice low, almost reluctant, "you know I care about Sadie like she's the brightest star in the sky. But after all the talk about Esther... well, I have to think about this."

My stomach twisted, but I nodded slowly. "I understand."

Simon crossed his arms, his brow furrowing. "She's been through a lot, Caleb. And she's not the kind of girl you court unless you're absolutely sure. You mess this up, and it's not just her who'll be hurt—it's her family, her reputation. Everything."

"I know," I said, the weight of his words settling heavily in my chest. "I wouldn't be here if I wasn't sure. I..." I trailed off, struggling to find the right words. "She means more to me than I know how to say."

Simon's sharp gaze softened slightly, but the hesitation didn't leave his face. "Sadie's not here, you know. She's at home helping her *mamm* today. Otherwise, I'd send you straight to her, so she could make her own decision."

Relief mixed with regret as I processed his words. On one hand, I wasn't sure I was ready to face Sadie yet. On the other, I hated that she wasn't here to hear what I was trying to do—for her, for us.

Simon exhaled slowly, breaking the silence. "All right, here's what I'll do. I'll think on it, pray on it. And I'll give you my answer at church on Sunday. If I agree, the rest will be up to Sadie. It's her choice, Caleb. Her happiness is what matters most."

His words were a double-edged sword—offering a sliver of hope while reminding me just how much was at stake. I nodded again, swallowing hard against the knot in my throat. "*Denke*, Simon. Truly."

Simon studied me for another moment before stepping forward and clapping me on the shoulder. "You'd better clean up before you make any more moves, Stoltzfus. You're shedding hay all over my storeroom."

Despite the tension in the air, I felt a wry smile tug at my lips. "I'll take care of it," I said, brushing at my shirt halfheartedly. More hay fluttered to the ground, but it seemed a losing battle.

Simon shook his head with a faint chuckle, the lines of worry easing from his face. "*Gut* luck, Caleb. And if my *dauchtah* agrees to give you the time of day, you better make the most of it."

As I stepped out into the sunlight, the weight of Simon's words stayed with me. Sunday felt like a lifetime away, and I had no idea how I'd face Sadie if Simon said no—or worse, if Sadie didn't want me at all.

Chapter Sixteen

SADIE

The wooden bench beneath me creaked as I shifted, trying to find a more comfortable position. My *kapp* felt tight today, as though it were another layer pressing against my already restless thoughts. Bishop Yoder's voice carried through the room, steady and deliberate, each word a thread meant to stitch our lives closer to *Gott's* will.

"Be completely humble and gentle; be patient, bearing with one another in love," he said, quoting from Ephesians. "Make every effort to keep the unity of the Spirit through the bond of peace."

The verse hung in the air, weighty and certain, and my stomach twisted. Humble and gentle. Patient. Bearing with one another in love. Was I those things? I didn't feel patient, not lately. And gentle? No, I'd been as brittle as the frost-bitten grass outside. Bearing with one another felt like a cruel joke, especially when one of those "others" was Caleb Stoltzfus.

My gaze flicked to where the men sat on the other side of the room, across the invisible line that separated us during worship. My eyes found him before I could stop them. He was seated near Levi, his hat perched on his knee, his posture rigid. Even from this distance, I could see the tension in his shoulders, the way his jaw worked as if he were grinding his teeth through the sermon.

What can he possibly have to be so cross about when the most sought after woman in the county is prepared to sacrifice everything just to serve him? I thought bitterly, tearing my gaze away and fixing it on my hymn book. It wasn't like he had to endure Hannah practically throwing her sister's name at him every chance she got. Or listen to Esther herself weave yarns about how Caleb relied on her in ways he never had with anyone else. And he certainly didn't have to sit through Edna's meddling, or hear the whispers in the quilting circle.

But I couldn't hold onto the anger, not when Bishop Yoder's voice softened, speaking of forgiveness and trust. "We must remember," he said, "to seek *Gott's* will, even when it feels unclear. His path is not always easy, but it is always right."

A lump formed in my throat. Did that mean I had to forgive Caleb? Did it mean I had to let go of this ache that had settled in my chest since that disastrous lunch at The Baker's Nook?

The final hymn began, and I stood with the rest of the women, the familiar words rising around me like a prayer. As I sang, I risked another glance toward Caleb. His head was bowed, his lips moving with the hymn, and for a fleeting moment, he looked almost peaceful. My heart squeezed.

When the hymn ended, we all sat down in unison, the soft rustling of fabric filling the silence. As the Bishop dismissed us, Caleb lifted his head, his eyes locking onto mine. It was like being caught in a beam of sunlight after a long, cold winter. His expression was open, raw, and so full of something I couldn't name that my breath hitched.

But I broke the connection first, looking away as quickly as I could. My hands trembled as I gathered my shawl, my mind whirling with thoughts I wasn't ready to face.

The familiar rhythm of shuffling feet and low murmurs filled the room as people began to file out of the benches. I busied myself with straightening my shawl and clutching my hymn book, avoiding any chance of meeting Caleb's gaze again. My heart raced, and I didn't trust my voice not to betray me. Emma trotted off to speak to one of her friends.

"Sadie," *Mamm* said softly, placing a gentle hand on my shoulder. "Are you ready to go?"

"*Jah, Mamm,*" I replied quickly, stepping closer to her side. *Dat* was already at the door, exchanging words with the Future Farmers leader, Amos Byler, about something that didn't reach my ears. Greta darted ahead, giggling about who would sit by the window in the buggy.

I followed in her wake, the cooler air outside a welcome distraction from the heat crawling up my neck. My steps quickened as I weaved through the crowd, keeping my head down. But even in the chaos, I could feel him behind me, his presence like a weight that refused to shift.

"Sadie," his voice called from somewhere nearby, and my stomach twisted. I didn't slow down. If I stopped now, I'd break. I couldn't face him—not here, not with my family watching and the weight of his gaze like a question I didn't have an answer for.

Mamm glanced at me as we reached the buggy. "Is everything all right, *dauchtah*?" she asked, her tone laced with concern.

"Fine, *Mamm,*" I said, pasting on a smile that felt more like a grimace. I climbed into the buggy beside Greta, who was still arguing with Emma over the window seat. Their chatter was a welcome cover for the storm raging in my chest.

Through the corner of my eye, I saw Caleb emerge from the meetinghouse, his stride purposeful as he scanned the crowd. He looked like a man on a mission, but before he could reach us, *Dat* joined *Mamm* at the lines, and the buggy lurched forward. Relief mixed with a sharp pang of regret as I watched Caleb's figure grow smaller in the distance.

As the buggy rolled down the familiar path toward home, I leaned my head against the window, the cold glass a balm against the heat in my cheeks. I thought of the way Caleb had looked at me during the hymn—so open, so earnest. It was the kind of look I'd dreamed of once, but now, it felt like a cruel joke. How could I trust it after everything? After the way he'd let me twist in the wind while Esther, Hannah and Edna painted me as little more than a charity case?

"Sadie," *Mamm* said gently, pulling me from my thoughts. "You seem troubled. Do you want to talk about it?"

I shook my head, blinking back the sting of tears. "*Nee, Mamm*. It's nothing."

But it wasn't nothing. It was Caleb. It was always Caleb.

Once we got home, *Dat* went to put the horse and buggy away. *Mamm* puttered about the kitchen before placing a steaming cup of chamomile tea in front of me and sitting down across the table. The kitchen was quiet, save for the faint hum of the clock on the wall and the occasional creak of the wooden floorboards. My *schweschders* were off playing somewhere, leaving me and *Mamm* alone in the warm, sunlit space.

"Now," *Mamm* began, her hands folding neatly on the table. "Out with it, *dauchtah*. You've been distracted all morning, and your face during the sermon looked like someone had stolen your favorite apron. I know you, and I know when something is troubling you."

I gave a weak laugh, but the sound didn't even convince me. "It's nothing, *Mamm*," I murmured, staring down into my tea. The amber liquid swirled like the confusion in my chest.

"Sadie," Mamm said gently, reaching across the table to touch my hand. "If something is weighing on your heart, it's better to share it. You don't have to carry it alone."

Her words loosened something in me, and before I could stop myself, the truth came tumbling out. "It's Caleb," I admitted, my voice barely above a whisper. "He feels like... like he could be the one, *Mamm*. But he keeps holding back, and I don't know if I can keep letting him hurt me like that."

Mamm's expression softened, her blue eyes filled with understanding. "What makes you think he's holding back?"

I hesitated, tracing the edge of the tea cup with my finger. "It's the way he looks at me sometimes, like I matter to him. Like he sees me in a way no one else ever has. But then there's the other side of him—the closed-off, gruff Caleb who doesn't know how to let anyone in. And when he doesn't speak up, when he doesn't stand up for me..." My voice broke, and I took a shaky breath. "It makes me feel like I'm not worth it to him."

Mamm tilted her head, her lips pursed thoughtfully. "Do you believe Caleb has feelings for you?"

"*Jah*." The word left me before I could second-guess it. "I do. But feelings aren't enough, are they? He has to show them. He has to open up."

Mamm nodded slowly. "You're right, Sadie. Love isn't just a feeling. It's a choice—a choice to trust, to share, to grow together. And sometimes, it takes a bit of courage to make that choice."

I sniffled, wiping at my eyes with the edge of my sleeve. "But what if he never does? What if I'm just fooling myself?"

Mamm's hand tightened around mine. "Then that's something you'll have to ask *Gott* for guidance on. But do not despair, if Caleb truly is the one *Gott* has chosen for you, I believe he'll find his way to your heart."

Her words settled over me like a balm, soothing the ache that had been building all morning. "Do you really think so?"

"I do," she said softly. "But remember, Sadie, love takes patience. For both of you."

After my chat with my *mamm*, I read a book on the screened in front porch for a while. Then the faint murmur of voices floated in from the kitchen—*Dat's* low rumble and *Mamm's* gentle tone blending into a comforting hum. I caught a few words, something about "he walked all the way here," and my heart skipped. Before I could piece it together, the screen door creaked open, startling me.

I turned to see Caleb standing there, his shoulders broad and stiff, his hat clutched tightly in his hands. He looked like he'd just walked a mile uphill in the rain, even though the sun was setting gently over the fields behind him.

"I was hoping we could talk," he said, his voice low and rough, like it hurt him to ask. "Just for a moment."

I hesitated but nodded, stepping outside and closing the door behind me. The cool evening air brushed against my skin as Caleb gestured toward the tire swing hanging from the old oak tree in the yard. It was far enough away from the house that we would have privacy. He walked ahead, his boots crunching softly over the gravel path, and I followed, unsure if my heart was racing with dread or hope.

When we reached the tree, Caleb turned, his expression shadowed and unreadable in the golden light. "Sadie," he began, gripping his hat tightly, "I know I haven't been... easy."

That was an understatement, but I held my tongue, watching him wrestle with his words. If he wanted to open up to me—to let some of his walls fall down—now was the time.

"I'm not good at saying the right thing," he admitted, his voice softening. "I've spent so much time trying not to feel anything that... I don't know how to show what I feel for *you*."

My breath caught, and I wrapped my arms around myself, trying to keep steady as his words sank in. He took a hesitant step closer, his hat dangling from one hand.

"But I want to try," he said, his voice growing firmer. "If you'll let me, Sadie, I want to court you."

The words hung in the air, a fragile promise, and I felt the tears welling up before I could stop them. "Caleb, you've hurt me," I whispered, my throat tight. "I can't pretend you haven't. You weren't there for me in a way that a man who cares about a woman would be."

His shoulders sagged, and for a moment, I thought he might turn and walk away. But instead, he nodded slowly. "I know. And I hate that I've hurt you. But I promise, I'll do everything I can to be better. For you."

The sincerity in his voice cracked something inside me, and before I could second-guess myself, I reached out, my fingers brushing his. His hand twitched, and he stared at me, wide-eyed, as if he couldn't believe what was happening.

"May I?" he asked, his voice barely audible.

I nodded, and his hand closed over mine, warm and strong and trembling just like mine was. The world seemed to shift around us, the quiet of the evening growing heavier, more intimate. His thumb brushed over the back of my hand, a small, tentative motion that sent my heart tumbling into freefall.

I looked up, meeting his gaze, and the emotion there—so raw, so unguarded—stole my breath. For a moment, it was just us, our hands clasped between us like a lifeline.

"Sadie," he murmured, his voice breaking. "I'll never take this for granted. Never."

And I believed him.

Caleb walked me back toward the house, our hands still clasped together, as if neither of us dared to break the connection. The quiet stretched between us, but for once, it wasn't heavy. It felt safe. Whole. Like maybe we could find our way through this together.

When we reached the porch, I hesitated, not ready to let the moment end. Caleb seemed to feel the same, his hand lingering in mine as he looked down at me, his gray eyes catching the faint glow of the lantern light.

"Sadie," he said softly, his voice carrying a weight that made my heart flutter. "I'd like to take you to the singing next week. I know it's not much, but..." He hesitated, his thumb brushing over my knuckles. "I'd like to show the community that... that we're something."

Something. The word echoed in my mind, full of possibilities and promise. My chest tightened, the idea of standing beside Caleb, claiming this tentative, fragile connection in front of everyone—including Esther—both thrilling and terrifying.

"I'd like that," I said, my voice barely above a whisper. "But only if you promise not to let Edna corner us. I heard she's chaperoning."

A grin tugged at his lips, softening his expression in a way that made my heart ache. "I'll make sure she doesn't upset you," he promised, his tone light, but his gaze steady and serious. "You have my word."

We stood there for a moment longer, the night wrapping around us, the crickets singing their quiet symphony. When Caleb finally released my hand, it felt like letting go of something vital, but the warmth lingered, settling deep in my chest.

"I'll see you at the store this week," he said, stepping back. "We'll figure out the details then."

I nodded, unable to find the right words to express what I was feeling. He tipped his hat, his gaze lingering for just a moment longer before he started walking down the lane. I stood there and waved until he disappeared from sight.

Inside, the house was quiet, my family already settled in for the evening. I closed the door softly behind me, leaning against it as I pressed my hands to my cheeks, my skin still warm where his hand had held mine. My heart felt too big for my chest, full of a hope I wasn't sure how to contain.

But then the doubt crept in, curling around the edges of my happiness like a shadow. What if I wasn't enough? What if Caleb, with all his steadfastness and strength, realized he needed someone more refined, more capable—someone like Esther?

I shook my head, forcing the thoughts away. *Mamm's* words from earlier echoed in my mind: If Caleb is in your heart, you must give *Gott* the chance to work.

And I would. I had to. No matter how much it scared me.

As I climbed the stairs to my room, a quiet determination settled over me. Next week at the singing, we would take our first step together. And I prayed that *Gott* would guide us, no matter where this path led.

Chapter Seventeen

Caleb

The steady rhythm of the horse's hooves against the packed dirt road was the only sound between us at first. The air was crisp, the kind of cool that bit at your cheeks but felt invigorating all the same. I stole a glance at Sadie beside me, her hands folded neatly in her lap, the soft fabric of her dress brushing against her wrists. She was quiet, but not the kind of quiet that meant peace. It was a silence that carried weight, like she was holding something back.

I cleared my throat, gripping the reins a little tighter than necessary. "You don't have to be nervous about tonight. Whatever happens, I will protect you."

Her head tilted toward me, her expression guarded. "Who says I'm nervous?"

"You're quiet," I pointed out. "You're never quiet unless something's on your mind."

Sadie let out a soft laugh, but it didn't reach her eyes. "Maybe I just like the sound of the road."

"*Ach*, Sadie," I murmured, shaking my head. "You're not fooling me."

She hesitated, then turned her gaze out to the horizon, the fields stretched out in shades of gold and green under the fading light. "I suppose... it's just a lot, you know? The charity drive, the garden, the singing. I wonder if I'm trying too hard to prove something."

"Prove something to who?" I asked, genuinely curious.

"To everyone," she admitted softly, her voice barely louder than the breeze. "That I'm capable. That I can do more than just—" She broke off, shaking her head. "Never mind."

"Sadie." I pulled the reins slightly to slow the buggy. Duke snorted but obeyed, the wheels creaking softly as we rolled to a stop. "You don't have to prove anything to anyone. Least of all me. I think you're perfect just the way you are."

Her eyes met mine then, wide and filled with something I couldn't quite name—hope, maybe. Or fear. "Maybe I do. Or maybe it's not about proving something to you. Maybe it's about proving it to myself."

I leaned back, letting her words settle between us. "What is it you think you need to prove?"

Sadie sighed, looking down at her hands. "That I can make a difference. That I can do something worthwhile. I've always felt like... like I was meant for more, but I don't know what that 'more' is."

Her vulnerability caught me off guard, and for a moment, I didn't know how to respond. Then, almost without thinking, I said, "You're already doing more than most. The charity drive, the way you care about people. That's more than enough, Sadie. You spread joy to everyone. What could be more important?"

She blinked, clearly startled by the earnestness in my voice. "Do you really think so?"

"I wouldn't say it if I didn't mean it," I replied firmly. "And you? You're the reason I'm even out here trying to be better."

Sadie's lips parted, her cheeks flushing slightly, but before she could respond, the horse shifted, jolting the buggy slightly. The moment broke, but something lingered, a thread of understanding between us that hadn't been there before.

We pulled into the clearing where the singing was being held, the buggy wheels crunching over gravel. Lanterns hung from posts, casting a soft golden glow over the gathering crowd. Sadie shifted beside me, her fingers fidgeting with the hem of her apron. I opened my mouth to reassure her, but before I could get a word out, Levi appeared out of nowhere, leaning against the buggy like he owned it.

"Well, well," he drawled, his grin wide enough to make my fists itch. "Look who decided to show up together. About time, *bruder*."

"Levi," I said warningly, hopping down from the buggy. "Don't you have somewhere else to be?"

"Not when there's entertainment like this," he shot back, tossing Sadie a wink. "Nice to see you, Sadie. You're a brave one being seen in public with Mr. Frowny-face."

Sadie laughed softly, her cheeks pink. "It's not so bad. Most of the time."

I scowled, reaching up to offer Sadie my hand as she climbed down. "Ignore him. He's been a nuisance since birth."

"*Ach*, you wound me, Caleb," Levi said, clutching his chest dramatically. "But I'm not the only one who's noticed this little... development."

"Development?" came a sharp, familiar voice. Becca stepped into the lantern light, her arms crossed and her gaze fixed firmly on Levi. "The only thing developing here is your overinflated ego."

Levi's grin widened, clearly unfazed. "Becca, always a pleasure. Don't you have some poor soul to harass? Or are you here to grace us with one of your 'insightful' observations?"

Becca raised an eyebrow, unimpressed. "I'm here to enjoy the singing. Unlike you, I don't need to insert myself into other people's business to feel important."

Sadie stifled a laugh behind her hand, and I sighed, already regretting ever leaving the farm. "Can you two not do this tonight? Just once? You've turned bantering into an art form. Kind of like an old married couple."

"Really?" Becca asked innocently. "I'm just pointing out that Levi's mouth moves faster than his brain."

"And you're just mad you can't keep up," Levi retorted, his smirk unwavering. "Admit it, Becca. You missed me."

"Missed you?" Becca snorted. "I'd miss an infested splinter in my toe before I'd miss you."

Sadie couldn't hold back her laughter this time, and even I felt the corner of my mouth twitch despite myself. Levi glanced at her, then back at Becca, his grin turning sly. "See? Even Sadie thinks you're full of hot air."

"That's because Sadie has a sense of humor," Becca shot back, turning to Sadie with a wink. "Unlike some people here."

"All right, that's enough," I said firmly, stepping between them before things could escalate further. "If you're both done, maybe we can all just... enjoy the evening?"

Levi held up his hands in mock surrender. "Fine, fine. I'll behave. For now."

Becca rolled her eyes but didn't argue, turning her attention back to Sadie. "Come on. Let's find a good spot before Levi tries to steal the best seat."

As they walked off, I shot Levi a look. "You have a death wish, don't you?"

He grinned, clapping me on the shoulder. "What can I say? She brings out the best in me."

The singing had begun in earnest, the familiar harmonies weaving through the crisp night air. Sadie sat beside me on one of the benches, her voice blending seamlessly with the others. Her *kapp* caught the soft glow of the lantern light, and her profile—serene, focused—had me completely transfixed.

She looked so beautiful. Most of all, she looked like *mine*.

Unfortunately, my admiration wasn't as subtle as I thought.

"You know, Caleb," Jonah muttered, leaning toward me from his spot on the bench behind us, "it's called singing, not silent prayer."

I blinked, realizing I hadn't sung a single note of the last verse. My lips had been moving, sure, but sound? Not so much.

"Back off," I hissed, my face burning. "I was singing."

Jonah snorted quietly. "Sure you were. Except I'm pretty sure the rest of us are supposed to hear it. Not just *Gott*."

Sadie turned slightly, catching my eye as she passed me the next song sheet. Her smile was soft but curious, like she'd noticed my distraction. I gave her a tight nod, hoping it masked my embarrassment, and pretended to read the words on the page. The last thing I wanted to do was make her disappointed in me on our first outing together.

Jonah, of course, wasn't done. "You're lucky Sadie's too polite to call you out. If it were me, I'd have announced to the whole group that Sheriff Stoltzfus forgot how to breathe."

"Jonah," I growled under my breath, "keep it up, and you'll be singing solo."

He grinned, clearly enjoying himself. "Don't be mad. I get it. It's hard to think straight when your head's so far in the clouds. Or should I say, in the *kapp*?"

I glared at him over my shoulder. "You've got a lot to say for someone who couldn't even hold a harmony last week."

Jonah smirked, unfazed. "Yeah, but at least I'm honest about it. Unlike you, lip-syncing your way through the hymns like some lovesick fool."

My jaw tightened, but the truth of his words stung more than his teasing. He wasn't wrong. I was distracted, more than I cared to admit, and it was all because of the way Sadie's presence wrapped around me like a gentle pull I couldn't resist. It wasn't just her voice or the way she sang with such sincerity—it was everything about her. For the first time in years, I was looking forward to the future.

I glanced at her again, trying to be subtle. She caught me looking this time, her eyebrows lifting in mild curiosity. *Ach*, I was making a mess of this. I turned my attention back to the song sheet, determined to focus on the next verse.

Jonah leaned in one last time, his tone laced with faux seriousness. "Hey, if you need a voice coach, I'm available. Just say the word."

"Jonah," I muttered, barely keeping my voice steady, "if you don't shut your mouth, I'll give you a reason to stay quiet."

He chuckled softly, falling silent just as the next hymn began. But his words stayed with me, a reminder that no matter how much I tried to play it cool, Sadie Miller had me completely undone.

The hymn ended, and the room buzzed with the soft hum of conversation. I managed to shake Jonah's teasing off, focusing on the moment. Sadie was smiling as she set her song sheet aside, her eyes catching mine briefly before she looked away, her cheeks coloring slightly. My chest tightened at the sight.

Before I could say anything, Becca appeared out of nowhere, sliding onto the bench beside Sadie with a conspiratorial grin. "Well, Sheriff, you surprised me. Didn't think you had such a decent singing voice in you."

I frowned. "It's Caleb."

Becca ignored me, her grin widening. "But you're definitely more tolerable than I expected. Sadie, maybe there's hope for him after all."

Sadie giggled, and I felt the tension in my chest ease just a bit. "He's not so bad," she said softly, her voice carrying a note of quiet defense.

"Well," Becca said, tilting her head, "maybe you're rubbing off on him."

"Or maybe he's always been a diamond in the rough," Edna interjected from a nearby bench, her tone carrying just enough warmth to surprise me. She stood and made her way over, her ever-watchful eyes settling on me. "Sometimes, a person needs the right encouragement to show what they're capable of."

I blinked, not expecting her words to land like they did. Edna had been a thorn in my side more often than not, but there was no denying the truth in her statement. I had been holding back for so long—afraid to take a risk, afraid to open myself up. Maybe Sadie's presence, her kindness, was what I'd needed to start loosening those reins.

Sadie shifted beside me, her hand brushing the edge of her skirt as if she were about to reach for mine but stopped short. "That's... wise," she said cautiously, glancing between Edna and me.

Edna nodded, her sharp gaze softening. "I might meddle, but it's only because I want what's best for my community. Sometimes, it's hard to see what's best for ourselves."

Her words hung in the air, and for a moment, I couldn't help but feel the weight of them. She turned to Sadie, her tone lightening. "You've done well tonight, dear. Your voice adds something special to these gatherings. Keep that up, *jah*?"

Sadie's smile widened, her cheeks flushing a soft pink. "*Denke*, Edna."

With a curt nod, Edna walked off, leaving the bench feeling oddly emptier without her imposing presence. Becca leaned in closer to Sadie, lowering her voice. "Okay, she might've just given you the nicest thing you'll ever hear from her. Needlepoint it and then frame it."

Sadie giggled again, and I couldn't stop the faint smile that tugged at my lips. Becca caught the expression and raised an eyebrow at me. "See? He does smile. Must be a full moon."

"I smile plenty," I muttered, though the warmth in my chest wasn't entirely unwelcome.

For once, Edna's meddling hadn't soured the mood. Instead, her words left me with something to think about—a reminder that I could be what Sadie needed.

The night air was cool as we stepped out of the hall, the lanterns casting a soft glow over the gathering buggies and quiet conversations. Sadie walked beside me, her steps light but deliberate. I couldn't stop glancing her way, trying to find the right words for what I wanted to say.

The moment she slipped her hand into mine, my thoughts scattered like chaff in the wind. Her fingers were small, warm, and they fit perfectly against my calloused palm. My heart stumbled over itself, the simple gesture speaking louder than any words could.

"*Denke*, Caleb," she said softly, her voice almost a whisper. She didn't look at me, her eyes focused on the path ahead, but her grip on my hand tightened just slightly. "For... tonight. For everything. I can't tell you how much it meant to me."

Her words hit me square in the chest, a rush of warmth and pride surging through me. "You don't have to thank me, Sadie," I said, my voice rougher than I intended. "I promised I'd stand by you, and I meant it."

She turned to me then, her eyes catching the light of the lanterns. They were soft, vulnerable, and filled with something I didn't quite know how to name but felt deeply. "I know you did," she said. "That's why it meant so much."

The rest of the walk to the buggy was quiet, but the kind of quiet that felt full, like the air after a storm. The stars stretched above us, and the faint sounds of crickets and distant laughter carried on the breeze. I wanted to say more, to tell her that seeing her smile made every word and glance tonight worth it, but the moment felt sacred, and I didn't want to shatter it with my clumsy tongue.

When we arrived at her house, I tied off the horse and walked her to the door, my heart pounding harder with every step. She turned to me, her cheeks glowing in the faint porch light. For a second, I thought she might say something more, but instead, she leaned in, her lips brushing my cheek so softly it felt like a whisper of the breeze.

It wasn't much—just a brief press of warmth—but it sent a jolt straight through me. Before I could respond, she pulled back, her eyes wide with something between shyness and boldness. "Goodnight, Caleb. See you soon," she said, her voice unsteady but sweet, before she turned and darted inside, the door closing softly behind her.

I stood there, frozen, my hand instinctively rising to touch the spot where her lips had been. The warmth lingered, seeping into my skin and spreading through my chest like the sun rising over the fields.

Ach, what was happening to me? I'd spent my life avoiding this kind of vulnerability, but with Sadie, it felt like a risk worth taking. My heart was falling, and for the first time, I didn't want to stop it.

Chapter Eighteen

Sadie

The hum of voices greeted me as I stepped into Grace Hall, the familiar sound wrapping around me like a well-worn quilt. Women clustered around the long tables, bustling with dishes of every variety—freshly baked pies, loaves of bread, and jars of pickled beets. Children's laughter echoed from the far corner, where they darted around like fireflies, weaving through the legs of their elders. I took a deep breath, the scent of cinnamon and freshly churned butter mingling with the tang of vinegar.

"Sadie!" Edna's voice rang out before I saw her, sharp enough to cut through the chatter. She bustled toward me with the determination of a woman on a mission, her shawl slipping slightly from her shoulders. "There you are, young lady. I've been looking for you."

I schooled my face into what I hoped was a welcoming expression. "*Hallo*, Edna. It's nice to see you."

"*Ach*, you're a busy bee these days," she said, her sharp eyes softening as they landed on me. "But I'll say this—you've done well for yourself, Sadie. Caleb's a fine man."

I blinked at her, startled. More kind words from Edna? That wasn't something you heard every day. "*Denke*," I managed, my voice wavering just a little. "That means a lot. But we've just started courting, you know. We can't go putting the buggy before the horse."

She nodded, crossing her arms. "You've handled everything with grace, especially with all the gossip flying around. Not many girls would've kept their composure." Her gaze narrowed slightly. "And Caleb—he's lucky to have a girl who sees past his stubborn ways. A man like him needs someone steady."

The knot in my stomach loosened just a fraction. "I appreciate that, Edna."

"*Jah*, well, don't let it go to your head," she said briskly, but there was a hint of a smile tugging at her lips. "I'll see you later. Make sure you grab a piece of Ruth's shoofly pie before the menfolk eat it all."

With that, she turned and strode off, leaving me standing there, blinking after her. Did Edna Zook just give me her blessing? The thought sent a warmth through my chest, though I wasn't entirely sure what to make of it.

"Sadie, over here!" Becca's voice pulled me from my thoughts. She was waving me over to a table near the windows, where the light spilled in, golden and warm. I made my way toward her, the chatter and laughter rising around me, and for the first time that day, I felt a glimmer of calm.

I settled into the seat next to Becca, letting the warmth of the sunlight and her familiar presence calm my nerves. Becca, of course, wasted no time diving into conversation.

"You're glowing," she teased, nudging my arm. "I don't know whether it's love or the reflection off all these pie tins, but either way, it's working for you."

I laughed, rolling my eyes. "You're impossible."

"*Ach*, don't be modest. We all see it, Sadie. You and Caleb... it's like a storybook ending." She smirked, but there was a softness in her tone that caught me off guard. "Maybe someday I can be as fortunate."

Before I could reply, a soft voice interrupted. "Sadie? Could I... could I sit with you for a moment?"

I turned to see Esther standing nearby, her hands clasped tightly in front of her, her cheeks faintly pink. It was the first time I'd seen her so tentative, so unsure of herself.

"Of course," I said, gesturing to the seat across from me. Becca's brows rose, but to her credit, she didn't say anything. She just leaned back slightly, watching the interaction with barely concealed interest.

The words took me by surprise, but there was a sincerity in her eyes that softened me. "Esther, you don't have to—"

"*Jah*, I do," she interrupted, meeting my gaze. "I... I let myself get caught up in what I wanted, without thinking about how it might affect others. You and Caleb, you're clearly meant for each other. And I shouldn't have tried to... insert myself where I didn't belong."

Her words were like a balm to a wound I hadn't realized was still tender. I nodded slowly. "*Denke*," I said, meaning it. "That means a lot, Esther."

A small, tentative smile crossed her face. "I'm happy for you, truly. And for what it's worth, I hope you'll forgive me."

"Of course," I said gently. "Forgiveness is important to me. I believe in second chances."

Becca, ever the firebrand, cleared her throat. "Well, that's settled then. Now we can all enjoy our baked goods."

Esther chuckled softly, her tension easing. "I'll leave you to your conversation," she said, standing gracefully. "I just... wanted to say my piece."

As she moved back toward another table, Becca leaned in, her eyes narrowing. "Well, that was unexpected. You think she really means it? That she wasn't just trying to butter you up, so she could sabotage you later?"

I glanced at Esther, who was now chatting with another group of women, her face relaxed in a way I hadn't seen before. "*Jah*, I think she does. And I'm glad for it. There's been enough tension to go around."

Becca smirked, folding her arms. "You're a better woman than me, Sadie Miller. I'd have let her stew a little longer. I'm still not sure she deserves the benefit of the doubt."

I just smiled, though I knew Becca would've done the same in my place. Sometimes, peace was worth more than pride.

As the hum of conversation picked up around the room, Ruth Lapp strode in with the kind of commanding presence that only came with years of running gatherings like this. She clapped her hands once, and the chatter quieted down immediately.

"All right, ladies," she began, her voice steady and warm. "Let's get started. We've got a lot to plan and not much time to do it. The Herschberger wedding is only three weeks away, and the family will need all the help we can give."

There was a murmur of agreement, and Ruth smiled, gesturing toward a long table laden with paper and notebooks. "We'll split into groups. Some of you will handle the cooking plans, others the decorations, and the rest will oversee the cleaning and upkeep schedule for the bride's home."

Becca leaned closer to me, whispering, "Bet you anything I get stuck peeling potatoes."

I suppressed a smile. "Maybe if you volunteered for decorations, you could avoid it."

She rolled her eyes. "*Ach*, fine. But if they put me in charge of ribbons, you're helping."

As the groups started to form, Ruth approached our table. "Sadie, I'd like you to help with the decorations. Your eye for detail will be a blessing to us."

I nodded, grateful for the assignment. "Of course, Ruth."

"And Becca," Ruth continued, her tone light but firm, "you can join her. Between the two of you, I'm sure we'll have the prettiest wedding Grace Hollow has ever seen."

Becca groaned softly but nodded. "Guess I'm doing ribbons after all."

As Ruth moved to the next table, I glanced at Becca, who was already doodling swirls on a scrap of paper. "It won't be so bad. Think of it as a chance to show off your creative side."

She raised an eyebrow. "Sadie, I've been creative exactly once in my life, and it involved sneaking apple dumplings out of *Mamm's* kitchen without getting caught."

Despite myself, I laughed, the sound easing the lingering tension from earlier. But as the laughter faded, my thoughts drifted back to Caleb.

I couldn't help but wonder what he was doing right then. Working on the farm, most likely, his broad shoulders bent to the task, his expression as serious as ever. My heart tightened as I thought of the way he'd looked at me during the singing—like I was the only person in the room.

"Earth to Sadie," Becca said, snapping her fingers in front of my face.

"Sorry," I mumbled, flushing.

Becca smirked. "Let me guess. You were thinking about Caleb."

I opened my mouth to deny it, but the words caught in my throat. Becca's smirk softened into something more understanding. "He's got you *gut*, doesn't he?"

I nodded, barely able to meet her gaze. "*Jah*, I suppose he does."

The gentle hum of activity in Grace Hall filled the air as Ruth Lapp gathered the decorations group together. She set a jar of wildflowers on the table and smoothed her apron.

"As we plan for the Herschbergers," Ruth began, her tone warm and purposeful, "remember, this isn't just about a single day. A wedding is the start of something bigger—a life shared, a family built, and a union that strengthens the entire community."

Her words settled over the group like a blessing, and I couldn't help but imagine what it might feel like to hear someone speak about Caleb and me in such a way. The thought made my chest tighten with longing and uncertainty.

"We're fortunate," Ruth continued, her gaze sweeping the room. "The Herschbergers chose to stay here in Grace Hollow. It's not every day we have a young couple committing to build their lives within our community. Let's do our best to make their day as beautiful as the life they're beginning."

A murmur of agreement rippled through the group, and Ruth smiled. "Now, let's talk decorations. Sadie, Becca, you'll handle the celery arrangements. Esther, I'd like you to assist with the table settings."

"Now," Ruth said, her smile widening, "let's make this wedding a day to remember."

The meeting began to wind down, the air in Grace Hall buzzing with warm anticipation for the upcoming wedding. Everyone's spirits were lifted, and even Becca looked slightly less annoyed as she gathered her notes into a neat pile.

Ruth clapped her hands gently, drawing everyone's attention one last time. "You've all done such wonderful work today. I'm confident this wedding will go off without a hitch. *Denke* all for your efforts."

A chorus of murmured thanks followed, and chairs scraped against the wooden floor as people began to gather their belongings. I lingered near the table, running my fingers along the edge of a scrap of fabric, lost in thought.

Becca sidled up to me, her eyes sharp but kind. "Sadie," she said, tilting her head, "you've been quiet. Everything alright?"

"I'm fine," I replied, forcing a smile. "Just a lot on my mind."

Her eyebrow lifted, and I knew she didn't believe me, but she didn't press. "Well, don't let Edna hear you say that, or she'll be planning your wedding next."

I groaned softly, but before I could respond, Ruth approached with a kind smile. "Sadie, I wanted to thank you for stepping up with the decorations. Your touch always adds something special."

"*Denke*, Ruth," I said, feeling a bit lighter under her praise.

Ruth's gaze softened, and she placed a hand on my arm. "And about Caleb… he's a good man, steady and strong. If he's the one *Gott* has chosen for you, trust in His plan."

Her words sank into me, carrying both comfort and weight. "I hope so," I said quietly.

As the room emptied, I caught sight of Esther helping to stack chairs. She glanced my way and offered another tentative smile, and for the first time, I returned it.

The crisp evening air greeted me as I stepped outside, the stars beginning to twinkle in the sky. Becca fell into step beside me as we made our way toward the buggies.

"You know," she said, her tone lighter now, "for someone who claims to be nonchalant about starting to court Caleb Stoltzfus, you sure spend a lot of time looking like you're thinking about him."

"I am not!" I protested, though my face heated under her knowing look.

"If you say so," she teased, her laughter carrying into the cool night.

As we reached the buggy, I glanced back at Grace Hall, its windows glowing warmly in the dark. A small flicker of hope sparked within me, fragile but growing.

Maybe Ruth was right. Maybe, just maybe, there was a path forward for Caleb and me, one step at a time.

With Becca's laughter still ringing in my ears, I climbed into the buggy, a faint smile tugging at my lips despite everything. Tonight hadn't been perfect, but it felt like the beginning of something good—something real.

Chapter Nineteen

Caleb

The sun climbed higher, its warmth spreading across the fields as I guided the team of horses along the rows of fresh-turned soil. Mornings always carried a particular rhythm—steady, predictable, comforting in their way. Today, though, my thoughts churned, a far cry from the tranquility surrounding me. The handles of the plow pressed into my palms, grounding me in the familiar task, but no matter how hard I focused, my mind kept wandering back to Sadie.

"Up early and brooding. Must be Tuesday," Levi's voice rang out, too cheerful for my liking. He leaned against the fence, his grin as easy as the breeze. "Thinking about your date, Sheriff?"

"*Ach*, Levi, don't you have anything better to do?" I snapped, though my tone lacked real heat. The endorphins rolling through the body could do that to a man. He was relentless, always poking and prodding until I either laughed or wanted to throttle him. Today, I was leaning toward the former for a change.

Levi hopped over the fence with the grace of a cat and strolled toward me. "I'm just saying, you've got a big night ahead. Taking Sadie out to dinner is no small thing. A man's got to prepare. You've got flowers, right?"

I groaned, stopping the horses and wiping the sweat from my brow. "Of course, I've got flowers. I'm not a complete dolt."

"Could've fooled me," Levi teased, his smirk widening. "You're pacing yourself too slow, Caleb. Girls like Sadie don't wait around forever."

I stiffened, gripping the reins tighter. "What's that supposed to mean?"

Levi held up his hands, feigning innocence. "Nothing. Just that she's got options. Plenty of folks think she's wonderful, and for *gut* reason."

The thought struck a nerve I didn't know was so raw. Sadie with someone else? I shook my head to clear it, but the image lingered, gnawing at me. "She agreed to go out with me, didn't she?" I said, my voice sharper than I intended.

Levi chuckled, slapping me on the back hard enough to jolt me forward. "Relax, *bruder*. I'm just trying to light a fire under you. You're courting her, not tilling a field. Move faster, or you'll lose her before you even get started."

He walked off, leaving me standing there with dust swirling around my boots. As much as I hated to admit it, he had a point. I had no idea what Sadie truly wanted out of life—or even out of this relationship. And if I was honest with myself, I wasn't entirely sure what I wanted, either. All I knew for sure is that I wanted *her*.

I guided the horses back to the barn, the plow bumping along the uneven ground. Somewhere between the rows, I made a decision. Tonight wasn't just about taking Sadie out for dinner. It was about figuring out if we could build a life together—and what that life might look like.

I had questions, plenty of them. But one thing I was sure of: if Sadie Miller wanted a life with me, I'd do whatever it took to make it happen.

*****

By late afternoon, I stood in front of the mirror in the washroom, tugging at the collar of my best Sunday shirt. It felt stiff and foreign, like I was trying to squeeze into someone else's skin. Levi leaned against the doorframe, arms crossed and his grin downright insufferable.

"Still time to back out, you know," he said, his voice laced with mock concern. "Just tell Sadie your buggy wheel broke. Or that the bishop called you for emergency prayer. Or your shirt burst at the seams from your bulging muscles."

"Levi," I warned, glaring at him through the mirror.

He held up his hands, palms out. "Fine, fine. I'll behave. But it's not every day I see my big *bruder* acting like a lovesick schoolboy."

I turned, smoothing the front of my shirt with a sharp exhale. "I'm not lovesick. I'm just... careful."

"Careful?" Levi snorted. "You've been 'careful' for twenty-seven years, Caleb. Maybe it's time to be something else."

I didn't have a response for that, so I focused on grabbing the small bouquet of daisies and wildflowers I'd picked earlier. They weren't extravagant, but they were bright and cheerful—just like Sadie. My stomach twisted at the thought of her reaction. Would she like them? Or would she think I hadn't put enough thought into it?

"Those'll do," Levi said, nodding at the bouquet. "Simple, but thoughtful. Classic Caleb Stoltzfus. Practical. Measured. Highly *un*romantic."

I ignored him, stepping past to grab my hat. "I'll be back late. Don't wait up."

Levi's laughter followed me all the way to the porch, where I stood waiting for the Amish taxi. The driver, an older *Englischer* with a kind face, tipped his cap as I climbed in. The ride to Sadie's place felt longer than usual, the hum of the tires on the road a steady rhythm to the anxious thoughts spinning in my head. I replayed every interaction we'd had since our courtship began. She'd agreed to go out with me, but what if she regretted it? What if tonight just proved I wasn't the man she needed?

When the taxi pulled up in front of her house, I wiped my damp palms against my trousers, my heart hammering in my chest. I gave myself a moment to breathe, straightening my hat and smoothing my shirt before stepping out. The gravel crunched under my boots as I made my way to the porch, where the warm glow of light spilled from the window.

Sadie stepped out just as I reached the steps, and my breath hitched.

She wore a light blue dress that made her eyes look even brighter, her *kapp* tied neatly under her chin. She smiled shyly, smoothing her apron as if she needed something to do with her hands.

"*Hallo*, Caleb," she said softly, her voice like a balm to my nerves.

"*Hallo*," I managed, holding out the bouquet. "These are for you."

Her cheeks flushed as she took the flowers, her fingers brushing mine for the briefest moment. "They're beautiful. *Denke*."

I nodded, unable to find my voice for a moment. When I finally spoke, it came out gruff. "You ready?"

She glanced back at the house, where her *mamm* waved from the doorway, before looking back at me with a small smile. "*Jah*, I'm ready."

As we climbed into the vehicle, I couldn't shake the feeling that tonight was more than just an outing. It felt like the start of something bigger—something that could change everything.

The ride to the restaurant was quiet at first, the kind of quiet that made me hyper-aware of every roar of the engine and every breath I took. Sadie held the flowers carefully in her lap, her fingers brushing over the petals like they were something precious. It made my chest tighten, seeing her treat them that way. It wasn't much—just some wildflowers I'd picked along the fence line—but the way she looked at them made me feel like I'd handed her the moon.

"So," she said finally, breaking the silence. Her voice was soft, but there was a hint of teasing in it. "Do you always pick such pretty flowers for the girls you're courting, Caleb Stoltzfus?"

I glanced at her, the corner of my mouth twitching. "You're my first, so I wouldn't know."

She looked at me, her eyes wide with surprise before her lips curved into a smile. "Your first? Really?"

"Really," I said, glancing out the window. "Never had much time for it before. Between the farm, the family... well, you know how it is. I guess I never felt that inspired. Until now."

She nodded, her expression softening. "I do. I think that's one of the reasons I..." She hesitated, glancing down at the flowers. "One of the reasons I agreed to let you court me. I know how much your family means to you. And family is important to me."

Her words hit me harder than they should have, and for a moment, I didn't know what to say. So I said the only thing I could think of. "You mean a lot to me too, Sadie."

The air between us shifted, heavier and yet lighter at the same time. She didn't say anything, but the way her fingers tightened around the bouquet told me she'd heard me.

We reached the restaurant just as the sun dipped below the horizon, casting everything in a warm, golden light. The Amish taxi driver tipped his hat as he helped Sadie out of the car. He gave me a knowing look, one that said he'd seen plenty of young couples like us over the years. I cleared my throat, ignoring the heat rising to my face as I followed Sadie inside.

The restaurant was simple but warm, with wooden tables and chairs polished to a soft shine. The smell of fresh bread and roasted vegetables filled the air, making my stomach growl despite my nerves. Sadie glanced around, her eyes lighting up as she took in the cozy space.

"This is lovely," she said, turning to me with a smile. "*Denke* for bringing me here."

I shrugged, shoving my hands in my pockets. "Figured you deserved something nice."

She laughed softly, her hand brushing my arm as she leaned in. "Well, I appreciate it very much, Caleb Stoltzfus."

The hostess arrived then, leading us to a small table near the window, the view of the fields beyond stretching out like a promise. As I pulled out Sadie's chair and watched her settle in, it struck me that this wasn't just about showing her a good time. Maybe I was just starting to realize what I wanted—and what I was willing to do to make it mine.

The conversation flowed more easily than I expected as we settled into our meal. The candlelight on the table flickered softly, casting a warm glow over Sadie's face. She was talking about an idea she had for the charity drive, her hands moving as she explained, and I couldn't help but watch her, caught between admiration and disbelief.

"How does your mind even work like that?" I asked, cutting into my roast chicken. "You've thought of things I wouldn't have considered in a year."

She tilted her head, her smile teasing. "It's all about seeing the bigger picture, Caleb. You're so focused on the details—and don't get me wrong, that's a good thing—but sometimes you have to step back and imagine what could be."

I grunted, chewing slowly. "Never been much for imagining. I like things laid out plain."

Sadie leaned forward, resting her elbows on the table as her chin perched on her hand. "Maybe that's why we make such a good team. You keep everything grounded, and I..." She paused, her eyes sparkling. "I help it fly."

The words hung between us, softer than a whisper but heavier than they should've been. My fork froze halfway to my mouth, and I cleared my throat, breaking the spell. "You're *gut* at that," I said, setting the fork down. "Making things better."

Her smile softened, her fingers trailing over the rim of her glass. "You give me too much credit, Caleb."

"Don't think so," I muttered, the words slipping out before I could stop them. "I've never met anyone like you, Sadie. And I don't think I ever will."

Her cheeks flushed, and she looked down, fiddling with the napkin in her lap. I knew I was being bold, too bold maybe, but the way she glanced up at me through her lashes told me she didn't mind. Not one bit.

The server returned to the table then, refilling our water glasses and offering a polite smile. "Everything to your liking?"

"Perfect," Sadie said quickly, her voice a touch higher than usual. I nodded in agreement, though the moment felt far from over.

As she moved to the next table, I leaned back, studying Sadie. "Do you ever think about the future?"

She blinked, caught off guard. "Of course. Don't we all?"

"What do you see?" The question felt too big, too loaded, but I couldn't stop myself.

She hesitated, her eyes searching mine. "I see... a family. A home. A life filled with purpose and love." Her voice softened, her gaze dropping to the table. "I see a lot of things, Caleb. But it's all blurry right now."

I nodded slowly, her answer stirring something deep inside me. "Blurry can be good. Means it's still taking shape."

She smiled then, small but genuine. "Maybe."

As the plates were cleared and the meal wound down, I realized I wasn't just thinking about my future anymore. I was thinking about ours.

The ride back to Grace Hollow in the Amish taxi was quiet at first, the soft hum of the tires on the road filling the space between us. Sadie held the bouquet in her lap, her fingers brushing over the petals as though committing their softness to memory. I wanted to say something—anything—but the words knotted in my throat like tangled twine.

Finally, she broke the silence. "This was... a lovely evening, Caleb."

Her voice was soft, and for a moment, I could only nod. The glow from the headlights cast warm shadows across her face, making her look even more radiant than she had at dinner. "It was my pleasure," I said, my voice gruffer than I intended. "I'm glad you enjoyed it."

She turned to me then, her gaze steady and searching. "You're different tonight. Not in a bad way," she added quickly. "Just... different."

I tightened my grip on the seat, unsure of how to respond. "Different how?"

"Lighter," she said after a moment, her lips curving into a small smile. "Like you're finally letting yourself breathe."

I chuckled, though it sounded hollow even to my ears. "Maybe that's your doing."

She tilted her head, curiosity flickering in her eyes. "How so?"

I didn't answer right away, too focused on the headrest in front of me. But the truth pressed at me, insistent and unrelenting. "You make me feel like... maybe I don't have to carry everything alone. Like it's okay to want something just for me."

Her smile softened, and she reached over, her hand brushing mine briefly. The touch was fleeting but enough to send warmth coursing through me. "That's what love is, Caleb," she said quietly. "Sharing the burdens and the joys."

The word love hung between us, weighty and unspoken. I glanced at her, my heart hammering in my chest. Did she mean it? Did she feel it, too? But before I could ask, the lights of Grace Hollow came into view, their warm glow marking the end of our night.

I asked the driver to stop outside her home, the house dark save for a single lantern glowing in the window. I climbed out first, stepping quickly to open the door for Sadie. She stepped down carefully, her skirts brushing lightly against my arm as she exited. She still held the bouquet, the blooms a vivid contrast against the deep shadows of the night.

"I'll walk you to the door," I said, my voice steady despite the storm brewing inside me.

She nodded, her steps light as we made our way up the path. At the door, she turned to face me, her expression unreadable. "Thank you again, Caleb. For everything."

Before she could step away, I reached out, my hand brushing her arm, stopping her in her tracks. She turned back to me, her eyes wide and searching. For a moment, I didn't know what I was doing—only that I couldn't let her go just yet.

Slowly, as if testing some invisible boundary, I raised a hand to her face, my fingers trembling as they brushed against her cheek. Her skin was impossibly soft, warm against the cold night air. Sadie froze, her breath hitching, her lips parting just slightly as she looked up at me, and the world around us seemed to fall away.

"I don't... I don't have the words," I murmured, my voice hoarse. "Not yet. But if I did..." My thumb traced the curve of her cheek, my chest tightening with every unspoken thought threatening to spill over. "If I did, I'd tell you that you're..."

I swallowed hard, the words lodging in my throat like a stone. Instead, I let my hand linger a second longer before pulling away, the loss of contact leaving my palm cold.

Sadie blinked, her lashes fluttering as if breaking from a trance. She didn't speak, but the shimmer in her eyes told me everything I needed to know.

With a shaky breath, she turned and slipped inside, the door closing behind her with a quiet click. I stood there in the stillness, staring at the empty space where she'd been, my hand still tingling from where it had touched her face.

I clenched my fist at my side, my jaw tightening as the weight of the moment settled over me. Sadie Miller wasn't just getting under my skin—she was changing me, pulling me toward something I wasn't sure I was ready for.

But ready or not, I was hers.

Completely.

Chapter Twenty

Sadie

The soft blush of dawn crept through the curtains, painting my room in shades of gold and pink. I knelt beside my bed, my hands clasped so tightly they ached. My whispered prayer carried the weight of the ache in my chest. "*Gott*, guide me. Show me the path You've laid before me, and grant me the courage to walk it."

As I rose, the quilt beneath my fingers felt smooth, familiar—a small comfort against the swirl of feelings I didn't quite know how to name. My eyes drifted to the small jar on the dresser where Caleb's wildflowers still sat, their petals just beginning to wilt. Even as they faded, they held something alive, something precious. A promise, maybe.

Last night had been... overwhelming. Standing on the porch with Caleb, his hand on my cheek, the way his voice had softened, breaking through his usual reserve—it made me feel things I'd never felt before. Things I'd never even thought about feeling. My heart had pounded so fiercely it felt like it might leap from my chest, and I'd barely managed to breathe when he'd looked at me like that, like I was the only person in the world who mattered.

I pressed a hand to my face, my skin still tingling where his fingers had brushed against me. It was more than a moment. It was a shift, a quiet breaking open of something inside me I hadn't known was locked away. I didn't just want Caleb to hold my hand or brush my cheek. I wanted... *ach*, I wanted to be his. To stand beside him as his wife. To be the person he turned to when the weight of the world bore down on his shoulders.

But those thoughts felt too big, too bold, and I tried to shove them back where they belonged. He hadn't said the words, hadn't promised anything beyond the touch of his hand and the warmth of his gaze. Still, something in me whispered that he wanted it too, even if he wasn't ready to say it aloud.

"Caleb Stoltzfus," I murmured, a faint smile tugging at my lips. "What are you doing to me?"

The words lingered in the stillness of the room, unanswered but heavy with meaning. Whatever this was between us, it was growing, deepening. And I wasn't sure if I wanted to stop it—or if I even could.

Downstairs, the smell of fresh bread greeted me, warm and comforting. *Mamm* was already in the kitchen, her hands a blur as she kneaded dough. "Good morning, *dauchtah*. You're up early."

"Morning, *Mamm*." I reached for the bucket near the door. "Thought I'd get a head start on the hens."

She looked up, her knowing gaze pinning me in place. "You've been thinking about Caleb. I trust your outing went well?"

Heat crawled up my neck. *Mamm* always had a way of cutting straight to the truth. "It was lovely," I admitted, gripping the bucket tighter. "And Caleb, he's... he's trying, isn't he?"

Her smile was soft. "He is. But trying isn't always enough. A man needs to know what he's working toward."

Instead of answering, I excused myself and stepped outside, the cool morning air brushing my face. The world felt quieter at this hour, as if everything was waiting. The hens clucked softly when I entered the coop, their feathers rustling as they shifted on their perches.

As I worked, scooping feed and collecting eggs, my mind circled back to Caleb time and again. By the time I finished, the sun was climbing higher, casting a warm glow over the yard. I paused by the fence, watching the fields stretch out toward the horizon. Somewhere out there, Caleb was probably working already, his broad shoulders bent to the task like always.

The rhythmic creak of the screen door brought me back inside, where the warmth of the kitchen wrapped around me like a familiar quilt. *Mamm* was humming a hymn as she set the bread dough to rise. The smell of yeast filled the air, mingling with the faint woodsmoke from the stove.

Before I could set my basket of eggs on the table, the sound of hurried footsteps outside caught both our attention. Before I could open the door, Becca burst in, cheeks flushed from the cool morning air. "Sadie! I need to talk to you."

"*Hallo*, Becca," *Mamm* said with a smile, wiping her hands on her apron. "Would you like some tea?"

Becca shook her head, her braid swinging. "*Nee, denke*, Mrs. Miller. I won't be long. Sadie, can we talk outside?"

I glanced at *Mamm*, who gave me a small nod. "Go on. I'll keep an eye on the bread."

Curiosity prickled at me as I finally set the basket down and followed Becca to the porch. She leaned against the railing, a sly grin already spreading across her face. "So. You and Caleb, hmm?"

My cheeks warmed instantly. "What about us?"

Becca tilted her head, giving me a look that said she wasn't letting this go. "Oh, don't you play coy with me, Sadie Miller. The whole town's buzzing about your dinner outing only one town over. What was it like? Romantic? Awkward? *Ach*, please tell me the Sheriff wasn't so stiff he spent the evening talking about crop rotation."

I laughed, shaking my head. "It wasn't like that at all. He was... kind. Thoughtful." My voice softened, the memory of his quiet smile making my chest feel full. "He even brought me flowers."

"Flowers?" Becca clutched her chest dramatically, her eyes wide with mock astonishment. "Caleb Stoltzfus? Our Caleb? The man who probably considers marigolds frivolous?" She leaned in, lowering her voice. "So, did he kiss you? Or is he still building up the nerve?"

"Becca!" I swatted at her, but I couldn't help the way my face lit up. "*Nee*, there was no kiss. Caleb is very respectful of our Amish ways. But..." My voice trailed off, and I looked down at my hands.

"But what?" Becca pressed, practically bouncing on her toes. "Don't leave me hanging, Sadie. You're glowing like a lantern, and I need to know why."

I bit my lip, hesitating for just a moment before the words tumbled out. "There was this moment... right before he left. He touched my face, Becca. Like he was afraid I'd disappear if he didn't hold on." My voice dropped to a whisper. "It felt like the world just... stopped."

Becca's teasing grin softened into something warmer, more genuine. "Oh, Sadie. That sounds... perfect."

"It was," I admitted, my fingers brushing the porch railing. "For the first time, I could see it—all of it. A future with Caleb. Being his wife. Building a life together."

Becca leaned in, her tone lighter again. "Well, if you're already daydreaming about walking down the aisle, you'd better brace yourself. Edna's probably halfway to writing your wedding invitations. And even though she was your biggest nemesis, she'll take all the credit."

I groaned, covering my face. "Don't remind me."

Becca laughed, the sound bright and infectious. "I wouldn't worry. Caleb might be slow to show it, but the man's clearly smitten. Just don't let him talk you into a courtship that drags on until we're both old and gray."

I smiled, the knot in my chest unraveling bit by bit. Becca had a way of making everything feel less overwhelming, even when the road ahead felt uncertain.

"Sadie," she said, her voice quieter now. "You deserve this happiness. Don't let anything—or anyone—make you doubt it."

I nodded, her words settling deep into my heart. "*Denke*, Becca. Truly. For your friendship, and for always having my back."

As we stepped back into the kitchen, the warmth of the moment stayed with me, like a promise of what was yet to come.

Mamm returned then, carrying a sack of flour. "Becca, will you stay for breakfast?"

Becca snorted. "Will Greta be there to torment me?"

When *Mamm* just laughed, Becca went on to say, "*Denke*, Mrs. Miller, but I should get back." Becca pulled her shawl tighter around her shoulders. "Besides, I think Sadie has some thinking to do."

As Becca left, I leaned against the counter, her words echoing in my mind.

"Sadie," *Mamm's* gentle voice broke through my thoughts. "Becca's a good friend. But matters of the heart take time. I know your excited after your supper last night, but don't rush it."

I nodded, staring at the dough in front of me. "I just... I don't know how to do that."

"Then pray about it," *Mamm* said simply. "Ask *Gott* for clarity. And trust that He will guide you."

I swallowed hard, the lump in my throat making it difficult to respond. *Mamm's* faith was so steady, so unshakable. I wanted to borrow some of that strength, to believe that everything would work out as it should.

But for now, all I could do was knead the dough and hope I didn't get ahead of myself.

As the afternoon sun dipped lower, casting long golden rays across the yard, I found myself drawn to the small flower patch by the edge of the garden. My marigolds had been struggling lately, weeds creeping in where they didn't belong, threatening to choke the life out of the delicate blooms. I hadn't had the time or heart to tend to them properly, not with all the turmoil in my mind.

But now... now they were perfect.

I stopped in my tracks, blinking at the patch of flowers. The weeds were gone, pulled out cleanly, leaving the marigolds standing tall and proud, their bright petals glowing like tiny suns. The soil around them had been freshly turned, the edges of the bed carefully defined. It looked like someone had spent hours tending to them, but I had no idea who.

My heart thudded as I stepped closer, my gaze sweeping over the meticulously weeded bed. And then I saw it—a small piece of paper, tucked neatly under a smooth stone at the edge of the garden. My fingers trembled as I picked it up, unfolding the note.

Sadie,

Before I left last night I saw your marigolds. I thought they could use a little care. The blooms deserve to thrive, just like you do. Thank you for bringing so much light to Grace Hollow—and to me.

—Caleb

My breath caught, the simple words hitting me like a wave. He'd done this. After the Amish taxi had driven away, he'd taken the time to tend to my flowers, to leave this note—quiet, thoughtful, and undeniably Caleb.

And then he'd walked all the way home.

I pressed the paper to my chest, my heart racing. The Caleb I'd been so frustrated with, the man I'd accused of not standing by me, had done this. And not because anyone told him to, but because he cared. About me.

The memory of his steady hands at the singing, the way he'd positioned himself between me and Edna, the way he'd held my hand like it was the most natural thing in the world—it all came rushing back. He wasn't perfect, but he was trying. And that mattered more than anything.

Tears pricked the corners of my eyes as I crouched down by the marigolds, brushing a petal with my fingertips. "Why do you have to be so confusing, Caleb Stoltzfus?" I whispered, a half-laugh escaping me.

The sound of *Mamm* calling from the kitchen broke through my thoughts. "Sadie! Breakfast's nearly ready!"

I straightened, tucking the note carefully into my apron pocket. My steps felt lighter as I walked back toward the house, my mind whirling with a hundred thoughts, each one more complicated than the last.

Caleb had left his mark here—on my marigolds, on my heart.

Breakfast passed in a blur, the usual chatter around the table fading into the background as my thoughts churned. *Mamm* asked if the biscuits were too salty; I nodded automatically, though I hadn't tasted them. *Dat* mentioned something about repairing the fence in the south field, and I murmured agreement, my mind miles away. Greta and Emma teased each other about nothing.

All I could think about was the note tucked safely in my apron pocket and the sight of my marigolds, free from weeds, standing proud and golden in the late afternoon sun. Caleb's careful handwriting lingered in my mind, the words replaying over and over like a hymn.

After the dishes were washed and the kitchen tidied, I slipped outside, needing a moment to breathe. The morning air was cool and crisp, carrying the faint scent of freshly tilled earth. The quiet settled around me, the only sound the faint rustle of leaves in the breeze. For the first time in days, my heart felt lighter, like some of the weight had been lifted. I didn't have all the answers, but I knew one thing for certain: Caleb Stoltzfus wasn't just a part of my life anymore. He was becoming the center of it.

With one last glance at the marigolds, I turned back toward the house. The warm glow from the kitchen window spilled out onto the porch, inviting me back inside. Tomorrow would bring its own challenges, its own moments of joy and doubt. But tonight, for the first time in a long time, I felt hope blooming alongside those golden flowers.

And that was enough. For now.

Chapter Twenty-One

Caleb

The air inside the feed store was thick with the scents of hay, grain, and the faint mustiness of old wood. I hefted a bag of seed onto my shoulder, but my mind wasn't on the task. It was back on the porch with Sadie—the way the lantern light caught the softness of her features, her voice low and full of something I couldn't name. When I'd reached for her face, I'd felt like I was crossing some invisible line, one I hadn't even known existed until that moment.

And then she smiled at me. Not just any smile, but one that made my chest feel tight, like I'd been standing too close to the edge of a cliff. I'd walked away when I should've stayed—gotten into that Amish taxi when I should've kissed her. But the thought of her watching me leave, still holding that bouquet, had gnawed at me the entire ride home.

So I'd done what any sensible man wouldn't—I paid the driver and got back out. The miles between our farms didn't matter. I just knew I had to do something. She'd poured so much of herself into that patch of marigolds, and I'd seen how it stung her when they didn't thrive. So I'd weeded the garden by moonlight, hands dirty and knees in the soil, because it was the only way I could say what I didn't have the courage to speak aloud.

The thought of her seeing it the next morning, maybe smiling to herself as she noticed the difference, was enough to pull me through the monotony of the day. I'd scrawled a note on a scrap from my wallet, and then walked all the way home alone with my thoughts and my body pulled tight as a bow string. But now, standing in the feed store surrounded by bales of hay and bags of grain, I couldn't stop wondering—did she know it was me? And if she did, did that mean anything to her?

But before I could think too far ahead, my ears caught something that yanked me back to the present.

"I don't know what I'm going to do, Agnes," *Grossmamm* said, her voice low but tremulous. I ducked around the corner of the aisle, careful not to be seen. She stood near the counter, leaning on it like the weight of her words might otherwise knock her down. "The loan... *ach*, it's too much. The payments keep climbing, and they've started sending notices. If I lose the farm, Agnes—" Her voice cracked. "It's been in my family for four generations. And young Caleb is working so hard to keep it going. What will people think?"

"*Gott* above, Ruth," Agnes replied, her hand on *Grossmamm's* arm. "Why didn't you tell anyone?"

Grossmamm shook her head, her *kapp* trembling slightly with the motion. "What could I say? I signed the papers. I thought I could manage, but... it's not right. The terms, they keep changing. The banker says I should've read more carefully." Her laugh was bitter. "As if I could understand all that fine print."

My stomach dropped. *Grossmamm*? A predatory loan? The two ideas didn't fit together, not in my head. She was the backbone of our family, the pillar of our community. She was unshakable. But here she was, breaking right before my eyes.

"They'll take everything," she continued, her voice now barely above a whisper. "The barn, the fields. Even the house. I'll have nowhere to go."

"No, that can't happen," Agnes said fiercely. "Caleb can help you, surely, there has to be a way—"

"*Nee*, there's no way," *Grossmamm* cut in, her tone final. "And I can't involve Caleb. He's already done so much. He's been my rock when Eli should have been here handling things. And now when he's about to embark on his own life journey with Sadie? *Nee*. I can't hold him back because of my stupidity. I've prayed for a miracle, but miracles don't come to foolish old women who sign away their lives because they don't know better. I should have brought Abraham with me, but I was so convinced I could handle it myself."

I stepped back, my chest tight. My hands curled into fists at my sides as the full weight of what I'd just overheard settled on me. *Grossmamm*, the woman who taught me everything I know about resilience and faith, was ashamed. Ashamed enough to hide this from all of us. Most of all from *me*.

I wanted to storm in, to tell her she wasn't foolish, that it was the banker who should be ashamed. But I didn't move. I couldn't. My feet felt like they were nailed to the floor, and my head spun with a thousand questions. How could this have happened?

When I finally managed to step out of the store, the fresh air hit me like a slap. My family was on the verge of losing our legacy, and *Grossmamm* had been carrying it alone. My heart burned with anger—at the banker, at myself for not knowing sooner, and at the world for letting this happen to someone like her.

But there was someone or *something* else I was even more angry with.

After getting out of the feed store undetected and stowing away my bags of grain, I headed toward the bank. The buggy ride felt endless, though I'd driven the path countless times before. Each clop of Duke's hooves seemed to echo my racing thoughts. *Grossmamm's* voice replayed in my mind—her anguish, her shame. How had none of us noticed? And how could I have been so preoccupied with my own future that I'd missed something this big? Instead of out galivanting around with Sadie, I should have been at home taking care of my family.

The bank loomed ahead, its red brick façade clean and orderly, standing in stark contrast to the chaos brewing in my chest. I tethered Duke and walked inside, the scent of varnished wood and ink hitting me as I stepped onto the polished floor. A clerk greeted me, but I brushed past him toward the desk of the man I knew *Grossmamm* had dealt with—Mr. Gilbert.

He was seated, flipping through a ledger, his glasses perched low on his nose. When he noticed me, he set the book aside, smiling like he wasn't the villain in someone's story. "Caleb Stoltzfus. What brings you here today?"

I clenched my fists, forcing myself to stay calm. "I need to discuss a loan."

His brows lifted in interest. "A loan for yourself? Or is this on behalf of someone else?"

My jaw tightened. "I need to understand the terms of the loan you gave my *grossmamm*, Eliza Stoltzfus."

His smile faltered, replaced by a wary look. "Eliza's loan? That's a private matter, Caleb. I couldn't possibly discuss it with you."

"Not when it threatens to destroy her farm," I snapped. "She's been a member of this community her whole life, and you're telling me you thought it was fair to trap her with terms she couldn't possibly meet?"

Mr. Gilbert sighed, leaning back in his chair. "The terms were laid out clearly. She signed willingly."

"Willingly?" My voice rose. "Do you honestly think she understood the fine print? You took advantage of her trust. And now you're planning to take the farm?"

"There are people in the state that think that land is ripe for development." He held up a hand, his expression cool. "This isn't about taking advantage of people, Caleb. It's about business. I'm not responsible for how much someone chooses to take on."

The words felt like a slap. Development? The thought of my family land being ripped up for some *Englischers* mansion left me nauseated and weak.

"You're responsible for knowing when someone is vulnerable and acting ethically," I shot back. "Instead, you saw an opportunity and took it. That farm isn't just land; it's her life. Her legacy. It's been in my *muder's* family for generations!"

His gaze hardened, and for a moment, we locked eyes in a silent standoff. "If you're here to discuss your own loan, we can proceed," he said finally. "But Eliza's situation is settled."

"Settled?" I hissed. "By ruining her life? When she's at the end of it?"

I stood abruptly, my chest heaving. Every instinct screamed at me to do something—anything—but I knew I was out of my depth. I couldn't fix this with words alone.

Turning sharply, I left the desk and headed for the door, the weight of the encounter pressing down on me. My mind raced with plans, none of them fully formed. But one thing was clear: I wasn't walking away from this, no matter what it cost me.

The buggy ride home was a blur, the reins gripped tight in my hands as Duke trotted along familiar paths. But the ache in my chest and the whirlwind in my head were anything but familiar. *Grossmamm* was drowning in a sea of debt, and I had no idea how to pull her out without sinking myself in the process.

When I reached the farm, the stillness of the fields mocked me. Normally, the sight of the orderly rows of crops and the steady rhythm of chores gave me peace—a sense of purpose. But today, all I could see was a future unraveling. *Grossmamm's* farm, gone. Her smile, faded. And me, powerless to stop it.

I unhitched Duke and led him into the barn, my thoughts circling like vultures. The loan I'd originally wanted to inquire about for Sadie and me—our future together—now felt like a selfish indulgence. How could I think about building a life with her when *Grossmamm* was on the brink of losing everything? How could I face *Mamm* and tell her that I hadn't made this situation my priority.

Dropping the reins, I slumped against the barn wall, the cool wood pressing into my back. I couldn't even bring myself to wipe the hay off my clothes. I just sat there, staring at the ground, the weight of the world pressing down.

My thoughts turned to Sadie, and guilt twisted in my gut. She'd looked so happy the last time we'd been together, talking about the future like it was a bright, endless horizon. But now? What kind of man was I to dream about a future with her while *Grossmamm's* very life was being stripped away?

The sharp sound of footsteps broke through my haze. Levi's voice called out, light and teasing as usual. "You planning to take root in the barn, Caleb? Or are you just giving the hay a closer inspection?"

I didn't answer, and Levi's tone shifted, softening. "What's going on?"

I dragged a hand over my face, trying to keep my voice steady. "It's *Grossmamm*. She's in trouble."

Levi crouched beside me, his usual smirk replaced with something more serious. "What kind of trouble?"

"Money trouble," I admitted, the words tasting bitter. "The farm... she might lose it."

Levi's face darkened, his brows pulling together. "Why didn't she say anything?"

"She's ashamed," I said quietly. "Doesn't want to burden anyone."

Levi let out a low whistle, leaning back on his heels. "So what are you going to do?"

"I don't know," I admitted, my voice cracking. "I thought about getting a loan for myself, even had it on my list of things to do, but... how can I focus on Sadie and me when *Grossmamm's* farm is hanging by a thread? If our family lost that land..."

Levi studied me for a moment, then clapped a hand on my shoulder. "Caleb, you're not the only one who cares about this family. You don't have to carry it all yourself. Why don't we go in right now and ask *Dat* for advice?"

His words landed like a lifeline, but the storm inside me didn't calm. Levi might be right, but I couldn't shake the feeling that if I didn't step up, no one else would. And the stakes were too high to risk failure.

*****

The following morning, I arrived at the bank before the doors opened, my resolve as rigid as the chilled air around me. The small building loomed ahead, its sign swinging faintly in the breeze. Inside, it was quiet, save for the rustling of papers and the muted sound of a clerk stamping documents. The air smelled faintly of ink and polished wood—a far cry from the earthy warmth of the farm.

My jaw tightened as I approached the counter, catching the eye of a young clerk who looked up with a startled expression. "I'm Caleb Stoltzfus. I need to speak to the manager," I said, keeping my voice steady but firm.

She nodded quickly, disappearing through a door behind the counter. Moments later, a man emerged—a balding *Englischer* with a pinched expression and glasses perched precariously on his nose. He carried himself with the kind of authority that made my skin crawl, like he thought he owned the place. Maybe he did, in more ways than one.

"Mr. Stoltzfus," he said, forcing a tight-lipped smile. "What can I do for you?"

I stepped forward, the weight of my frustration bubbling just beneath the surface. "I'm here to discuss my *Grossmamm's* loan. Eliza Fisher. I want to know the terms."

His smile faltered, and he adjusted his glasses. "I'm afraid I can't discuss another client's financial arrangements with you. It's a matter of confidentiality."

"Confidentiality?" I echoed, my voice rising despite my attempt to keep calm. "I'm her kin. I work her land. The land that's been in my family for generations. You didn't seem too concerned about confidentiality when you pushed her into a loan she couldn't afford."

He stiffened, his expression turning defensive. "Mr. Stoltzfus, I assure you, this institution operates within the bounds of the law. If your grandmother misunderstood the terms—"

"She didn't misunderstand anything," I snapped, stepping closer to the desk. "You took advantage of her. She trusted you, and you've put her entire farm at risk."

The banker's face reddened, a vein pulsing at his temple. "Sir, I must ask you to lower your voice. We don't tolerate accusations of this nature without evidence."

"Evidence?" I leaned over the desk, my hands flat against the polished surface. "I overheard her yesterday, talking about how she didn't fully understand what she was signing. She's ashamed to even tell her family, and you're sitting here pretending this is business as usual."

The clerk behind the counter froze mid-motion, her wide eyes flicking toward us. The banker cleared his throat, adjusting his tie as if the fabric was choking him. "Mr. Stoltzfus, if you have concerns, you're welcome to seek legal counsel. But I must insist that—"

"Tell me what she owes," I interrupted, my voice sharp enough to cut glass. "How much, and what will it take to save her farm?"

His lips pressed into a thin line, but he finally rifled through a stack of papers. "Her balance is considerable. Even if we were to renegotiate, the payments would remain... challenging."

"Challenging?" I repeated, the word like bile on my tongue. "You didn't think to explain that to her before she signed?"

His silence answered for him.

I straightened, my fists clenched at my sides. "Forget it. I'll figure something else out."

"Sir—"

As I stormed toward the exit, my mind a tangled mess of frustration and resolve, I nearly collided with Edna Zook, who was standing by the counter, purse clutched tightly in her hands. Her eyes widened, sharp as ever, as she took in my stormy expression and the tension that practically radiated off me.

"Well, Caleb Stoltzfus," she said, her tone dripping with curiosity. "What's got you all riled up in a place like this?"

I didn't answer, couldn't answer, not with my emotions threatening to boil over. But her pointed gaze followed me all the way out the door, and I had no doubt she'd caught every word of my conversation with the banker. Edna didn't miss much, and when she did, she made it her mission to fill in the gaps.

This wasn't over—not by a long shot.

I didn't say one word. Turning, I strode out of the bank, the weight of the injustice settling heavily on my shoulders. I had to find a way to fix this. For *Grossmamm*. For our family. For my own soul.

The buggy wheels creaked under the strain of the uneven road as I drove home, the fields blurring past me. My chest felt hollow, like a cruel winter wind had carved me out from the inside. *Grossmamm's* sweet face haunted me—the quiet dignity with which she bore her shame, the farm she fought so hard to hold onto crumbling under the weight of betrayal. And now, I had to choose between the life I'd dreamed of with Sadie and the responsibility that had been thrust upon me just like all the responsibilities before it.

My fingers tightened around the reins, the leather digging into my palms. The memory of Sadie's smile flashed in my mind, bright and full of hope, and it made the ache in my chest unbearable. She'd looked at me like I was her future. Like I was someone who could make her happy.

But how could I make her happy when my own foundation was crumbling? What kind of man would I be if I put my desires above my family's needs?

I pulled the buggy to a stop at the edge of a field, the wind biting at my face as I climbed down. The sky was a muted gray, heavy with the promise of rain. I sank to my knees in the brittle grass, the cold seeping through my trousers as I clasped my hands together.

"*Gott*," I murmured, my voice breaking. "I need your help. I don't know what to do. I love her—I love Sadie more than I ever thought possible. But how can I keep her when my family needs me? How can I hold onto her without failing them?"

The words hung in the still air, carried away by the wind. I stared at the horizon, waiting for an answer, a sign—anything to tell me what to do. But there was only silence, vast and unyielding.

Tears burned at the corners of my eyes, but I refused to let them fall. Instead, I stood, my legs trembling under the weight of my decision. I knew what I had to do. It wasn't fair to Sadie to keep her tethered to a man who couldn't give her everything she deserved. She needed someone who could build a future with her, not someone drowning in the past.

The thought of telling her tore at me, but it was the only way. I would break her heart before I let my burdens drag her down. And in doing so, I would break my own.

I climbed back into the buggy, the reins slack in my hands. The road home felt endless, each step of Duke's hooves a reminder of what I was about to lose. I would never forget the way Sadie looked at me, her eyes full of trust. And I would never forgive myself for breaking that trust.

But this wasn't about forgiveness. It was about duty. And I would carry that duty, no matter the cost. Because loving Sadie meant putting her happiness above my own. Even if it meant letting her go.

Chapter Twenty-Two

SADIE

The clatter of dishes echoed softly in the kitchen as I dried the last of the breakfast plates, setting them in neat rows on the rack. The familiar motions of tidying usually brought a sense of calm, but today, my hands felt heavy, my thoughts even heavier. Caleb was on my mind—how his hand felt when it held mine, the way his voice softened when he spoke. I could still hear his laugh, rare and quiet, but so precious.

The distant rumble of a buggy caught my attention, pulling me from my thoughts. I set the towel down and wiped my hands on my apron, a nervous flutter stirring in my chest. I glanced out the window, catching a glimpse of the familiar broad-shouldered figure climbing down. My heart leapt, then stalled. Caleb.

Before I could compose myself, there was a firm knock at the door. I took a deep breath and opened it, my pulse racing.

"Caleb," I said, his name barely a whisper. "I wanted to let you know how much I appreciate all that weeding..." My words faltered as my throat constricted. His hat was clutched tightly in his hands, his expression strained. Something wasn't right.

"Sadie," he said, his voice low. "Can we talk?"

I nodded, motioning toward the porch, but he shook his head. "Somewhere private."

A chill ran through me as I stepped aside and led him toward the sitting room, bracing myself for whatever he had to say. The usual warmth in his eyes was gone, replaced by a distance that made my stomach drop.

The heaviness in his step filled the room before he even crossed the threshold. "Is everything all right?" I asked, though I already knew it wasn't.

The weight of the moment pressed heavy as he chose the armchair across from me, leaving the empty space on the sofa untouched. The distance between us, though only a few steps, felt like an unbridgeable chasm. He avoided my gaze, his eyes fixed somewhere near the floor. When he finally spoke, his voice was low and strained. "I've been thinking. About us."

A chill ran through me, making me clutch the edge arm of the sofa. "And?"

He set his hat on the end table, his hands lingering as if they needed something to hold on to. "I don't think we should continue courting."

The words hit like a punch to the chest. My breath caught, my heart stumbling over itself. "What?" The question tumbled out before I could catch it, sharp and disbelieving. "Why?"

Caleb looked at me then, but his eyes were guarded, his jaw tight. "It's... complicated. My family needs me. I have responsibilities—ones I can't ignore. It wouldn't be fair to you."

"Fair?" My voice rose, trembling. "You think this is fair? Caleb, we were building something. I thought..." My words faltered, my throat tightening. "I thought we were a team. I thought you trusted me."

His gaze flickered, the faintest crack in his stoic mask. But he shook his head, his voice clipped and distant. "This is for the best, Sadie. You deserve someone who can give you everything. I can't."

I leaned back, crossing my arms as if that might shield me from the blow he was delivering. "You don't trust me enough to tell me what's really going on, do you? Or is it that you don't believe in us?" My voice broke on the last word, and the look in his eyes nearly undid me. "That you don't believe in *me*!"

"I'm sorry, but this is for the best," he said, his tone flat, hollow. "I have to go."

And just like that, he stood up and turned his back on me, leaving a silence so thick it felt like the walls themselves were closing in. My chest constricted, every breath shallow and sharp, as though the air had been sucked from the room. I couldn't move, couldn't think, couldn't do anything but watch him walk away, the sound of his boots fading like the last thread of hope unraveling. My heart shattered, each jagged piece cutting deeper as the realization sank in—he wasn't just leaving my house. He was leaving us. And I wasn't sure if I'd ever know how to put the pieces back together.

*****

The familiar hum of Grace Hall felt like a balm at first, wrapping me in the comforting noise of purposeful work. Women bustled around, preparing for the upcoming wedding of yet another couple, their laughter and chatter filling the air. But my heart felt like it was being crushed under the weight of Caleb's words. I sat with an unfinished quilt before me, every stitch I took feeling like a desperate attempt to sew my broken pieces back together.

I tried to keep my head down, to stay unnoticed, when Edna's voice rang out, as sharp and clear as a bell. "*Ach*, Sadie, there you are! I was just saying how it's good to see young people like you keeping busy."

Her gaze zeroed in on me like a hawk's. I forced a weak smile and focused on the fabric in front of me. "*Jah*, it's a blessing to have work to do."

Edna didn't sit. She perched, her weight on one foot, leaning closer. "You look a bit... drawn, dear. Is something troubling you?"

I stiffened, my hands faltering mid-stitch. "*Nee*. Just a long morning, is all."

She clucked her tongue. "Well, sometimes *Gott* gives us these burdens to show us the way, doesn't He? Like with young Caleb." Her tone turned pointed, and I braced myself. It sound as if she knew something about Caleb that I didn't. "He's always been a good boy, but *ach*, it seems he's found himself at a crossroads, hasn't he? But I fear it's in his DNA, my dear, to always put his family before anything or *anyone* else. He just can't cut the apron strings."

The needle pricked my finger, sharp and stinging. Had someone told her about Caleb's visit this morning? I pressed it against my skirt to stop the bead of blood before it stained the fabric. "I'm not sure what you mean."

Edna's voice lowered, though not enough to keep it from carrying to nearby ears. "Oh, you know. Sometimes the heart needs a nudge in the right direction. Like with Esther. Such a sweet girl, that one. She would live with Caleb on the Fisher farm for years while he looked after Eliza until her dying day, if that was want Caleb wanted. She would sacrifice everything for him. Can you say the same?"

My throat felt tight, words tangling before they could escape. "Esther?" I managed, though my voice sounded as thin as paper.

Edna nodded, clearly pleased with herself. "*Jah*, Esther. It's no secret she's always had a soft spot for Caleb. And who could blame her? Such a strong, dependable man. And she, well... she has all the qualities a good man looks for in a wife. Sweet, demure, *obedient*. She understands that *Gott's* plan for a woman is to submit to a man. His wants and needs become hers."

The words sliced through me like a blade. Sweet. Demure. Obedient. None of which I'd ever been accused of being. I swallowed hard, but the lump in my throat didn't budge. Was Esther's apology that day nothing but a ruse? "Excuse me," I whispered, rising to my feet and heading for the restroom before the tears could fall.

As I passed the hallway, I heard Edna again, her voice loud enough to echo. "Caleb and Esther would make such a fine match, don't you think? A classic beauty, a kind heart. None of that stubborn independence. It's what a man like him needs, so he can focus on what's important to him."

The walls blurred around me, the sting of tears too much to fight. By the time I reached the restroom, my hands were shaking. I splashed cold water on my face, but it did nothing to cool the ache burning in my chest. I couldn't stay there. Not like this. Not now.

I splashed cold water on my face, hoping to cool the fire raging beneath my skin. The restroom's dim light did little to soften the redness in my cheeks or the tremble in my hands. Caleb's words, Edna's barbs—it all churned in my mind, threatening to unravel me. The older woman *knew* something. But how? With a shaky breath, I straightened my *kapp* and smoothed my skirt. I couldn't fall apart here. Not now.

As I stepped back into the hallway, the faint hum of voices drifted from near the kitchen. I wouldn't have noticed if it weren't for the distinct lilt of Esther's voice, as sweet and sticky as honey left out in the sun. My steps faltered, and before I could stop myself, I leaned closer, just enough to hear.

"*Ach*, Caleb is such a good man," she said, her tone carrying the kind of practiced humility that always seemed to draw people in. "So strong and dependable. It's no wonder he needed someone to confide in, someone who understands his burdens. Someone who will stay quietly by his side and not make waves when it comes to family matters."

My chest tightened, the words hitting like a slap. My fingers curled into fists at my sides, the fabric of my skirt bunched between them. Confided in? What burdens? Caleb hadn't shared anything with me—no, he'd shut me out completely. Then he'd willfully pushed me away.

Esther continued, her voice dipping lower, coaxing the small group of women closer. "I've tried to be there for him... in ways Sadie might not have been able to." There was a pause, and then a light laugh, as if she'd said something charming. "Sometimes, it takes the right kind of person to shoulder that kind of weight."

A hot flush crept up my neck. The insinuation wasn't subtle. Esther was weaving her tale with precision, planting seeds of doubt where they would grow the quickest. And she wasn't just talking to the women gathered around her—she was speaking to me, I was sure of it. Had he held Esther's hand too? Had he touched her? Kissed her?

Bile made its way back up my throat again, the nausea almost bringing me to my knees. I stepped back, my heels clicking against the polished wood floor. Esther's gaze flicked toward the hallway, and for a moment, our eyes met. Her smile widened, syrupy sweet, the kind that made my stomach churn. She knew I'd heard her. Her former apologies meant nothing, and I felt like such a fool to have trusted her.

I turned sharply, retreating down the hall before my composure crumbled. My breaths came fast and shallow, my heart pounding so loudly it drowned out the hum of the gathering. By the time I reached my seat, my knees felt weak, and I lowered myself carefully onto the hard wooden chair.

The needle and thread sat untouched in my lap, but my mind was anything but still. Esther's words looped in my head, twisting the knife

Caleb had already lodged there. Had he really turned to her? Found solace in her presence while leaving me in the dark? I felt like a laughingstock, and worse, I could feel the weight of others' smirks settling on me, as if they knew, as if they believed her.

I gripped the fabric tighter, blinking back the tears that threatened to spill. Esther might've been spinning a web, but I was the one trapped in it.

The walls of Grace Hall seemed to press in on me, the once-comforting hum of conversation now suffocating. I couldn't stay. Not another moment. Gathering my things with trembling hands, I muttered a quick, barely audible goodbye to the room and hurried toward the door.

The cool evening air hit my face like a slap, and I gulped it in, desperate to steady the storm raging inside me. I climbed into the buggy, my movements stiff and mechanical, and urged the horse forward. My grip on the reins was as tight as the lump in my throat, my vision blurring with tears I could no longer hold back.

The rhythmic clatter of hooves against the dirt road should've been soothing, but instead, it amplified the ache in my chest. Esther's voice echoed in my mind, her honeyed tone dripping with confidence and insinuation. Caleb had chosen her. Or worse, he'd turned to her when he should've turned to me.

A sob broke free, shattering the fragile calm I'd tried to maintain. I let it out, the tears flowing unchecked as I clung to the reins. The horse trotted on, oblivious to the chaos unraveling within me. How could Caleb not see that we were meant to be? How could he doubt what we had shared?

The familiar curve of the road leading to home came into view, but instead of relief, a wave of dread washed over me. What would I say to *Mamm*? To *Dat*? What if Emma teased me about my pain? What if Greta laughed at me? How could I explain the whirlwind of emotions crashing through me when I didn't even understand it myself?

By the time the buggy rolled into the yard, my tears had dried, but the ache in my chest remained, heavy and unyielding. I climbed down, my legs trembling beneath me, and tied the reins to the post with fingers that barely obeyed.

The door creaked as I stepped into the quiet of home. The familiar scent of fresh bread and lavender soap filled the air, but it did nothing to comfort me. I set my bag down on the table, my hands trembling. *Mamm* looked up from her chair by the fire, her knitting needles pausing mid-stitch as her eyes scanned my face.

"Sadie," she said softly, setting the yarn aside. "What's the matter, my dear?"

I shook my head, willing the tears to stay put, but the moment she stood and opened her arms, I crumbled. I rushed to her, burying my face in her shoulder, my sobs coming out in broken gasps. "Caleb... he ended it. And—and everyone thinks it's because of Esther."

Mamm's hands rubbed soothing circles on my back. "Shh, child," she whispered. "Breathe. Tell me what happened."

I pulled back, wiping my face with the edge of my apron. My voice cracked as I spoke, the words tumbling out like a dam had burst. "He said we can't be together, that he has too much on his shoulders, and that I deserve better. But he won't tell me why! And now Esther—Esther is telling everyone that she's been 'there' for him, that she understands him in ways I don't. Edna's spreading it around like it's gospel truth, and I feel so... so humiliated."

Mamm's face softened, her eyes full of quiet understanding. "*Ach*, my sweet, sweet *dauchtah*. People will talk, especially those who thrive on stirring the pot. But you know the truth in your heart, don't you?"

I shook my head. "I thought I did. But now... I don't know. Maybe Caleb does care for her. Maybe I wasn't enough."

Mamm cupped my face, her hands warm and steady. "Sadie Miller, listen to me. You are more than enough. Caleb's struggles are his own, and until he shares them, you can't take his burdens onto yourself. But I know this—love, true love, fights through storms. It doesn't give up when the clouds roll in."

I bit my lip, her words a balm to the ache in my chest. "But what if I can't fight anymore? What if I've lost him?"

Her gaze didn't waver. "Then you pray, child. You pray for *Gott's* guidance, for the strength to keep your heart open, and for clarity. Sometimes the answers come when we least expect them."

I sank into the chair by the fire, my hands clasped tightly in my lap. *Mamm's* faith was unshakable, and part of me wanted to believe her, to hold on to the hope she offered. But the weight of Caleb's absence, of Esther's lies, felt too heavy to carry.

"I don't know if I have the strength," I whispered, more to myself than to her. "Perhaps I am meant to walk the path of life alone."

Mamm leaned down, brushing a strand of hair from my face. "You do have the strength. You are stronger than you think. Stronger than you give yourself credit for. And whatever is meant to be, *Gott* will guide you to it."

Her words lingered as I closed my eyes, a flicker of hope lighting somewhere deep inside me. But would it be enough?

Chapter Twenty-Three

Caleb

The clang of buggy wheels and the low hum of voices reached me long before I stepped into the town square. A crowd had already gathered, spilling out from the benches near the auction platform. Bishop Yoder had asked all the men of Grace Hollow to meet in the town square to discuss the next barn raising. It was the kind of gathering you couldn't ignore, even if you wanted to, and I wasn't one to ignore it. Not today.

I kept to the edges, tipping my hat in silent greetings as I scanned the faces. Levi fell in beside me, his usual grin notably absent. "Quite the turnout," he muttered. "You ready for whatever this is?"

"Ready as I'll ever be," I said, though my gut churned. I didn't know what I expected, but the tension in the air wasn't promising.

Bishop Yoder stood at the front, his broad frame commanding attention even before he spoke. He raised a hand to quiet the murmurs, but before a word left his mouth, a voice sliced through the gathering like a scythe.

"Bishop, if I may."

Eli Fisher.

I stiffened, the name alone enough to set my teeth on edge. He strode into the square as if he owned it, his jacket too fine for a man supposedly struggling and his smirk too confident for someone with so much to answer for. His arrival drew immediate whispers, heads turning in unison to watch him.

Levi leaned closer, his voice low. “Brace yourself, bruder. He’s about to spin a yarn thicker than Mamm’s Sunday stew. Because that’s just he does.
“

I said nothing, but my fists clenched at my sides. Whatever Eli had planned, it wasn’t going to be good.

“Thank you, Bishop,” Eli said, his voice carrying with a practiced ease that made my skin crawl. “I’ve come back to Grace Hollow to clear up some misunderstandings. There’s been talk about my dealings with Eliza Fisher, my muder, and I’d like to set the record straight.”

The crowd shifted, a ripple of curiosity and unease spreading through it. I felt the weight of their stares, though I kept my own eyes locked on Eli.

He continued, his voice dripping with sincerity. “I understand some of you believe I pressured our dear Eliza into taking a loan. I assure you, nothing could be further from the truth. In fact, the loan was her idea—a way to ensure the farm would continue to thrive for future generations. But Caleb—” He turned, his gaze locking onto mine like a challenge. “—he seems to think I’ve done her wrong. That I am the kind of man who would throw his own muder underneath the wheels of a runaway buggy.”

The crowd gasped, the accusation hanging heavy in the air. My jaw tightened as murmurs broke out around me, the tide of public opinion shifting dangerously.

“You’ve got to say something,” Levi hissed, elbowing me sharply. “Don’t let him get away with this.”

I drew a slow, measured breath, my pulse hammering in my ears. Not yet. Not until he'd hung himself with his lies.

Eli's smirk grew as he looked around the crowd, feeding off their unease. "Caleb's jealousy blinds him. He can't stand the idea that someone else might want to help his grossmamm, that someone else could do what he couldn't."

The smugness in his voice was my breaking point. My boots moved before my mind caught up, and I stepped into the open space between us.

"Stop!" My voice rang out, cutting through the murmurs and turning every head. "You've said your piece, Eli. Now let's talk about the truth."

All eyes turned toward me, the weight of their stares pressing heavy on my chest. But I didn't falter. Not this time. I wouldn't let Eli twist the truth into knots while Grossmamm's name—and our family's honor—hung in the balance.

"Eli," I began, my voice steady despite the anger simmering beneath it, "you're good at weaving stories, I'll give you that. But let's talk about the truth for once."

He smirked, crossing his arms over his chest. "The truth, Caleb? As if that's something a selfish no-account such as yourself has ever dealt in. Please, enlighten us."

I stepped forward, the distance between us closing with every step. "The truth is, Grossmamm took that loan because you convinced her she had no choice. You fed her lies about needing money to buy a farm of your own, saying it would secure the future for the family. But you never intended to pay it back, did you?"

Eli's expression flickered—just for a second—but it was enough. "That's absurd," he said, though his voice lacked its earlier confidence. "I told her it was an opportunity. One she agreed to."

"Did she agree to losing the farm that's been in our family for generations?" I shot back, my voice rising. "Because that's what's about to happen."

Gasps rippled through the crowd. A few people whispered, their eyes darting between us. Bishop Yoder raised a hand for silence, but it wasn't enough to quell the tension.

Eli's smirk returned, though it was thinner now. "You're blowing this out of proportion, Caleb. Muder knew the risks. She made her own decision."

"And I suppose she made that decision without any pressure from you?" I asked, my tone sharp enough to cut glass. "No promises of making things right for the family? No guilt-tripping about how it was her duty to help her youngest son?"

"Enough!" Eli's voice cracked as he shouted, his mask slipping. "You think you're better than me, don't you? Always the good, obedient one, always the favorite. Her little liebling. Well, guess what? I've done what I had to do to survive."

"And that's what this is about, isn't it?" I said, my voice cold. "It's never been about the family. It's always been about you."

The men of Grace Hollow murmured louder now, their judgment turning like the tide. I caught Edna's sharp intake of breath as she stood on the porch of the General Store and clutched her shawl, her eyes darting between us. For once, she looked unsure, like she wasn't certain whose side to take.

Before Eli could respond, a new voice broke through the tension. "I believe I can clarify a few things."

The crowd parted as Mr. Gilbert, the banker, stepped forward. His presence silenced the whispers instantly, and I could feel the weight of his gaze as he approached.

"Mr. Stoltzfus," he began, addressing me directly, "you're correct. The terms of Eliza Fisher's loan were... aggressive, to say the least. And the reasoning behind the request was questionable."

Eli stiffened beside me, his face pale.

"After further review," Mr. Gilbert continued, "I believe this matter deserves reconsideration. It's clear there were... extenuating circumstances."

The crowd erupted, their voices a mix of shock and outrage. I turned to Eli, who looked like he might bolt at any second.

"Now who's spinning stories, Eli?" I said, my voice low enough for only him to hear.

Eli's face had drained of color, but his lips were pressed into a thin line, like he was grasping for some way to regain control. The crowd was no longer whispering—they were openly staring, their judgment heavy in the air. Mr. Gilbert adjusted his tie, glancing between Eli and me like a schoolteacher waiting for a confession.

"You lied," I said, my voice quiet but cutting. "You lied to Grossmamm, and you lied to the gut people of Grace Hollow. And you did it for your own selfish gain."

Eli scoffed, a bitter laugh escaping him. "You think you're some kind of saint, Caleb? You think working yourself to the bone on that farm makes you better than me? At least I had the guts to go after what I wanted."

"And what you wanted," I snapped, stepping closer, "was to take advantage of your own family. You convinced Grossmamm to sign that loan knowing full well she couldn't handle the payments. You let her carry the weight of your deceit while you ran off to live your life without a second thought."

Eli opened his mouth to argue, but before he could, Bishop Yoder raised a hand. "Enough," the bishop said, his voice steady but firm. "This is not how we handle matters in Grace Hollow."

The bishop turned to Eli, his gaze stern. "Eli Fisher, you've brought shame upon your family and this community. Your actions have shown a lack of repentance and an unwillingness to honor the trust placed in you. You will leave Grace Hollow immediately and will not return unless you seek reconciliation through honest repentance."

Eli's face twisted in anger, but he didn't argue. He glanced at the crowd, his gaze briefly landing on Edna. Her eyes were wide, her mouth opening and closing like she didn't know what to say. For once, it seemed she wasn't sure whose side she was on.

"Good riddance," Levi muttered behind me, loud enough for only me to hear. I shot him a look, but I didn't entirely disagree. "Uncle or not, that man is bad news."

As Eli turned to leave, Mr. Gilbert cleared his throat. "I should add that the bank has reviewed the terms of Eliza Fisher's loan, and we've restructured it to something more manageable."

A murmur ran through the crowd, but this time it was softer, more approving. Relief washed over me, though it was tempered by the weight of everything that had happened. Grossmamm's farm would be safe, but the damage Eli had done wouldn't heal overnight.

"I'll handle it," I said, meeting Mr. Gilbert's gaze. "Whatever needs to be done, I'll see it through."

Mr. Gilbert nodded, his expression unreadable. But then he reached out to shake my hand. "I believe you will, Mr. Stoltzfus."

As the banker walked away, Edna finally found her voice. "Well," she said, her tone unusually subdued. "It seems there's been quite a misunderstanding."

I turned to her, my patience worn thin. "This didn't have to happen, Edna. I know you think you know what happened in the bank that day, and you relayed the story like a childhood game of telephone. But you had it wrong. Gossip hurts people—families. Maybe it's time we all think about the weight of our words."

She blinked, clearly unprepared for the rebuke. For once, she had nothing to say.

As the crowd began to disperse, their murmurs fading into the background, I stood rooted in place. My heart pounded, adrenaline coursing through me, but the weight pressing on my chest felt a little lighter now. I'd said what needed saying. Eli was gone, and the truth was out. Still, I couldn't shake the lingering tension, the feeling that the ground beneath my feet wasn't quite steady yet.

Levi clapped me on the shoulder, his usual grin softened with something like pride. "You did good, bruder. Grossmamm would be proud."

I nodded, swallowing hard. "It wasn't about pride. It was about making things right."

Levi tilted his head, studying me with that unnervingly perceptive look of his. "Making things right with Grossmamm, sure. But what about with Sadie? Or with yourself?" He leaned against the porch railing, crossing his arms. "You know, bruder, no one in this family is putting all that pressure on you. You do that yourself. You don't leave room for the rest of us to step up, because you're too busy taking it all on. Maybe it's time you let go a little. Trust that we can carry some of the load too."

Sadie's name hit me like a gust of wind, sharp and unrelenting. My gaze drifted toward the general store, where Sadie had disappeared after I'd arrived. I hadn't seen her since, but I'd felt her presence like a thread pulling at my heart the entire time.

"I don't even know if she'll talk to me," I admitted, my voice low. "Not after what I said to her."

Levi shook his head, his grin returning, this time with a hint of mischief. "Ach, Caleb, you're as dense as a hay bale sometimes. Go talk to her. You don't fix things by standing around feeling sorry for yourself."

Before I could respond, a voice behind me made me freeze. "He's right, you know."

I turned to see Edna, her expression uncharacteristically thoughtful. She clasped her hands in front of her, avoiding my gaze at first. "I've been wrong before, Caleb, and I won't pretend I haven't hurt people with my words. But today... today you showed us something important. It takes strength to stand up for what's right, even when it's hard. Sadie's lucky to have someone who cares for her the way you do."

Her words stunned me, the rare sincerity in her tone leaving me momentarily speechless. She turned and walked away before I could muster a response, leaving me alone with Levi once again.

"Well, that was unexpected," Levi said, smirking. "Maybe she's human after all."

I shook my head, a faint smile tugging at the corner of my lips despite everything. "Maybe."

But Levi's teasing faded into the background as I spotted Sadie emerging from the store. Her arms were full of parcels, her face turned away from me, but even from a distance, I could see the tension in her posture, the careful way she carried herself.

"Go," Levi said, giving me a nudge. "And don't mess it up."

Taking a deep breath, I started toward her, each step feeling heavier than the last. When I reached her, she looked up, her eyes widening slightly as she saw me. For a moment, neither of us spoke, the weight of everything between us hanging in the air.

Chapter Twenty-Four

SADIE

The parcels in my arms felt heavier than they should have, as if they carried the weight of my heart along with them. Despite the spectacle I just witnessed, I kept my gaze focused straight ahead, unwilling to meet Caleb's eyes, though I could feel his presence closing in behind me. Even after finding out why he had ended things with me, I couldn't stop. I wouldn't. My steps quickened without conscious thought, the uneven rhythm of my boots against the cobblestones echoing my jumbled emotions.

"Sadie, wait!" His voice, deep and pleading, cut through the cool evening air.

No. I just wasn't ready to deal with him right now. Not when my heart and my nerves were both still so raw. I wanted to think, to process. My grip tightened around the packages as I veered toward the community garden, my only thought to get away, to find some space where I could breathe without the memory of his rejection suffocating me. The marigolds swayed gently in the breeze as I stumbled into the rows, their vibrant hues almost mocking in their brightness.

"Sadie!" His voice was closer now, desperate and filled with something I didn't want to name. I didn't look back.

My knees hit the soft soil before I realized I was falling, the parcels tumbling to the ground. My hands fisted in the earth, the dampness grounding me even as my chest heaved with the effort of holding back tears. Why had he followed me? Why couldn't he just let me be?

"Sadie." His voice was softer this time, almost broken. A shadow fell over me, and I felt him beside me, his presence overwhelming. I didn't move, didn't speak. What was there left to say?

"I know I hurt you," he began, his tone raw and uneven. "I've done everything wrong, and I don't deserve your forgiveness. But I can't let you walk away thinking I don't care. I care more than I've ever cared about anything."

I closed my eyes, the words twisting something deep inside me. How dare he say these things now, after everything? "Then why did you break my heart?" I whispered, my voice cracking under the strain. "Why tell me you were quitting me if you felt this way?"

His breath hitched, and for a moment, all I could hear was the rustling of the marigolds around us. Then his hand, calloused and familiar, rested lightly on the top of my *kapp*. "Because I thought it was the right thing to do. I thought... I thought I was protecting you."

I looked up then, finally meeting his eyes. They were stormy and filled with regret, but they didn't soothe the ache in my chest. "Protecting me from what? From you?"

His shoulders slumped, his hand curling into a fist. "From everything. From the mess I made, from the shame my family's facing, from... from me failing you."

The vulnerability in his voice cut through my anger, leaving behind only raw, aching confusion. "You didn't even give me a chance to help you,"

I said, tears slipping free despite my best efforts to hold them back. "You didn't trust me enough to stand by your side."

"I was wrong," he said simply, his voice heavy with conviction. "I see that now. And I'll do anything to make it right. Anything."

Caleb shifted closer, his knees sinking into the damp earth beside me. His hand hovered over mine, unsure, as if he knew I might pull away. "Sadie," he said, his voice thick, trembling with something I hadn't heard from him before—fear. "I don't know how to say this the right way, but I need you to hear me. *Bitte*."

I didn't look at him, keeping my eyes fixed on the marigolds that swayed softly in the breeze. They were sturdy, resilient, their blooms bright even in the fading light. Unlike me. "You've said enough, Caleb. What more could there be?"

"I never wanted to hurt you." The words rushed out like a confession. "I thought I was doing what was best for everyone. For my family, for *Grossmamm*, for you. But I see now... *ach*, Sadie, I was so wrong."

His voice cracked on the last word, and I risked a glance at him. His hat had fallen beside him, his dark hair mussed and damp with sweat. His eyes, stormy and searching, locked onto mine, and for the first time, I saw not just regret but desperation.

"Wrong about what?" I asked, my voice breaking. "About us? About me?"

"About everything," he admitted, his hand finally settling over mine. His touch was warm, steady, the kind of touch that used to make me feel safe. "I thought I had to carry it all on my own—the weight of *Grossmamm's* loan, the shame of Eli's betrayal. I thought letting you go would protect you from it all. I thought I didn't deserve happiness. That I didn't deserve you."

Tears blurred my vision, but I refused to let them fall. "You thought I couldn't handle it. That I wasn't strong enough."

"*Nee*," he said quickly, his grip tightening on my hand. "That's not it at all. Sadie, you're the strongest person I know. You've been my light, my anchor. I just didn't want to drag you down with me."

I shook my head, the ache in my chest threatening to consume me. "Do you even hear yourself, Caleb? Do you know what it's like to love someone, to give them everything you have, only to be told you're not enough? That they don't trust you enough to let you help carry their burdens?"

His face crumpled, and he leaned forward, his forehead nearly touching the soil. "I was a fool. I thought I was protecting you, but all I did was hurt the one person who matters most to me. Mercy, Sadie. Tell me there's a way to make this right."

The marigolds blurred as fresh tears filled my eyes. I wanted to stay angry, to cling to the hurt he'd caused, but his words—raw, unpolished, true—pierced through my defenses. "You can't undo what's been done, Caleb," I said quietly. "But maybe... maybe you can prove you won't do it again."

"I will," he said fiercely, sitting up straighter. "I'll spend the rest of my life proving it to you. Just... just don't give up on me, Sadie. Don't give up on us."

Caleb's hands trembled as he reached for mine again, his rough fingers brushing against my skin. "Sadie, I love you," he said, the words falling from his lips like a prayer. "I think I've loved you from the moment you first smiled at me over that counter in your *dat's* store. I didn't know it then—I didn't know what it was—but I know now. You've filled every empty part of me."

My breath hitched, the weight of his confession wrapping around my heart and squeezing tight. For so long, I'd wanted to hear those words, and now that they were here, they felt both like a balm and a wound.

"Do you know how hard it was to let you go?" he continued, his voice thick with emotion. "When I walked away, it felt like I was leaving my own heart behind. I thought I was doing the right thing, that if I hurt you now, it would spare you greater pain later. But all I did was create a void I couldn't fill."

I shook my head, a mixture of anger and sorrow bubbling to the surface. "And what about me, Caleb? What about my choice in all this? You made the decision for both of us without even giving me a say."

He winced, the truth of my words landing squarely. "You're right. I was selfish. I thought I was being noble, but I wasn't. I was scared, Sadie. Scared of not being enough for you, of failing you the way Eli failed *Grossmamm*. I didn't want you to see that weakness in me."

Tears streamed down my face now, and I didn't bother to hide them. "Don't you see, Caleb? Loving someone means seeing all of them—their strengths and their weaknesses—and still choosing them. You didn't trust me enough to let me in."

"I do now," he said earnestly, his hands gripping mine as if they were the only things tethering him to this moment. "I've been a fool, Sadie. But if you'll let me, I'll spend the rest of my life making it up to you. I'll show you that you can trust me, that I'll never shut you out again."

His words hung in the air between us, raw and vulnerable. For a moment, all I could hear was the soft rustle of the marigolds around us, their golden heads swaying gently in the breeze.

"Do you mean it, Caleb?" I whispered, my voice trembling. "Do you mean every word?"

He leaned closer, his eyes locking onto mine with an intensity that sent a shiver down my spine. "With everything I am, I mean it. You are my heart, Sadie. And I'll do whatever it takes to prove it."

I swallowed hard, my chest tightening as his words broke down the last of my defenses. "Then you'd better start proving it now," I said softly, my voice cracking under the weight of my emotions. "Because I'm scared too, Caleb. But I think... I think you're worth the risk."

Caleb's hands tightened around mine, his grip warm and grounding, even as his voice wavered with emotion. "You don't have to be scared anymore, Sadie. I'll carry that fear with you. Just... let me show you."

Releasing one hand to reach into his pocket, he fumbled slightly as if the moment had caught him off guard. Caleb pulled out a small, wooden box, its surface gleaming. My breath caught as he held it out, the warm, honey-colored wood glinting in the light. Intricate carvings of marigolds adorned the lid, their petals so delicately etched they seemed to bloom beneath my fingertips.

"I made this for you," he said quietly, his voice thick with emotion. "I didn't have much time, but it felt... right. Like something I needed to do."

I hesitated before lifting the lid, my hands trembling. Inside lay a simple treasure—a small, hand-carved token shaped like a heart, its edges worn smooth. Tears prickled at my eyes as I glanced up at him, my heart swelling with a mixture of awe and disbelief.

"Caleb, this is... *ach*, it's beautiful. I didn't know you could..." I trailed off, still staring at the craftsmanship.

He gave me a sheepish smile, rubbing the back of his neck. "I've always loved working with wood. Before *Dat's* accident, I'd planned to make it my trade. But life... well, life had other plans." His gaze softened as he reached for my hand, his thumb brushing gently over my knuckles. "I've been thinking, though. It's time I start making space for the things that bring me joy. And you—Sadie—you've shown me that it's okay to want things for myself. It doesn't make me selfish. It makes me... better."

My chest tightened at his words, the sincerity in his tone wrapping around me like a warm embrace. "You deserve that, Caleb. You deserve to find your joy."

"And I want to share it with you. Because you've made me believe in something I thought I'd lost. I've thought about this moment a thousand times," he admitted, his voice shaking. "But every time, it felt like I wasn't ready. Like I didn't deserve you yet. But standing here now, with everything that's happened, I know I can't waste another second."

He rose to one knee in the soft soil, his gaze never leaving mine. The marigolds surrounded us, their golden glow a stark contrast to the storm of emotions swirling inside me. He looked up at me, his expression raw, unguarded, and so achingly sincere that it stole the breath from my lungs.

"Sadie Miller," he said, his voice firm despite the tremor in his hands. "I love you more than words can ever say. I want to spend the rest of my life proving to you that I'm worthy of your love. Will you marry me?"

For a moment, the world seemed to hold its breath. The wind stilled, the rustling of the plants fading into silence as his words hung in the air between us. Tears blurred my vision, but through them, I saw the hope and fear etched into his features, his heart laid bare before me.

"Caleb." My voice trembling as my fingers reached for his, gripping them tightly as tears streamed down my cheeks. "You don't have to prove anything to me. You've already shown me everything I need to know."

His breath hitched, his lips parting in stunned silence as I smiled through my tears.

"*Jah*," I said softly, the single word carrying every ounce of love and hope I felt in that moment. "*Jah*, I'll marry you."

Relief and joy flooded his face as he cupped my cheeks, his touch reverent. "You've just made me the happiest man in Grace Hollow," he whispered.

And for the first time in days, the ache in my chest eased, replaced by a warmth that felt like the first rays of sunlight after a long, dark storm.

Caleb's hands lingered on mine as we knelt together, the world around us forgotten. The entire garden swayed gently in the breeze, a testament to the new beginning taking root between us. For a moment, neither of us moved, both lost in the enormity of what had just happened.

"I can't believe this is real," I whispered, staring at the delicate box Caleb had carved for me. The marigold etching caught the sunlight, its beauty almost too perfect to be true.

"It's real," Caleb said, his voice steady, yet filled with awe. "And it's just the beginning, Sadie. I promise you, I'll spend every day making sure you never regret becoming my *frau*."

I tilted my head to look at him, the raw sincerity in his eyes wrapping around my heart like a warm blanket. "You're not the only one making promises, Caleb Stoltzfus. I won't let you carry every burden alone. We're in this together."

A slow, genuine smile broke across his face, one that made my heart swell. He brushed his thumb across my cheek, wiping away the tears I hadn't even realized were still falling. "Together," he repeated softly.

We stood, the marigolds brushing against our legs as we steadied ourselves. Caleb held out his hand, and this time, I didn't hesitate. After I slid his gift into my apron pocket, my fingers slipped into his, and the warmth of his touch sent a shiver up my spine. Holding hands might have seemed simple to others, but to us, it felt monumental—an unspoken vow of unity.

As we left the community garden and walked toward Caleb's buggy, the street was quiet save for the soft murmur of voices from a few lingering people. At the edge of the general store, Caleb slowed, his hand tightening gently around mine. He glanced down the street, then back at me, his expression shifting as though he were fighting some inner battle.

"Come with me," he murmured, his voice low but steady.

Before I could question him, he led me into the narrow alley beside my family's store, the scent of fresh hay and cedar crates filling the air. The shadows cast by the setting sun danced across the walls, giving us a cocoon of privacy away from curious eyes.

There, hidden from view, Caleb stopped, turning to face me. His thumb brushed over my knuckles, his gaze locking on mine with an intensity that sent a shiver through me. "Sadie," he said, his voice barely more than a whisper, "I know this won't be easy. There's still so much to figure out, but I need you to know—I've never been more certain of anything in my life."

My breath hitched, the weight of his words pressing against my chest. "Caleb..." I started, but the look in his eyes silenced me.

He reached up, his calloused fingers grazing my cheek as though I might shatter under his touch. "You're everything I didn't know I needed," he said, his tone reverent. "And I'm not letting you go again."

Before I could respond, he leaned in, his forehead brushing lightly against mine. His breath fanned against my skin, warm and steady, as his other hand settled gently at my waist. My heart thundered in my chest, every nerve sparking to life as the world around us seemed to fade into nothingness.

And then, his lips found mine—soft, tentative, but filled with every unspoken word we'd held between us. The kiss deepened, slow and sure, a promise in its own right. When we finally pulled apart, his hand lingered at my waist, his thumb tracing gentle circles there.

"I love you, Sadie," he said, his voice low but unwavering. "And I'll spend the rest of my life proving it to you."

I couldn't speak, couldn't do anything but nod as my heart swelled with a joy I hadn't thought possible. In that quiet, hidden moment, everything else fell away, leaving only us.

"I should go," he said reluctantly, his fingers tightening around mine as if he didn't want to let go.

I shook my head, a teasing smile tugging at my lips. "Not without one more promise."

"What's that?" he asked, his brow furrowing slightly.

I stood on tiptoe, wrapping my arms around his waist. His eyes widened in surprise, his hand flying to the spot as if to capture the moment. "Promise me you'll never stop fighting for us," I said softly.

His voice was steady, filled with quiet determination. "That's a promise I'll never break."

Chapter Twenty-Five

CALEB

The barn hummed with life, the congregation's hymn rising and falling like a tide, wrapping me in a familiar comfort. Lanterns cast soft golden light across the gathered community, illuminating the faces of those who had shaped our lives. At the center of it all stood Sadie, her back to me as she faced Bishop Yoder. Her dark blue dress fell in clean lines, and the white covering pinned over her hair reflected her quiet strength and faith. She turned as the bishop beckoned me forward, her gaze finding mine, steady and filled with something that made my chest tighten.

I stepped beside her, aware of every eye in the room, but hers were the only ones that mattered. Bishop Yoder's voice filled the space, solemn and steady, speaking of faith, commitment, and the sacred covenant we were about to enter. I barely heard the words, my focus caught in the softness of Sadie's expression. When the bishop paused, his question carried weight that grounded me.

"Caleb Stoltzfus, do you take Sadie Miller to be your *frau*, to walk beside her in faith and love, through all that life may bring?"

My voice came out stronger than I expected. "*Jah*. With all that I am."

Sadie smiled, and for a moment, the room seemed to hold its breath.

"Sadie Miller," the bishop asked, his tone gentle, "do you take Caleb Stoltzfus to be your mann, to honor and cherish him as you walk this path together?"

"*Jah*." Her voice was soft, but the conviction behind it resonated deeply. "Always."

I reached for her hands, warm and small in mine, and the world seemed to fade. This was it—the moment when everything shifted.

As the ceremony ended, the congregation broke into song, their voices filling the barn with praise. Sadie and I turned to face them, her hand still clasped in mine, and their smiles reflected the joy coursing through me. Levi was beside me, and Becca was beside Sadie, their grins wide enough to rival the sun.

Sadie and I lingered at the front of the barn, her hand still warm in mine. Guests began approaching, offering congratulations and blessings, their faces lit with joy.

Bishop Yoder clasped my shoulder firmly. "It was a beautiful ceremony," he said, his tone reverent. "May *Gott's* blessings guide your life together."

"*Denke*," I replied, feeling the weight of his words settle over me. Sadie dipped her head in gratitude, her soft smile speaking volumes.

Levi and Becca were next, their approach as subtle as a storm.

"Well, you did it, Sheriff," Levi said, clapping me on the back. "Perfect delivery. You didn't even stumble over your lines. Guess that means I'm next in line, jah?"

I rolled my eyes, but Sadie laughed, the sound spilling over like a ripple of sunlight.

"Good luck finding someone to put up with you," Becca shot back.

I smirked, nudging Levi. "She's got a point."

Sadie laughed, a sound that drew their gazes to her. "I think Levi just likes the attention," she said, her eyes sparkling with mischief.

Levi grinned unabashedly. "Not wrong. But I'll leave you two lovebirds to it. Don't forget to breathe, Caleb. It's just a party, not a barn-raising."

As they wandered off, Sadie turned to me, her expression softening. "They mean well."

"They always do," I said, my voice quieter now, meant just for her. "But none one else here is half as important as you."

Her cheeks flushed again, that endearing pink that never failed to make my heart lurch. "You keep saying things like that, Caleb Stoltzfus, and you'll have me thinking you're a romantic."

I leaned closer, letting the warmth of her presence draw me in. "Maybe I'm starting to learn."

The day unfolded like a dream, the tent alive with energy. The tables buzzed with conversation, and laughter filled the air as children darted between benches. The smells of roasted chicken, fresh-baked bread, and spiced apples mingled with the crisp autumn breeze.

The barn itself carried a weight of significance, a rare exception granted by Bishop Yoder. Tradition dictated that weddings be held at the bride's family home, but he'd understood the unique circumstances that tied us to *Grossmamm* Fisher's place. It wasn't just where we'd celebrate today—it was where Sadie and I would begin our lives together, tending the land *Grossmamm* cherished. I'd already been running the farm, ensuring it thrived through each season, and once *Grossmamm's* time came, the property would pass to us as her legacy. The bishop's decision felt like a blessing, not just for the wedding but for the future we were already building here.

Sadie and I shared stolen moments amidst the bustle. At one point, I caught her adjusting the flowers at the center of our table, her fingers deftly arranging marigolds.

"Are they not perfect enough?" I teased, leaning closer.

"They could always be better," she replied, her smile soft but determined.

Sadie and I were sitting at the head table, the "*Eck*," surrounded by our families and the bridal party. Plates piled high with traditional Amish wedding fare like creamed celery passed between hands, the air alive with laughter and the clink of glasses.

Leaning closer, I whispered, "If one more person offers me creamed celery, I might start hiding it under the table."

Sadie giggled, nudging me with her elbow. "Don't you dare. *Mamm* would never forgive you."

"Let her," I said, unable to keep from smiling. "You're the only one I want to please today."

Her cheeks flushed a delicate pink, and she reached for my hand under the table, her fingers brushing mine in a quiet moment of connection. The noise and movement around us faded as we shared a look that said everything words couldn't.

This was it. Our beginning.

At one point, Levi stood, tapping his glass to draw attention. "I'd like to propose a toast," he announced, his voice carrying over the hum of conversation. "To Caleb and Sadie. May your life together be filled with love, faith, and the strength to face whatever comes your way."

A chorus of agreement followed, and glasses were raised in unison. I felt a lump form in my throat, moved by the outpouring of support and affection from those around us.

As the meal drew to a close, platters of homemade pies were brought out—apple, cherry, and shoofly—each slice a sweet conclusion to the feast. Sadie and I took turns serving pieces to our guests, a gesture of our appreciation for their presence and support.

As the sun dipped toward the horizon, casting a warm, golden hue over the farm, the atmosphere shifted from the structured meal to a more relaxed and joyous celebration. The tables were cleared, and benches were rearranged to create an open space within the barn, inviting guests to gather for an evening of fellowship and entertainment.

Children, freed from the confines of the meal, darted about the yard, their laughter ringing through the crisp autumn air. Some engaged in games of tag, while others gathered around elders who shared stories and gentle admonitions. The sight brought a smile to my face, a reminder of the continuity of life and tradition within our community.

Sadie stood beside me, her hand resting lightly on my arm. Her eyes sparkled with happiness, reflecting the lantern light that illuminated the barn. "It's beautiful, isn't it?" she murmured, her voice filled with contentment.

I nodded, squeezing her hand gently. "*Jah*, it is. I couldn't have imagined a more perfect day."

As the evening progressed, various members of the community took turns leading songs, each selection reflecting a piece of our shared heritage. Some were lively tunes that had us clapping along, while others were solemn hymns that brought a reflective hush over the gathering. The ebb and flow of the singing mirrored the tapestry of our lives—moments of joy interwoven with times of contemplation.

At one point, Levi approached with a mischievous glint in his eye. "Caleb, how about a game of horseshoes?" he suggested, nodding toward the makeshift pit set up near the barn.

I chuckled, recognizing his intent to lighten the mood. "You're on," I replied, rolling up my sleeves.

A small crowd gathered to watch as we took turns tossing the metal shoes, the clinking sound punctuating the evening air. Laughter erupted with each near miss and triumphant ring, the friendly competition adding to the camaraderie of the night. Sadie cheered me on, her laughter a melody that warmed my heart.

As the game concluded—Levi claiming victory by a narrow margin—we returned to the barn, where the singing had resumed. I noticed Edna sitting alone near the back, her usual sharp demeanor softened in the glow of the lanterns. Feeling a nudge of compassion, I approached her.

"Edna," I greeted, offering a smile. "I'm glad you could join us today."

She looked up, surprise flickering across her features before she returned the smile. "*Denke*, Caleb. It was a beautiful ceremony."

We exchanged a few more words, the conversation light but meaningful. It was a small moment, but it felt like a step toward healing old wounds, a reminder of the importance of grace and forgiveness within our community.

As the night wore on, the energy began to wane, the songs turning softer, the conversations more subdued. I found myself standing at the edge of the barn, looking out over the fields bathed in moonlight. Sadie joined me, slipping her hand into mine.

"It's been a long day," she said softly, leaning her head against my shoulder.

"A perfect day," I replied, pressing a kiss to her head. "The first of many."

We stood there in comfortable silence, the weight of the day settling into a peaceful contentment. Surrounded by the love and support of our community, we felt ready to face whatever the future held, knowing we would do so together.

As the evening's festivities drew to a close, the barn gradually emptied, leaving behind the soft echoes of laughter and song. The lanterns cast a gentle glow, their light flickering against the wooden beams, creating a warm and intimate atmosphere. Sadie and I stood side by side, watching as our guests departed, each farewell accompanied by heartfelt well-wishes and embraces.

Levi was among the last to leave, his usual grin softened with genuine emotion. "Take care of each other," he said, pulling me into a tight hug. Turning to Sadie, he added, "Welcome to the family, Sadie. We're blessed to have you."

"*Denke*, Levi," Sadie replied, her voice tinged with gratitude. "I'm blessed to be part of it."

With a final wave, Levi joined the others, the sound of departing buggies fading into the night. The farmstead grew quiet, the stillness wrapping around us like a comforting blanket.

I turned to Sadie, taking her hands in mine. "It's just us now," I said softly, the weight of the day's events settling into a profound sense of peace.

She met my gaze, her eyes reflecting the same depth of emotion that swelled within me. "Jah," she whispered, a smile playing at the corners of her lips.

Hand in hand, we walked toward the house, the path illuminated by the soft glow of the moon. The air was cool, carrying the faint scent of flowers and freshly turned earth—a reminder of the life we were beginning together.

Inside, the house was quiet, the remnants of the day's preparations neatly tidied away. We made our way to the small room that had been prepared for us, its simplicity a reflection of our shared values. A handmade quilt adorned the bed, its intricate patterns telling a story of love and dedication.

Sadie paused at the doorway, her hand resting on the frame. "Caleb," she began, her voice trembling slightly, "I want you to know how grateful I am—for today, for you, for everything."

I stepped closer, cupping her face gently in my hands. "And I am grateful for you, Sadie. You are my heart, my partner, my love. Today was the beginning of our journey, and I am honored to walk it with you."

Tears glistened in her eyes, and she leaned into my touch, her breath warm against my skin. "I love you, Caleb," she whispered, the words a balm to my soul.

"And I love you, Sadie," I replied, my voice thick with emotion.

We stood there for a moment, the world outside fading away, leaving only the two of us in the quiet sanctuary of our love. With a gentle tug, I led her into the room, closing the door softly behind us.

The night stretched ahead, a canvas upon which we would paint the first strokes of our life together. In the stillness, we found solace in each other's arms, the rhythm of our hearts beating in unison. The future was unknown, but in that moment, we knew that whatever came, we would face it together, bound by the love and commitment we had pledged to one another.

As the first light of dawn began to creep over the horizon, casting a gentle glow through the window, I held Sadie close, a profound sense of contentment settling over me. Our journey had begun, and with her by my side, I felt ready to embrace all that lay ahead.

In the quiet of the morning, with the promise of a new day unfolding before us, we drifted into a peaceful sleep, our hearts entwined, our souls united, ready to face the world together.

Epilogue

SADIE

The early morning sun shone over Grace Hollow, painting the fields and hills in hues of gold and amber. I walked beside Caleb, the warmth of his hand in mine grounding me in the moment. It had become our ritual, tending to our little corner of the community garden every week. Though the plot was small, the marigolds we'd planted during those first tender days of our courtship had flourished, their bright blooms a symbol of everything we'd overcome.

"I still can't believe they let us have a prime spot," I said, smiling as I glanced up at him. Caleb chuckled, his deep, rumbling laugh filling the quiet morning.

"They probably just wanted to keep me busy," he replied, his eyes twinkling. "Idle hands and all that."

"*Ach*, Caleb Stoltzfus, you couldn't be idle if you tried." I squeezed his hand, feeling a surge of affection as he held the garden gate open for me. The scent of fresh earth and dew-drenched flowers greeted us, and I inhaled deeply, letting it calm the nervous flutter in my stomach.

The marigolds waved gently in the breeze, their golden petals catching the sunlight. I crouched down, brushing a stray leaf from one of the blossoms. The blooms were hardy, resilient—much like us. Caleb knelt beside me, reaching for a patch of stubborn weeds that had sprouted along the edges.

"How are you feeling today?" he asked, his voice soft with concern. His gaze, steady and warm, met mine. He'd been asking that question often lately, more attentive than ever, though he didn't know why.

I hesitated, my fingers brushing the rich soil. The words sat heavy on my tongue, waiting for the right moment to bloom. "I'm feeling... grateful," I said at last, looking up at him.

Caleb tilted his head, a small smile tugging at his lips. "Grateful?"

I nodded, my heart pounding in a way that had nothing to do with the work ahead of us. "For this. For us. For everything that's grown here." My voice wavered slightly, but I pressed on. "And for what's still to come."

His brow furrowed slightly, a flicker of curiosity crossing his face, but he didn't press. Instead, he reached for another weed, the warmth of his presence steady beside me. It was moments like this, quiet and unspoken, that reminded me why I loved him so fiercely.

Caleb shifted closer to me, his strong hands pulling weeds with practiced ease. The rhythmic tugging and the soft rustle of leaves filled the space between us. I glanced at him, his shoulders broad and steady, his nose slightly crinkled in concentration. The sight made my heart ache with affection. He was my partner in every sense—through trials, joys, and the simple beauty of mornings like this.

"You know," he began, his voice breaking the quiet, "when we started planting this garden, I didn't think much of it. Just another chore to keep busy." He paused, a small smile playing at the corners of his mouth. "But now, I can't imagine a better place to be. There's something about tending to things that grow. It reminds me that *Gott* always has a plan, even when we can't see it."

His words settled over me like a warm quilt. I felt my chest tighten, the truth I'd been carrying growing too big to hold any longer. I straightened, brushing the dirt from my skirt as I searched for the right way to say what I needed to.

"Caleb," I said softly, my voice catching his attention. He looked up, his gaze steady and curious. "Do you ever think about what else we might grow here? Not just flowers or vegetables, but... something more."

He tilted his head, his gaze narrowing slightly as he tried to piece together my meaning. "Something more?"

I nodded, my hands trembling slightly as I clasped them in front of me. "Like... a family."

The words hung in the air, and for a heartbeat, he didn't move. His eyes widened, the weight of my statement landing fully. Then, as if the realization clicked into place, his expression softened, his lips parting in surprise.

"Sadie," he murmured, his voice thick with emotion. He reached for my hands, his rough palms warm against mine. "Are you saying...?"

I nodded again, unable to hold back the smile that spread across my face. "*Jah*, Caleb. I'm saying that by spring, we'll have more than just marigolds to tend to."

My husband froze, his hands still wrapped around mine as if he were afraid letting go might make the moment disappear. His mouth opened, then closed, his usual steadiness replaced by a rare vulnerability. I watched as the realization settled over him, his eyes shimmering with a mixture of awe and disbelief.

"We're..." His voice trailed off, and he shook his head, a grin breaking free. "Sadie, are you saying I'm going to be a *dat*?"

I laughed softly, the sound trembling with my own emotion. "*Jah*, Caleb. You're going to be a *dat*."

His grip on my hands tightened, and then, as if overcome, he pulled me into his arms. The earthy scent of soil and marigolds filled my senses as I pressed my cheek to his chest, listening to the strong, steady rhythm of his heartbeat. It was racing, fast and full, much like my own.

"A *dat*," he whispered again, his voice thick with wonder. He pulled back just enough to look at me, his hands framing my face. "How long have you known?"

I ducked my head, suddenly shy. "Not long. A few weeks, maybe. I wanted to be sure before I told you."

Caleb's brow furrowed, his protective instincts kicking in almost immediately. "And you've been out here working, bending, pulling weeds?" His eyes scanned me as if looking for any sign that I shouldn't be here.

"Caleb," I said, a teasing lilt in my voice, "women have been doing this for generations. I'm fine."

He didn't look entirely convinced, his lips pressing into a firm line. "From now on, I'll handle the heavy work. You don't lift anything. Not a single thing. You hear me?"

I couldn't help but laugh at his earnestness. "You'll spoil me if you keep this up."

"*Gut*," he shot back without hesitation, his smile returning. "You deserve it. Nothing is more important to me than you. And now... our *boppli*."

For a moment, we stood there in the middle of the garden, the world around us quiet save for the rustle of leaves in the breeze. The marigolds swayed gently, their golden blooms a vibrant backdrop to a moment I knew I'd treasure forever.

"Sadie," Caleb said, his voice soft but filled with purpose, "I don't know if I'll ever be able to say it right, but... *denke*. For this. For you. For everything."

My throat tightened, and I reached up, brushing a stray lock of hair from his forehead. "You don't have to say it right, Caleb. You show it every day."

His smile deepened, and I saw the glimmer of tears in his eyes, a rare and precious sight. It wasn't often Caleb Stoltzfus let his emotions spill over, but when he did, it was like the first rays of sunlight after a storm—warm, bright, and full of hope.

We settled back into the rhythm of our work, though the atmosphere felt lighter now, the air humming with an unspoken joy. Caleb was quieter than usual, but every so often, I'd catch him glancing at me, his lips twitching like he was holding back a grin. It was as if he couldn't stop marveling at the idea of what was to come.

"You know," he said after a long stretch of silence, his voice teasing, "I hope this little one likes marigolds. They're going to be spending a lot of time here."

I laughed, brushing a stray curl from my cheek. "If they don't, they'll learn to love them. This garden's as much a part of us as anything else."

He nodded, his eyes scanning the rows of blooming flowers. "It's a good place to start a family. Feels like... hope."

I paused, the weight of his words settling in. Caleb wasn't a man who spoke lightly, and when he did, his words carried a depth that always caught me off guard. I reached over, placing my hand over his where it rested on the soil. "It does, doesn't it?"

We worked side by side, our movements in sync as we pulled weeds, adjusted stakes, and tended to the plants that had become symbols of our journey. The marigolds had grown thick and vibrant, their golden faces turned toward the sun. It felt like a promise, blooming bright and steady, no matter the storms we'd weathered.

As Caleb leaned back to admire a particularly stubborn patch he'd cleared, he turned to me with a thoughtful look. "Have you thought about names yet?"

I blinked at him, startled by the question. "Names?"

"For the *boppli*," he said, his smile softening. "Boy or girl, it doesn't matter. But I figure... we should start thinking about it."

Before I could respond, the sound of boots crunching over the gravel path reached us. Caleb and I both turned as Levi strolled into view, a cocky grin plastered across his face. "*Boppli*? Did I just hear '*boppli*'? As in, you're going to be a *daedi*?" He clapped a hand to his chest, mock-staggering like he might faint. "*Ach*, Caleb, I thought you were the practical one. Didn't you and Sadie get separate beds for your marriage, like proper Amish folks?"

My cheeks burned hotter than the midday sun as Caleb scowled. "Levi," he warned, his voice low and growly, though the corner of his mouth twitched.

"Separate beds, I say!" Levi crowed, ignoring his brother's glare. "Guess that didn't last long. It's a *gut* thing *grossmamm* is hard of hearing."

Before I could muster a retort, Becca appeared from behind Levi, her arms crossed and her face set in a look of feigned disapproval. "Levi, stop tormenting them. Sadie's face is about to match the roses."

"Oh, come on, Becca," Levi shot back, his grin widening. "Don't tell me you're not curious how Mr. Responsible here managed to get this done."

Becca smirked, leaning against the fence. "I'm more curious about how they're going to raise a *boppli* if Caleb doesn't stop acting like the Sheriff of Grace Hollow."

"That's funny, coming from the woman who can't get through one quilting circle without starting a scandal," Caleb fired back, his voice dry but teasing.

Becca gasped in mock offense. "I don't start scandals. I finish them."

"You're both impossible," I muttered, trying to fight a smile.

Levi threw his hands up dramatically, looking skyward. "*Gott*, hear my plea! Please let this *boppli* look like Sadie. It's the only chance the poor thing has!" He dropped to his knees in the dirt, clasping his hands together like a repentant sinner. "And if You can't manage that, at least give it her temperament. One grumpy Stoltzfus is enough!"

Becca burst out laughing, clapping her hands as she doubled over. "Levi, you're going to get struck by lightning one day, I swear. And I hope I'm there to see you turn black and crispy."

Caleb rolled his eyes but couldn't hide the grin tugging at his lips. "Get up, you fool, before you scare the marigolds."

Levi stood, brushing off his knees and winking at me. "Sadie, you're too good for him, *boppli* or not."

"I know," I said, smiling sweetly. "But someone has to keep him in line."

Becca snorted. "Good luck with that. I've been trying to keep this one in line for years." She jabbed a thumb toward Levi. "It's a losing battle."

Caleb pulled me close, his arm warm and steady around my waist. "Don't listen to them," he murmured, his voice low enough for only me to hear. "We've got all we need, right here."

After a round of farewells, Levi and Becca turned to leave, laughing and shoving each other.

Caleb pressed a kiss to my lips and wrapped his arms around me. And in that moment, standing among the marigolds enveloped in Caleb's strength, I knew he was right. We had everything we needed—and maybe a little extra chaos to keep life interesting.

In the quiet aftermath of our friends' departure, Caleb rested his forehead against mine, his breath warm and steady, grounding me in a way I didn't know I needed. The world felt small here in this hidden place—just the two of us and the unspoken promises stretching ahead like the first rays of dawn. The weight of the uncertainties fell away, replaced by the steady, unshakable truth in his eyes. This wasn't just a moment—it was the beginning of forever. And as he whispered my name like a prayer, I knew that within his strong arms, I'd found the safest place I could ever be.

Made in United States
Orlando, FL
14 June 2025

62124024R00146